Branthwaite's Lot

RICHARD MASON was born in 1962 and brought up on the family farm in the Lune Valley, north Lancashire. He left school at the age of 16 to work on the farm, and attended Myerscough Agricultural College. He ran the farm with his parents until his father's death in 1997. In 2004 he completed an MA in creative writing at the University of Lancaster. He has worked in sales and in social care, and currently earns his living in landscaping and garden maintenance. *Branthwaite's Lot* is his first novel.

RICHARD MASON

Branthwaite's Lot

A Novel

Marius Press

A *Marius Press* Book

Copyright ©Richard Mason 2012
This edition copyright ©Marius Press 2012

Richard Mason has asserted the moral right to be identified as the author of this work
in accordance with Section 77 of the Copyright, Designs and Patents Act 1988

A CIP catalogue record for this book
is available from the British Library

ISBN 978-1-871622-08-9

Author's Note
*All characters in this publication are fictitious and any resemblance to
real persons living or dead is purely coincidental. However, the meeting
between the farmer and the neurosurgeon is a real event. The farmer in
question was my grandfather, and I have used his real name; all other
characters in the scene are fictitious. With the invention of modern animal
medicines the operation described became unnecessary and subsequent
animal welfare legislation made it illegal..*

Typesetting and design by The Drawing Room Design, Over Kellet, Lancashire, UK
Printed in Great Britain by the MPG Books Group, Bodmin and King's Lynn, UK

Branthwaite's Lot

April 1992

1

Earth, or which is the same thing, 'tis the superficies of pores, cavities, or interstices of the divided parts of the earth, which are of two sorts, viz. natural and artificial.

Jethro Tull. The Horse Hoeing Husbandry (1733)

Branthwaite's Lot is a place of secrets; cold, marshy and sour at its lowest points where moss chokes out grass and heather, compresses under its own weight, darkens and turns to peat; an acrid world where death leads not to the dignity of transformation into soil but where acid and tannins leak into bodily canals, permeating through membranes and tissues, preserving them like grisly laboratory specimens, hidden away for decades, millennia, until some major event exposes them to the air. Huge oaks wait deep beneath the surface along with the bodies of beetles, small mammals and birds; unchanged and unseen.

At its summit the lot is capped with rock. Limestone paving running north to south and stretching along a ridge for half a mile forms the top of the escarpment, a treacherous expanse of cracks and crevices, fissures in the old rock, widened and deepened over time to create a criss-cross pattern of clefts and crannies up to a yard deep. At first glance it appears lifeless but looking down from directly above, a whole miniature world can be seen of wild geraniums, harts-tongue ferns and minute flowers in colours from yellow to magenta and blue. Hidden in their shrunken world, these organisms are protected from harsh winds that whistle over the tops of the rocks, forced up as air drawn off the sea meets the expanse of ridge.

The ridge itself falls away steeply to the west, forming screes and slopes so steep that only the most agile or desperate of grazers dare to climb them. On the eastern slope is pasture, exposed to hungry north-easterlies, browning the grass in winter, frosting new shoots in spring and, in the rare event of a hot summer, burning the grass where soil is thinnest.

In the spring of 1992, changes began to occur. Men with heavy boots and tripods crossed the lot, stopping briefly to take measurements, make notes and adjustments to details on old maps. They scrutinised the terrain, made judgements about blocks of limestone and deposits of clay, commented on the suitability of a landscape formed in a time when rock was quarried and ground by tons of ice; humans wore skins, scraped and stitched with tools of flint and bone.

The surveyors came and went without using gates or stiles, preferring to clamber over walls and wire fences as if these old boundaries and rights of way were nothing more than obstructions; smudges and scrawls of a cartographer's quill to be doused, dissolved and wiped away. They pointed, straight-armed to the horizon, followed invisible lines in their own imagination, made mental pictures of trenches cut through hillsides; streams piped and bridged.

Some days after the intruders had gone, a young man was mending a wall on the next ridge. He dragged out loose rubble and boulders, lined up top stones out in the grass, pulled unsteady edges till only sound wall remained. He breathed in damp air from the centre of the wall; soothed by the familiar knock of stone against stone.

A casual glance to the east caused him to stop, remain poised with a stone held ready to place. Something alien stood out on Branthwaite's Lot, a line of square pegs driven into the ground, spaced out with twenty yards between, the white wood contrasting sharply with browns and greys of heather and rock. From his position of elevation he could see the dotted line of pegs stretching past Branthwaite's boundary and across the fields to the north and south.

Somewhere beyond the southern end of the peg-line a

strange sound broke through the curlews' cries and lambs' bleats: the distant rumble of heavy machines. It resonated against a stand of conifers to the west and echoed across both valleys, becoming the background noise for the drama about to be played out. As the machines crept invisibly closer, the thunder separated into two sounds, the roar of diesel engines and a rhythmic pounding that could be felt through the ground almost before it was heard. Ewes raised their heads from grazing, called to their lambs and hurried them away to the farthest corners of their pastures, huddling in shadows, behind rocks and pressing so tightly against wire fences that the netting bowed, creaked and strained. Lapwings screamed and swooped, searching the hillside for the as yet unseen threat to their eggs and chicks. The ground itself seemed to tremble as the noise grew louder.

Two dark shapes appeared over the horizon; tractors moving slowly, relentlessly, about sixty feet apart, their huge front wheels biting into soft turf. As they rounded the top of the hill it appeared as if they were hurling spears from their cabs. They continued, following the row of wooden pegs and moving in line with each other. When they began to descend the steep slope, the trailers behind them came into view, each carrying a man and a large load of fence posts. The two men worked rhythmically, throwing out posts at ten feet intervals, silent beneath the engines' roar.

By the time the trailers were halfway between skyline and base, the source of the pounding came into view. Two more tractors with mechanical post-knockers were following the line of posts. Two more figures in overalls scurried ant-like, retrieving posts and positioning them in line with the vertical booms, dodging the huge descending weights as they drove each post into the ground, flinching at each detonation of steel against wood, ducking back to fetch the next post; men serving machines.

Half a mile to the north where the lot opened onto a lane, a Landrover roared into sight and its occupant, a burly man with grey hair, rushed to open the gate. He jumped back in, drove at high speed across the moss and heather, splashing through puddles, throwing up mud and water. The engine groaned up an incline, its note turning to a high pitched scream as the vehicle thundered across a ridge, racing towards the wall where the two tractors and trailers had stopped, engines idling, drivers smoking. The drivers nodded to each other and turned their gaze towards a digger that was trundling down the slope to demolish the wall.

The Landrover skidded to a halt and the burly man threw himself out, reaching behind the seat for his shotgun. He bundled over clumps of rushes and propped himself against one of the rusty old farm machines that had been lined up along the wall in the path of the tractors. He was panting, clutching his chest and reaching into his pocket. He brought out a small flat tin, flicked it open and popped a tiny black tablet under his tongue, leaned his back against the rusty bonnet of the ancient tractor and waited for the pain to subside. Sweat was trickling from under the brim of his cap, his jaw was set tight and as he breathed, gobs of spittle frothed from between his teeth.

He turned towards the men beyond the wall, levelled the shotgun on the bonnet of the tractor and took a large box of cartridges from his jacket pocket, placing it beside him within easy reach. He glared at the contractors and their machines less than twenty yards away. The greys of his eyes were circled in white and a vein pulsed above his collar. His lips were moving almost unconsciously and when the sound came it hissed like steam from a valve.

"Bastards."

✢

The whole scene was sheltered on three sides by rounded hills. To the north, the end of the escarpment hid the tractors and digger from farms and fields beyond so that the only witness to the events was the young man on the next ridge. He placed the final top stones and watched as the digger driver climbed out of his cab, turned back towards the top of the hill either for inspiration or hoping for someone to appear. Despite cold gusts lashing across the valley, the young man felt heat in his cheeks; a tingle that told him this wasn't his business. He looked at his watch and returned to his Toyota pickup that was parked a few feet away with the door open and the radio tuned into Radio 2. The engine started at second turn and he drove cautiously away towards the main road as if he was avoiding being seen or heard, only revving the engine when he reached the tarmacked road. Followed the signs for Lancaster, studying fields and other men's livestock as he headed towards town. His fingers tensed slightly on the steering wheel when he joined the one-way system and merged with city traffic. He passed *The Farmer's Arms*, a city pub, and stopped at a red light.

The woman on the pelican crossing could have been his grandmother, but then so could anyone else her age. She turned her head and smiled at him waiting patiently in the battered truck. The young man smiled back, creasing the corners of his face; tanned and weathered, the hallmark of working outdoors.

He turned across the traffic and up a ramp, stalling the engine between two large cars by the hospice door, climbed out, lifting the door as he closed it, and reached back through the open window for an envelope on the passenger seat. He bent to pick up an old chip paper that he'd accidentally kicked from the foot well, crunched it with his fist and tossed it in the back. Strode towards the entrance.

Through the heavy doors the air smelled of disinfectant and polish. He followed the corridor round to a desk where a young nurse sat typing awkwardly into a computer.

"Is Mr Waterford in here?"

Startled, she looked up.

"Oh, hello." She was staring him in the face. "Mr Thomas Waterford?" She was playing with her earlobe, eyeing him. He was in good shape from lifting stones. "Are you his son?"

"Just a friend." He looked beyond her at the door to the ward, content with his own company.

"Through there." The response was cold. She looked down at some papers, then at her nails.

"Thank you." He strode past and across to the room at the end where a patient was coughing weakly and swiping at his mouth with a tissue. Clear tubes ran from his nostrils to an oxygen bottle against the wall. The old man in the bed laboured at his breathing; intermittent gasps like a lamb that wouldn't live. He looked grey, as if the life had been sucked from his veins, or as if some strange force was destroying him from the inside. The young man glanced from the figure in the bed to the name written on a card on the wall. He tried not to look shocked. It wasn't that long since he'd seen him but Christ, he'd lost weight, lots of weight. For a much larger man it might have been an improvement but with Tom, who'd never carried any surplus, it left him looking like that iceman mummy they found in the Alps. His eyes had sunk into his skull. His arms were nothing but bones bound together with skin and sinew and there was so little disturbance to the covers on the bed that it was hard to believe there was a body beneath them. There was hardly anything left of the Tom he remembered; the quiet one in other men's tales of war, a name etched on a dozen trophies for dry-stone walling. Tom had won them all, could build across peat, moss and jutting rocks; walls so straight and true that they could have been guided by laser. He never used a line.

It's a sad day when y' can't trust yer eyes ... never trusted

*strings. They blow. Seen blokes usin' one in a wind ... ended up wi'
a curved wall. Spirit levels get knocked in yer toolbox ... always out
o' true.*

The old man's head turned towards him, a smile breaking
across the wasted face. The young man took a step forwards,
holding out his hand.

"Hello Tom. Happy birthday." He handed him the
envelope, turned his attention towards the cards on the
cabinet and all along the window ledge.

"Some bloody birthday, eh?" There was a whistling noise
as the old man breathed. He fought with the seal and pulled
out the card. On the front was picture of a shepherd with two
border collies. "Thank you, lad." His eyes had reddened and
moisture welled in the corner near his nose. It almost became
a tear.

The young man pretended to be studying the cards in the
window, fumbled with thickened fingers, left a smudgy mark
and put his hands behind his back. Tom dropped the envelope
in the bin and sneaked the card in front of the others on the
bedside cabinet. His visitor turned back to him.

"I brought you these." He reached into his pocket and held
out a crumpled bag.

"Humbugs." The old man reached in and tried to break
one away from the rest, failed and waved them away. "I'll have
one later. Anyway, how have you been?"

"Keeping busy. Putting up a wall gap for Smiths this
morning."

When he mentioned the name, a pained expression grew
on the old man's face as his mind drifted to a distant memory
across sixty years of regret. Changing the subject quickly, the
young man continued with his news. "I've been lambing for
Sedgwick's, then I'm lambing at Hawes till the end of May. I've
got a contract walling on the pipe track this summer."

"If they've finished."

"Money's too good to miss. I might have to lose some regular work to finish it on time."

"Put it off but don't lose any. It might not be easy to get it back."

"There's one or two jobs I wouldn't mind losing." The young man struggled with a smile.

"Oh, Bill Branthwaite's. I warned you about him." The old man began coughing and for a moment his companion looked embarrassed, unsure about how to react. "Bloody fags! You do right to keep off 'em. You wouldn't have made a fell runner if you'd smoked like I did when I was your age."

"You did Tom, and everyone says you were a good runner."

"Yes but they were all farm lads then, no club runners or amateur athletes. Locals couldn't catch me ... except Bill Branthwaite. He could have made a champion."

The young man looked at him; his brow crumpling. "But he's like a barrel!"

"He wasn't then. He was built like you. He was a popular young bloke, mild mannered, good-natured. Everyone thought he would take after his mother. His real mother was a lovely person. She died before the war. Old Mrs Branthwaite who you remember was her cousin. Like chalk and cheese those two." He was gasping for air.

"I can't imagine Bill Branthwaite as mild mannered, Tom. He punched young Charlie just for breaking a brush, and it was half-rotten. He gets me to repair his walls then stands over me telling me what to do."

"Well he is a bit of a perfectionist around the farm."

"A bit of a perfectionist? The man's mad ... and the way he has Dennis living in that old caravan ... ."

"Don't be so hard on him, lad. Dennis would've been locked up years ago if it weren't for Bill." Tom gazed out of the window towards the bay and the edge of Branthwaite's Lot. He knew that he would never smell the heather again. "You know, of all the strange things about Bill, I could never understand why he never drained his lot."

"The pipeline contractors are probably on his land right now. They were putting up the fences on Smith's place when I finished and the diggers were just moving in." He paused, unsure whether to tell the sick man what he'd just seen, settled for half a tale. "He's still insisting that they haven't got the right. He was even talking about stopping them himself."

"Oh dear." Tom was searching for a note of wisdom. "That's probably just talk. When they're finished he'll have it all to himself again. He never liked anyone going up there. Everyone felt sorry for him at first and made allowances, but after years of … ." He ran his fingers through the remains of his hair, sighed then asked quickly, "Where are you working next week?"

✣

Sergeant Mason was sitting at his desk wading through the endless paperwork that blighted his life as a village bobby. The report was half finished when the telephone rang. There was some kind of disturbance at Sandholme. A call had come through from some liaison officer for British Gas. Bill Branthwaite was trying to stop their contractors from entering his land up the lane towards Waverley Cottage. The farmer was in breach of a court order and things were in danger of getting out of control.

The policeman had an uneasy feeling as he grabbed his jacket and headed for the car. Branthwaite was an odd character. He must be in his seventies, still one of the most progressive farmers in the district and not well liked. He was one of those blokes who'd never been charged but could be capable of anything. The man wasn't a drinker, maybe even a teetotaller, but he had that red face which often went hand in hand with a violent temper. He'd never married. Some of the local women joked that this was probably the only charitable thing he'd ever done in his life.

Bill Branthwaite lived for profit. The sergeant had seen that when he'd been policing the local hunt. They weren't allowed on his farm. To Branthwaite, grass was a commodity and he talked about it like a city broker protecting his investment. He wasn't having anyone galloping over it and churning it into the soil ... whoever they were. Solicitors, businessmen, land agents; they all did the same amount of damage when sitting astride a horse and charging across productive grassland.

Mason thought this was unusual. Most farmers were afraid of upsetting the 'toffs." It might count against them in the courts or at a rent review, but Branthwaite treated them with the same contempt that he showed to anyone else who strayed onto his high land.

There'd been a story at the *Plough* a couple of years back. One of the regulars had told it so many times and with such detail that half the drinkers at Mason's local could tell it, and several of them claimed they'd been there.

A group of hunt saboteurs, believing that they'd found an ally, made the mistake of asking if they could cross Branthwaite's land. It was a crisp Saturday morning in January and the master of the hunt had outwitted them, leading the pack out of the back entrance of Friar's Hall, along a newly made track through the woods and behind the high deer fence. The hunt always started beyond Branthwaite's cow pasture away from footpaths and roads.

Branthwaite's reply to the saboteurs was to take them round the back of the buildings and shoot a guinea fowl in front of them. A female student burst into tears. It was her first day 'sabbing' and she'd probably pictured herself hiding on a hillside stroking a saved fox cub.

One of the guys in the crowd pushed forwards, a real

hardman-anarchist. He'd earned his reputation releasing mink from farms in Devon. It was rumoured he'd been behind an attack on a laboratory in Berkshire. A security guard had been beaten senseless and the whole complex had been burned to the ground. The security guard never recovered; he was pensioned off with blurred vision and nerves like a pheasant in the shooting season.

The thug faced Branthwaite. Stalked him, trying to stare him out, no qualms about beating up a man twice his age. He pulled down the neck of his T-shirt, pointed to a tattoo on his neck. A dotted line with the words, "cut here."

When Branthwaite leaned to read the tattoo, the thug jerked his head forward in a mock head butt. Branthwaite didn't flinch. He merely picked up the bird and began plucking it, letting the feathers blow in the wind, the shotgun tucked under his arm. The thug was boiling. He grabbed Branthwaite by the shoulder, flung him against the wall and lunged forward to grab him by the throat.

Branthwaite's face stayed blank. In one motion, he snapped the barrel of the twelve-bore shut and brought it up under the thug's chin. The thug flinched as steel pressed into soft flesh. His lip trembled like a child's. He tried to regain control.

"You haven't got the bottle."

Branthwaite pushed the gun higher, raising the kid's head.

"I think you've just lost yours … Danny boy." The farmer watched the saboteur's face go white. "I know exactly who you are and where you live, so don't think you can come round here scaring me." He took a pace forward and pushed the kid into the crowd then ordered them back onto the road and followed them with the guinea fowl in one hand and the twelve-bore under his arm.

Charlie Watkins had watched the whole scene from the dairy doorway. He'd just finished feeding Branthwaite's heifers and was washing off his wellies before hurrying home for his rugby kit and playing hooker for the Vale. He met his boss marching back into the yard swinging the guinea fowl.

"How did you know who he was?"

"I didn't. I was watching 'em get out o' that minibus half an hour ago. I heard one o' them lasses call him Dan."

Young Watkins had been embellishing that story at the rugby club and in the village pubs until it became a local legend. Branthwaite's status might even have been raised to that of a hero if he hadn't been so unpopular in the first place.

There'd been another incident before that, when Sergeant Mason had been involved himself. Shelley Williams, a teacher's daughter from Over Keer, had been seeing one of the Barrett boys from Waverley Cottage. She'd met him in Lancaster one Saturday morning in the summer of eighty-four. They'd bought some tapes, had burgers and milkshakes at Macdonald's and travelled back to his place on the bus. His mum and dad had gone to a car boot sale in Blackburn. They wouldn't be back until after eight. Young Bobby Barrett had bought condoms from a machine in the shopping centre toilets. He hadn't told Shelley.

When he put the music on she'd been exploring the house. There were no books. The house didn't have a study. He talked her into sitting on the settee but she kept getting up and wanting to dance. When he started dancing close, she told him that she loved him and he said, "Yeah. So do I."

She missed his irony, thought she'd found a romantic. When he started touching her up she giggled and pushed him off. He carried on and she got upset. He showed her the condoms and she went quiet. Remembered what her friend Kate had said about the Barrett lads. Bobby was persistent. Shelley said she was leaving and tried to ring her mum. Her brother Jimmy answered; said she was out with Dad.

She told Jimmy she was walking home and left Bobby to

14

listen to his music and his hormones. When she saw a public footpath sign to Over Keer, she hopped over the stile and followed the wall. The footpath cut across to the opposite corner, so when she found the old hunting gate onto Branthwaite's lot she thought she was going the right way.

Branthwaite had parked the Landrover on the grass verge by the lot gate and was spending the afternoon stubbing Scots thistles with a spade. He was enjoying the peace and quiet when he saw the girl walking towards him along the ridge.

She looked up, saw him rushing towards her with the spade in the air, screaming at her to go. She raced down the hill and vaulted the wall into an old overgrown lane, and didn't stop running until she reached a cluster of houses that used to be Joe Moss's farm before he disappeared during the war. The young couple at the first house called her parents who'd just got home. Their daughter was so shaken up she could hardly talk. They called the police.

Sergeant Mason took a statement from Shelley Williams and called at Friar's Holme Farm. Branthwaite was standing in the dairy doorway watching him park the car and walk across the yard.

"I've come to ask you a few questions." He was studying the farmer's reaction and knew he could tell if the man had something to hide. He'd met the guy several times before, always complaining about the cost when he came in to renew his shotgun license. He seemed a bit abrupt but had no record of any sort. Probably fiddled a bit on his tax returns but none of the lads at the station had heard anything against him at that time, apart from PC Denby who said he was a grumpy old bastard.

"How can I help you?" The farmer hadn't flinched.

"Where were you at about two o'clock this afternoon?"

"Up on me lot. Stubbin' thistles."

"Did you see a young lass up there?"

"Yes I did. Looked like she was goin' somewhere in a hurry. She was runnin' down towards that old lane that comes out by Lane House Cottages. Is she in some kind of trouble?"

"She's made a complaint against you, said you chased her off with a spade, shouting."

The sergeant studied him, could tell he was running the afternoon's events through his head. A man looked different when he was trying to make something up. After nearly thirty years in the force, you knew these things.

The farmer laughed, shook his head.

"I chopped into a bees' nest in an old gorse branch and some dried out moss. There was a thistle growin' through it. I did some wavin' an' swingin' an' cursin' for a few minutes." He showed the policeman three stings on his neck and a couple on his arms. "Funny though, I thought that'd happened a long time before I saw that lass."

The sergeant rubbed his chin. He could see that Branthwaite was telling the truth, as he saw it.

"I guess she could have seen you and misunderstood."

He left the farmer to finish his work and headed back to the station. His stomach was rumbling and he wanted his tea.

On Monday he had a call from the girl's father, wanting to know what they were going to do about it. When Mason told him what he'd heard from Branthwaite, the guy started ranting and said the farmer had been running right at his daughter.

The policeman was always wary of parents who had a vivid picture of what their kids had been up to in their absence, especially those who took the moral high ground and insinuated that he wasn't doing his job.

The guys at the station said Mr Williams was a bit of a pillock, a left-wing radical who'd moved into one of the new houses behind PC Denby's. He'd caused a lot of trouble at parish council meetings, objecting to everything that came up. He didn't like farmers since one of them had given him a bollocking for letting his dog chase some sheep in lambing time. Mason told him he'd make more inquiries and call him back.

When he got home that night he asked his son if he knew a girl called Shelley Williams. Ryan laughed and told him that Bobby Barrett had taken her back to his place on Saturday afternoon. According to Ryan, young Barrett had tried to get his end away and the girl had run off. Sergeant Mason guessed that she'd been in a state and had blown the whole thing out of proportion. He'd rung Mr Williams and persuaded him not to press charges. After all, how would it have looked in court when all that came out?

The sergeant climbed into the patrol car, tugged at his lower lip and considered the quickest route to the lot, mouthed the words "Bill Branthwaite." There was something odd about Branthwaite's manner. Mason had seen it sometime before, but he was damned if he knew where. He clicked on his seatbelt and started the car.

1939–1941

2

*In all probability before the enclosure acts, fences as we
think of them today were relatively few and gave farmers
little worry.*

F. G. Beadon. Economic Farm Fencing. Farmer
and Stock-Breeder Year Book (1955)

Bill Branthwaite strode across the paddock and breathed in
deeply. The scent of growing grass hit the back of his nostrils.
It was a good smell. Together with the warmth on his back it
told him spring was here. Patches of ryegrass in the forty-acre
park in front of him were shining in the sun, and the duller
green clumps of cock's-foot were beginning to push up above
the sward. In the woods sheltering the fields a woodpecker was
drilling. Short rattling bursts echoed between the trees.
Somewhere, hidden in the branches, the cock bird was
attracting a mate.

Bill leaned on the gate; listened. Spring was definitely here,
and today was the best day of the year. He unhooked the chain,
swung the gate back against the iron railings and wedged it
with a stone. He knew that stone – a large cobble, river gravel
with a seam of quartz running through it. He'd been using it
to prop the paddock gate since he was big enough to pick it
up, and remembered dropping it on his foot when, at four years
old, he'd rushed to help his dad, keen to be doing real work.

A bawl from the shippen made him look back towards the
yard. Some of the cows knew what was coming and their
patience was fading. They'd been housed for six months, and
the smell of fresh grass was calling them out to graze. Bill
hurried back. Mary would be waiting, standing on the middle
rung of the gate waiting for the spectacle, or peering through
the lower bars wondering why the cows were still inside. He
ran, feeling the breeze on his brow lift his cap and fill his lungs,

warm and fresh. His boots creaked and the buckles of his leggings rattled as he scattered the hens under the chestnut tree. At the gate into the yard he remembered himself and walked across to the cowshed door.

"Where've y' bin?" Dennis was waiting. "Are we lettin' 'em go? Or are we leavin' 'em till next year?"

He liked Dennis for his superstitious ways, his simple wit and pearls of wisdom, even though they often came at times when you least wanted them. Since arriving with a pot of his mother's ointment six years ago, Annie Scowcroft's boy had become one of the fixtures, almost a part of the family, or as close as someone like Dennis could be. She'd brought him up in a stone cottage under the shadow of Hutton Roof crag where he'd spent his days wandering through the herb garden or playing in the steam from her pan of famous salve. The schoolmistress said he'd shown some promise but, with a nervous disposition, the son of the local herbalist had been met with taunts and derision until he stopped attending. On the three-mile walk to school there were much better places to hide from bullies than in the playground.

His days became lessons in ferreting rabbits or fishing for brown trout in the streams beneath the crag. At twelve, in a moment of inspiration, he'd poured vinegar on the chain of the school inspector's unattended bike so that he could hear it squeaking in pursuit behind tall hedges along narrow lanes.

His mother had seen that her son's ideas needed an honest direction. She'd seen Jack Branthwaite unloading the milk churns at the station and overheard him say he was looking for a lad to help out at hay time. She'd approached him with the guise of selling a jar of ointment. Dennis had been sent to deliver it and had returned after dark full of stories of hay turning and scaling. By the time he was fourteen he'd been taken on indefinitely and had his own room above the granary with a stove and iron bedstead.

The latch rattled on the back door and both Dennis and Bill turned towards the house.

"Let 'em go son." Jack Branthwaite was smiling as he stepped out. His daughter Mary appeared by his side.

"Daddy, can I watch the cows go out?" She'd been pestering since breakfast time.

"Come on Mary, but stay out of the way. We don't want you getting trampled."

Bill watched as his father picked her up and set her down in the back of the cart. As he marched into the shippen he felt his father's hand on his shoulder.

"All right, you let the first one go."

He felt himself growing. Releasing the first cow in spring had always been his father's preserve, as if it held a kind of status. This moment held in it the marking of a new season, the start of spring proper and with it the promise of summer with its long days of sweet smelling meadows and birds in the hedgerows.

Stepping into the stall beside the first cow he began to untie the band from its neck. The other cows waited, pricking up their ears and listening, then galloping up and down the passageway when they were released. A roan-coloured heifer skipped round the yard before racing back inside as if she was telling the others how good it was to be free again. Those waiting their turn shook their heads in an attempt to undo their neckbands, iron rings rattling against stone partitions.

His father was standing beside the next milker, squeezing a lump on her back. As he increased the pressure a hole in the lump began to widen, and a fat, white maggot, about the size of a child's thumb, popped out and rolled off the hide onto the floor. He stamped on it with his boot and rubbed the lump with his fist.

"Bloody warbles! She'll feel better for that."

They continued along the row of cows until Jack reached

the last one, a strong red animal, still with a numbered ticket on her rump – lot forty-three, Bentham Auction Mart.

"Now there'll be trouble. This one fancies herself as boss. I hope they can sort it all out without one losing an eye."

The newly-bought cow trotted out into the yard with her head high, stood sideways in the gateway and bellowed. The roan heifer tried to squeeze past and ignored her superior's warning. The older cow dug her horns hard into the heifer's ribs, forcing her against the gatepost. The heifer let out a bawl and ran off.

Bill closed the gate. By tonight the squabbles would be over. The cows would come in for afternoon milking with clean udders and smelling different. The musky dung of winter would be replaced with that fresh scent of cows at grass. Within a week they would be out at nights too, and by the time the youngest calves were released into the paddock summer would be here.

The following week was spent repairing fences and clipping out the ewes. Bill found himself studying Dennis. He couldn't be sure whether the actions he was seeing were new or a habit he hadn't noticed before. His work mate would mutter to himself as he brought a post from the cart, or move his head in a peculiar way each time he was told which job to do next. He came to the conclusion that this had been happening for a while but Dennis's habits and quirks seemed to be becoming more extreme.

As his father stooped over the last ewe from the riverside, clipping off the dirty wool from its tail, Bill spotted Dennis crossing himself whilst holding the sheep's head. He'd seen him do it with the last one, but thought he'd been adjusting his jacket.

Dennis was still on his mind as he walked the flock back across the park and down the lane to the steep land by the river. Many of the lads working on farms were said to be a bit simple or daft. Dennis wasn't daft. He was an oddity all right, but he was good with stock and could often see a simple way round a problem when everyone else was losing their temper and getting nowhere.

When one of the hens had started eating eggs last summer, Jack had suggested watching the nest boxes all day to find the culprit and ringing its neck, but Dennis came up with an easier solution. He'd asked Mrs Branthwaite for a couple of eggs, made two holes in each, blown out the contents and packed them with mustard. Before leaving them in the hen cabin, he'd tipped all the water out of the water trough and had laughed all afternoon about the fat young pullet he'd seen running to the stream for a drink. The egg eating stopped.

Dennis was fun. Even the way he would hand you the yard brush, then grip it tight as you tried to take it from him, could make you smile. He could brighten up the worst jobs on the farm. Mucking out loose-boxes and cleaning out ditches were games when you were working with Dennis. Bill, however, was becoming concerned. The behaviours he'd been noticing were more akin to the ways of the inmates at the Royal Albert. He'd heard stories from his uncle who managed the farm at the mental hospital. Grown men who hooted and chattered to themselves, or walked around imaginary barriers in the farmyard.

The last batch of ewes to be clipped out were up on the lot so Jack and Bill saddled up the two ponies and rode up the lane with Bill's dog trotting along behind. When they reached the lot, the heifers were crowding round the gate, jostling to get out. A strange bull prowled amongst them, sniffing each one and moving on to the next, lordly advertising his lack of breeding. Bill looked at it from over the wall, its crooked back legs and rough, yellowy hide. Heavy in the shoulders and slack in the back, the beast was a runt, a scrub bull unfit for breeding but left entire, uncastrated. Who in their right mind would breed from an animal like that? The answer came swiftly – "Moss."

Jack tied the ponies to a tree and climbed over the wall into Moss's pasture. Headed over the hill towards the farm. Bill followed, picking his way between gorse and brambles, stepping round bogs.

In Joe Moss's yard there was no one to be seen. The place was silent except for the cooing and croaking of a muddle of hens, scratching in the muck on the midden. A grey muzzled old dog, chained to a broken cartwheel was licking lazily on a long bone with the hoof still attached.

"They're feeding it a dead calf."

Jack looked at it expressionless, leaned towards his son's ear.

"It's not a good idea. It gives 'em worms."

Bill nodded slowly, said nothing. They passed the stable and out into the croft behind the buildings. In the shadow of the far wall Joe Moss, a fat little man was getting to his feet and rapidly shaking blood and mucus from his hand and forearm. Behind him a Herdwick ewe was lying on her side with a lamb's head and feet sticking out under her tail. A sullen looking boy was holding her head. Moss turned to the boy, shouting,

"It's no use. I can't get it. Go and get Bruce. Jump to it, lad. The bluffy sheep's gonna dee!"

Jack prodded his son and was turning to leave but Joe Moss spotted him and came waddling across the grass towards them, his face turning to a smile. He pointed back at the ewe.

"She's been lambin' since this mornin'. She's one of a batch I bought cheap off a dealer. They've been nowt but trouble. Lamb was comin' with its legs back. I've got 'em both but I still can't get it out. John's gone for Bruce. He's fencin' out back."

Jack Branthwaite ignored the talk.

"We've got a bull of yours up on the lot. It's chasin' round my heifers."

Moss's smile retreated. He blanked his face as if he was trying to look innocent.

"I've got a shorthorn bullock up there."

"This is a bull, an' a poor specimen at that. It's definitely not fit to breed off."

Moss looked away, at the ewe and then towards the gate.

"Ah. Here's Bruce. He'll get that lamb out. He's as strong as an ox." The boy was coming back with the farmhand. He was an ox. Dull black hair hung into his eyes. His huge shoulders swayed as he walked and his shirt blew open in the wind. Still carrying a heavy hammer, he said nothing, lumbered over to the ewe, dropped the hammer and gave a grunt. She still hadn't moved. He sat in the dirt behind her, his feet against her rump, grabbed the two tiny legs and pulled, leaning back and screwing his face. The ewe made a weak attempt to lift her head, let out a pleading bleat and gave up. Lowered her head and closed her eyes.

Bill's jaw dropped. His father looked away. Moss was becoming agitated.

"Leave it Bruce! Summat's wrong!" and when the ox kept pulling, "Leave it! Have a rest!"

He seemed to have understood that, let go and sat slumped with his elbows on his knees. Moss turned to Bill. The smile had returned. "I bet you're a handy young lad at lambin' sheep. Get your hand inside that yow and find out what's wrong." He turned and began walking back across the croft.

Bill took a step forward to follow him but his father grabbed his arm, spoke in a low growl.

"Leave it. That yow's a gonner." Then to Moss, raising his voice, "We haven't time to stand about here. We're going to get that bull out of my heifers before it does any more damage." He released Bill's arm and set off back across the yard at a train's pace. Bill followed, struggling to keep up. Moss was shouting.

"Nay! Nay! Jack, you're not gonna make me pay for a vet are you?"

By the time Bill had matched his pace, his father was half way across the front meadow, fists clenched, his eyes fixed on the hill. The adolescent was puzzled. The man spoke, gritting his teeth, still walking: a furious stride.

"They've pulled the shite out of that poor old lass! I reckon she's been on lambin' since last night. She's 'avin' twins. Stupid bastards 'ave got head from one an' forelegs from t'other. Yow'll be dead in an hour. Lambs'll've bin dead all mornin'. If you'd tried to help 'e would've blamed you for 'is disaster." He fell silent for a moment, shook his hands in frustration. "I saw Moss in Carnforth last week. He started tellin' me I shouldn't've bin rollin' on a Sunday. Said it wasn't Christian."

He wheeled round, eyes burning like a stallion's, stabbed a finger in the direction of Moss and the ewe. His voice was a roar. "There's no fuckin' Christianity in that!"

Bill followed his father's back towards the lot, heard him sniff and thought he saw him rubbing his eye.

3

Fine language will not fill a farmer's barn, Neither does truth need any embellishments.

Jethro Tull. The Horse Hoeing Husbandry (1733)

Agnes Branthwaite was not a warm woman. Christened Agnes Celia Patterson, and the only daughter of a naval officer, she started her life in Plymouth. Her mother had dressed her in satins, protected her from the rabble in the port and educated her at home under the charge of a governess by the name of Miss Beet. The young girl was disobedient to her mother, spent her days studying and her evenings reading the works of Dickens. As she grew to womanhood her interest spread to Lawrence. She was never close to her father.

He had spent his whole life in the navy, was promoted to Captain after the battle of the Falklands, and died at Jutland on the thirty-first of May 1916, Agnes's eighteenth birthday. She blamed her mother.

When the Great War ended, Agnes discarded her nurse's uniform and studied to become a teacher. In the summer of 1920 she travelled to north Lancashire to spend a month with her cousin Mabel and Mabel's husband Jack Branthwaite. In Agnes's eyes, Mabel had it all. She had a home in the country, a husband who was there every mealtime and, to cap it all, a baby on the way. Agnes became jealous, concealing it behind smiles and enthusiastic questions about making pasties and Eccles cakes.

She promised to return when the baby was due, and from then on it was understood that Agnes would stay with them every Easter and during the summer holidays.

After Bill was born Mabel had miscarried her next child and it was a full eleven years before she was able to conceive again. Agnes was present when Mary emerged. It had been a difficult birth and Mabel developed septicaemia. Her cousin had sat with her, following the doctor's instructions and working tirelessly round the house.

When Mabel died Agnes broke the news to Jack. Even though his wife was slipping away before him he had never even dreamt that she might die. He was confused, broken, did not know where to turn. Agnes had him in bed before Mabel's body was in the ground.

Mary had called Agnes 'mummy' from the start, but Bill had always felt uneasy around his stepmother. He didn't know what to call her. When his mother had been alive it was easy. He'd called her Aunt Aggie but when he'd seen his aunt with his little sister, he'd become confused. He'd heard Agnes saying 'Come to Mummy," and had wondered how his sister's mother could be his aunt. She definitely wasn't his mother. He'd never felt able to ask anyone about it so he'd spent the years since his mother's death not calling her anything. She seemed to take it as an insult and Bill read her abruptness as dislike or something worse.

His father had a more retiring nature. He would shy away from conflict whenever he could, often bit his lip and left Agnes to her moods. He was not prone to displays of emotion. The outburst in Moss's meadow had been a shock to Bill. It was the first time he'd heard his father swear.

At breakfast, Bill was still smarting from the ear bashing about Moss's ewe. He thought it was aimed at him and felt he was in some way to blame. He'd only stepped forward to help the man out of politeness. He'd been concerned for the ewe and lambs. Perhaps it had been a stupid thing to do.

His father's voice could make him wince, like the sting of a strap on his buttocks or a cane across his knuckles. Directions to do tasks on the farm could become punishments. Comments about the difficulty of a job often felt like chastisement.

"This ditch is takin' longer than I thought," was heard as

a criticism, as if he was being rebuked for working too slowly. At times he found himself wondering which of his misdemeanours he was being punished for when the next manual job was handed out. It came as no surprise to him when he was given an onerous task for the day.

"I want you and Dennis to fence along t'lot side today, one strand o' barb along that wall top. If Moss won't keep that bull at home we'll have to do it."

Bill finished eating and left the house to start loading up the posts, feeling the weight of each one as he threw it in the cart, the sharpness and roughness of the sawn points, his father's voice.

Up on the lot, the air was fresh with the smell of heather and peat. Bill led the horse along the wall side, picking out the driest route. The cart lurched sideways when a wheel hit soft ground and sank halfway up the spokes. Dennis rushed to turn the wheel as Bill tugged at the harness, coaxing the horse for more effort. He looked round to see Dennis splattered with peaty mud. The farmhand was grinning, smearing away the dirt with his sleeve.

"You didn't tell me you were going to bury me here."

"Not until I've drowned you in the stream first."

Dennis's smile vanished for a moment, and Bill realised that he'd been taken literally.

"Don't worry, Dennis. I'm not going to drown you. I was only pullin' yer leg."

They found the crossing place in the stream and helped the horse to heave its load up the other side. The cart was stopped half way along the boundary where the gap between the stream and the wall was wide enough for the wheels to pass safely. Bill strode out the spaces for the posts, five yards apart, and began making holes with a crowbar. The ground was stony. Sometimes he started three different holes for one post before he found a gap between the rocks. Dennis followed behind him, jamming posts hard into the holes, ready to be driven in with the heavy maul. When the cart was empty they returned to the start of the line and took it in turns, one holding the post and the other swinging the twelve-pound hammer. The posts were long. They started them off with both arms outstretched, balancing between the wall and the stream, the hammer held horizontally above their heads. Even for Dennis, who was taller, it was difficult to hit the posts squarely on top. The hammer's head kept landing with a dull thud, splintering the edges. Bill's arms ached, and as he handed the hammer to Dennis he saw him rubbing his biceps before starting on the next post. Dennis took a swing and miss-hit the post, sending chips flying into the grass. A cough erupted from above Bill's head. He looked up to see Moss watching them from the high ground behind the wall.

"Nay, nay. You're mekkin' a right mess o' that. Hit it on top, lad."

Dennis tossed the hammer over the wall.

"Hit it yer fuckin' sel' if yer think yer so bloody clever."

Moss reddened. Glared down at him.

"You watch yer language, lad! I'll be 'avin' a word with yer boss. You'll be out on yer ear at term end if I 'ave my way! Now git on wi' yer work."

Dennis shrank. His face was white. Bill jumped to his defence.

"You've got the bloody 'ammer. You knock it in."

Moss picked it up. Swung easily at the post, its top, level with his belly. The sound rang. He carried on hitting until the post hit hard ground and shuddered. "Theere. That's a' it teks." He stuck his chest out like a fat pigeon. Threw the hammer back. It landed in the stream, its shaft wet and slippy.

Bill, feeling defeat creeping up on him, retorted, "We wouldn't be 'avin' t' do this if you kept that runt of a bull at 'ome."

"I'll 'ave a word wi' your father, lad and 'e'll tek a strap to you if 'e knows 'is business."

When Bill looked up, the piggish face had gone. He stepped on a through-stone, peered over the wall. Moss was trudging away, but not towards his own house.

He climbed back down. Dennis had retrieved the hammer and was wiping the shaft with a wisp of hay from the bottom of the cart. He looked up, quavered as he spoke.

"D'you think 'e'll get me the sack?"

Bill shook his head. Tried to convince himself.

"I don't think so. I'm buggered if I'm doin' all t'muckin' out on me own." He breathed in. "I think I'm gonna cop it though."

Dennis was plodding back towards the wall. He looked as if the hammer had got heavier. Bill stopped him.

"Look. We're half way now. We can stand in t'cart to knock these in."

Dennis looked back along the line of posts. Turned and saw the track between the stream and the wall. He jumped in the cart.

"I'll do the first six. You do the next ten." His smile had returned. He swung the hammer. The ring echoed from the crag to the trees in the valley.

They returned to the farmyard with aching arms. Their triumph at finishing the job was shadowed by fear of what was to come.

Jack Branthwaite was standing by the dairy door. His eyes followed the cart across the yard. Bill climbed down, approached him, didn't speak.

"I hear you've been upsetting Mr Moss." The tone was cold.

A lump in his chest, Bill bit his lip, couldn't look his father in the eye.

"He tells me you've been using foul language, being

disrespectful. He says you should learn some of the scriptures. Honour thy mother and thy father. Respect your elders and betters. What do you have to say for yourself?"

Nothing. He looked up. Aware his eyes were getting moist.

Jack's voice softened.

"Elders and betters. Betters?" He broke into a smile. "I told the flarchy little sod to go home and practice what he preached." He slapped Bill on the shoulder. Winked. "Did you finish the posts?"

Bill nodded, felt relieved and tried to smile.

"You did all right. Go and get some tea."

He felt taller. Went to get Dennis.

4

*Do not mark or brand with tar. It cannot be effectively
removed from wool.*

British Wool Marketing Board. Farmer
and Stock-Breeder Year Book (1955)

Time in the valley was measured by seasons. Seasons were
governed by the weather. In a cold spring the seasons slowed
but in warm weather a week's growth could occur in little more
than a day. The mornings rang with bird song and a night's
warm rain burst the buds in the trees, hedges and gardens. The
woods up the lane towards the lot gained a green tinge
overnight and the best nesting sights were being claimed in
trees, bushes and farm buildings.

Bill stopped halfway across the yard, tilting his head at a
familiar chatter from somewhere high above the farm buildings.

"There!"

Dennis looked up from behind the pigsty wall.

"What?"

Bill had spotted it now and was pointing eastwards towards
the sun.

"A swallow." He dropped his hand and watched it dip and
land on the barn roof. It chattered and sang as its mate
appeared and swooped straight through the barn doorway and
into the rafters.

"They've woken up, then?" Dennis carried the last shovel
of pig muck from the sty and closed the door.

"Woken up?"

"That's right. They've spent all winter in the nooks and
crannies. Swallows is one of the seven sleepers; swallow,
watersnake, frog, hedgehog … ."

Ever since he'd first seen Dennis, he'd noticed that he was
different to everyone else. Bill had been at school for three

months. He'd seen a dark haired boy, older than himself, standing in the school playground, staring at a dead starling that had crashed against the school window. The boy (he said he came from near Hutton Roof) had spent all playtime looking down at the bird. He'd been reluctant to leave it when the head mistress rang the bell, and he sat in silence through arithmetic, his neck crooked towards a damp stain on the glass. A feather, stuck in congealed blood.

In drawing class the boy had drawn a perfect picture of the bird. He'd even made its eye, half-closed, look dead. The teacher was furious. She'd stood him in front of the rest of the class, bellowed at him, at the rest of the kids.

"When I tell you to draw the crucifixion, I expect you to do as you are told." She'd smeared away the drawing from his slate, made him start again. He'd drawn the same bird, identical, as if he'd traced the first one. Every feather, every drop of blood. The bird's wings outstretched. She grabbed him by the collar. Dragged him to her desk, caned his knuckles until his hand swelled.

Miss Taggart later told the class that she had slept badly that night. She'd dreamt she was on a green hill, staring at a dead bird nailed to a cross. She'd seen the symbolism, from a child she thought did not understand, or was just being disobedient. Awoke. Sweating. Crying. It was very dark. What had she done to the boy? She knelt on the rough mat by the bed. Prayed. Pleading for the Lord's forgiveness. Knew she would never find her own.

It had been almost two weeks later when the school inspector's bike squeaked into the schoolyard. Dennis walking in front. Head down like a recaptured slave. Or an escaped wether returned to the slaughterhouse.

Bill remembered seeing him stood before the rest of the school, wincing from the teacher's hand on his shoulder. Miss Taggart's voice, wavering.

"Two weeks ago I did something very bad." She was trying not to cry. "Dennis here, drew a picture of a dead bird, with its wings spread out, like Jesus on the cross. I punished him for it." She crouched by him, looked into his face. "It was the most beautiful picture I have ever seen." She wiped her eyes. "Will you draw us another one? On paper so that we can put it on the wall?"

The boy nodded, still looking at the floor.

She brought him paper, pencils and sat him at his desk. He was allowed to draw when the others were doing maths. When he'd finished, she brought him ink. He sat there, outlining every quill, detailing each exposed fluff, and when it was dry she framed it and hung it in the entrance. The drawing had been there in full view every time he walked into the school. The eye was different. It didn't look real.

Bill fed the pigs. The sow chomped and slobbered at the potato peelings, cabbage stalks and what was left of yesterday's porridge. He tipped in a scoopful of oatmeal and the piglets yelped and ran from the cloud of flour dust. He filled the trough with a bucket of water and went to find Dennis.

He was tilting the barrow against the midden wall. Bill had an idea.

"D'y' fancy comin' down to t' chippy tonight? All t' lads 'll be there. It's sports next Saturday."

Dennis looked away.

"I'm buyin'."

Dennis looked back.

"Thought that 'ud get yer interest. I'll tek it yer comin'."

"I'll think about it." The corners of his mouth twitched.

"Right! Go an' get two sacks. We've got to go an' pick meadows."

They started on the first field, Bill going clockwise and

Dennis, left-handed, going the other way. They picked up sticks. Pushed them into the hedge bottom. Followed round the hedge side, every now and again rolling a stone back onto the bank. Placing them out of the mower's reach, before the grass grew and hid them. Tidying up after the lambs had been moved out.

They met at the top of the field. Each had been watching the other, not wanting him to get ahead, hurrying up if they felt they were behind, slowing down if they were too far in front. It was a game, unstated. No one set the rules. But they both played and always met halfway.

"I saw a duck's nest under that holly tree." Bill was pointing. "Eight eggs. She flew off when I got close. Gave me a start, she did."

Dennis had a better one. "I found that axe you lost when we were hedgin'."

"I thought you lost it."

"It was on your length. Tucked behind a stump."

Bill remembered placing it there. Knew he was beaten. Shrugged.

They set off down the middle of the field, picking up bits of wool, stuffing them in their sacks.

The afternoon's milking was finished in daylight. Bill climbed over the partition in front of the cows and shoved the door open into the barn. It was nearly empty. The hay was almost gone. Only a wedge in one corner was left. Most of it had sweat to a copper brown colour. He grabbed armfuls and carried it to the cows. Shook it in front of them. A huge cloud of dust, fungal spores, erupted from each clump. As he stooped in the barn for another armful he reached for a strand away from the mould. Popped it in his mouth and chewed it. The taste was sweet. Bitter, like burnt sugar. By the time he'd finished feeding the cows, the air was so thick in the shippen that he couldn't see the far wall. The dust filled his nostrils and coated the inside of his mouth, turning the saliva to sludge. He sneezed. Spat out and hoped for a better summer. The cows would sleep outside tomorrow and wouldn't taste hay again until October.

Outside he listened to the evening calls of the birds and breathed in. He loved that feeling. The work was finished but there was plenty of day left. He looked round the yard. The granary door was open. Dennis had gone. He must be in his loft, hurrying to get changed and thinking about his fish and chip supper.

Bill hurried into the house, brushed past his stepmother without speaking. He stripped to the waist at the kitchen sink and washed himself with carbolic soap, grabbed the towel from the back of the door and went to change his clothes.

When he opened the back door, Dennis was waiting. Shifting from one foot to the other. As the door opened, he turned away quickly. Looked towards the garden and into the sky.

Bill suppressed a smile. "Are you ready?"

"Oh, er yeah. I thought I might as well come ... . If it's all right."

"Yeah. It's all right. Come on. Let's get there before t' rush." He smiled. Set off across the garden, vaulted the wall, Dennis hurrying to keep up.

On nights like this, Bill felt free. There were no cows calving, no sheep lambing and hay time was two months away. Usually he would be on his bike. Trousers clipped tightly to his shins. His best coat folded behind the saddle and his mind on the dance or whist drive in the next village. Sometimes he rode all the way to Kirkby Lonsdale or Caton. He stayed away from Carnforth. The railway workers were a different breed and could be relied upon to be brawling after the pubs shut. He'd heard tales of farm lads cycling into the middle of a brawl and being set upon by a mob in the dark streets. Town drunkards soon forgot their differences when faced by a lone outsider.

Tonight Bill was walking. Dennis didn't have a bike and he wasn't safe riding pillion so they strode towards the village, their low shoes crunching on the limestone road. Dennis was beside him, almost walking sideways, chattering.

"'Ave you got yer money?"

"Yes Dennis." He smiled at Dennis's concern.

"Enough for chips?"

"Yes, Dennis."

"Enough for two of us?"

"Yes, Dennis." He allowed himself a low laugh. "Enough for fish, chips, tea and bread and butter … for two of us."

"I … I don't mind. I'll just have chips … if you 'aven't enough."

Bill stopped. "You can 'ave the same as me. Dad gave me the money."

"Well, that's right good of 'im. I'll remember t' thank 'im in t' mornin', I will."

They crossed the humped bridge over the beck. Dennis stopped, peering down into the water. Bill paused.

"What're y' lookin' at?"

"That watter comes all t' way down off t' lot. Doesn't it?"

"Yes. Most of it."

"I bet there's trout in there." He was rolling up his sleeves.

"Another night, Dennis. Mrs Dobson's got fresh plaice, from Morecambe."

"Aye … . Another night." Nodding. "Fresh plaice, y' say? From Morecambe."

They rounded the corner to the first row of cottages. The door of the end one was open and a temporary sign stood outside on the pavement. Bill strode in and Dennis crept behind him. Eyes wide, staring at the ceiling and whitewashed walls, gripping his cap with both hands. Annie Dobson, a middle aged woman was squeezed between the counter and a cast iron stove. She liked chips.

"Hello, boys. What can I get you?"

Bill was at the counter.

"Fish, chips, tea and bread and butter, twice please."

Dennis pressed against his shoulder.

"Fresh plaice ... from Morecambe."

She smiled. "Aye, it is that. Bobby brought it on train this afternoon." She turned. Shook the basket in the chip pan. "I've just got started. Take a seat. I hope you don't mind waitin' a minute."

Dennis sat at the nearest table. Shook his head. "No. No, missus. Don't mind waitin'."

Three farm hands from the next village walked in, nodded across the counter, muttered a greeting to Bill and sat in the corner.

"I'll be with you lads in a minute." She was bustling. "You boys an' yer appetites. I can hardly keep up."

Bill listened. She said that every night. It was good for business.

Footsteps in the doorway made them look up. Tom Waterford had just stepped through the open door. Bill budged up to let him sit down and asked him if he was going to the sports.

"I wouldn't miss it. Someone's got to give you a bit o' competition."

They talked about runners and who might be there next Saturday. Chatted about cows and sheep. Tom's dad had finished rolling his meadows already.

Dennis peered round at the room full of faces, twitched.

"Don't mind waitin'. Nowt wrong wi' waitin'."

Annie Dobson seemed to sense his discomfort.

"How's yer mother, Dennis?" She handed him his plate.

"Thank you, missus. She's champion. Right champion."

Annie was passing a plate to Bill.

"I'm glad to hear that. I haven't seen her in a long time. Careful Dennis. Those chips are hot." She turned to get the bread and tea. As her back was turned Bruce from Moss's farm pushed into the shop, grabbed a handful of chips from Dennis's plate and stuffed them in his mouth. Dennis looked up, wounded. Annie Dobson turned and the bully tried to swallow. His eyes widened and he made a low groaning sound. She spun towards him, pointing the butter knife.

"I saw that!" Saw him clutching his throat. "Serves y' right." She faced him, eyes like stone. She was scared of no one. "Now tek' yer bullyin' ways 'n wait outside. I'll tell y' when y' can come in."

He wilted, turned and left.

Annie reached for the chip basket and tipped some onto Dennis's plate.

"Here,'ave a few more. You look like y' could use 'em."

He dug in and mumbled a thankyou through a mouthful of fish.

✛

The village sports had been held on the same day in the same field for longer than anyone chose to remember. On Saturday morning Bill set off for the cows in daylight. For a week now, he'd been opening the yard gate and the shippen door, then, instead of going through the paddock, he'd run out onto the road, up the lane and full length of the lot before descending through Moss's lot and front pasture, back onto the road and vaulting the fence into the top of the park; a round trip of two and a half miles. This morning he took the easier route, allowing himself a quiet jog to the top of the park. He wasn't tiring himself or risking a sprain. He wanted to win and knew that Tom Waterford would have been training. He'd likely run a couple of miles before going to the chip shop last Friday.

Bill would only enter the cross-country race. It was open

to all comers. Unlike many of the sack races, potato races and egg-and-spoon races, which were for locals only. He'd long since grown out of these. He had no passion for Cumberland wrestling. Bruce Crabtree had dominated that competition since he was twelve. He was a big fish in a pondful of minnows, never wrestled anywhere else but made sure the whole district knew he was champion at Sandholme. It was a 'locals only' competition. Sometimes there were only five entries; sometimes fewer. It often ended up with Bruce wrestling against the latest stable lad at Friar's Hall. They saw it as a kind of initiation. Get mauled by Bruce and then you were one of the lads. He never congratulated his opponents. They were usually half his weight and had to be either extremely brave or a bit stupid to step into the ring with him. He was big, ugly and strong enough to beat any of his contenders without hurting them, although it was well-known in the village that he usually did. Bill, like many of the other locals, really wanted to see Bruce get a pasting, but knew he wasn't the man to do it and concentrated on his running.

When he returned to the yard with the cows, his dad was waiting.

"I hope you haven't been racin' the cows on yer early mornin' jaunts."

Bill's cheeks burned. He didn't think anyone knew he'd been training.

"I'm only messin', son. I know y've more sense than that. Did Moss see ya, runnin' through his cow pasture?"

"No. I was up too early."

His father laughed.

Bill frowned. "There's one thing I was wonderin' tho'. Why 'ave all Moss's cows got a bare patch across their shoulders?"

"Hen shit!"

"What?" Bill was puzzled.

"He lets 'em roost on t' beams above 'is cows. Shit drops

in a line onto 'em, an' the ammonia in it burns their hides."

Bill tugged at his collar. Felt a prickle on the back of his neck. He finished the milking, ate breakfast and took the pony to check the stock.

When one o'clock came Bill was already on the sports field. The cows in Charlie Taylor's flat pasture had been moved out for the day and two rows of benches from the village hall had been placed about ten yards apart. A cotton rope, the finishing line, was laid on the ground, joining the ends of the two rows. The village's two cars were parked behind the benches and a group of small boys were peering through the windows. Bill heard them arguing.

"That's the brake."

"No, that's the gear lever."

Another one piped in "Where's the starting handle?"

"On the front. Don't you know anything?"

He left them to their disputes and wandered through the gathering crowd. A table had been set up in the barn doorway. Annie Dobson and Mrs Taylor were laying out chicken and ham sandwiches. Miss Taggart was fussing around and trying to help. Bill heard Mrs Taylor's voice, inquiring.

" Did I hear Mr Finch asking for someone to judge the baby show?"

The teacher's head turned.

"Oh? I wanted to see Mr Finch myself." She scurried off towards the crowd by the benches. Annie Dobson winked. Mrs Taylor's eyes creased. She put her hand over her mouth and turned towards her basket, shoulders shaking.

Bill went in search of Tom, spotted his rival standing by a huddle of men with dogs. He could hear raised protests from the men.

"Fair do's. Fair do's."

"Mek lads run later."

The silver grey head of Mr Finch the postmaster was

bobbing in the middle. As Bill approached he could see the little man holding up his hands and backing away then nodding and taking out his pencil and notebook. Tom beckoned him across.

"They're holding t' hound trail before t' cross country. Seems like our race messed up their scent trail last year."

Bill raised his eyebrows. "I don't suppose it'll make any difference to us." He glanced over to where the houndsters had retreated behind a hay cart. They were smiling now and swapping bundles of folded white paper. Tom flicked his head in the direction of the group.

"Looks like there's a lot o' money at stake. Don't tell Mr Finch or 'e'll 'ave a seizure."

The school bell rang. Norman Watterson had commandeered it for the afternoon. Miss Taggart was hovering at his shoulder, pleading with him not to ring it so violently. He wafted her away with his free hand as if she was a troublesome bee. He rang it again, more vigorously, and addressed the crowd. He was a Cumberland man.

"Ladies an' gentlemen! Boys an' garls! Welcome t' this years spooarts. We'll start wi' th' baby show. It'll be judged this year by Mrs Moss."

A scruffy looking woman standing by the table of sandwiches began to bundle herself across the field. One of the benches by the finishing line had been cleared. Six women and their offspring were settling onto them. Three of them were in traditional black dresses and bonnets. The babies shuffled in their lace bonnets and shawls. Mrs Moss paraded up and down the line. Touched her chin. Tom leaned to Bill's ear.

"That one on t' end 'll win."

"Never!" Bill looked at him and back at the burly woman with the pug faced toddler. Norman Watterson bellowed out.

"And the prize goes to ... Mrs Boon and Jonty!"

"Told you." Tom looked sideways and whispered. "She's

Mrs Moss's cousin."

The other mothers on the bench exchanged glances as Mrs Boon received her prize card. The crowd began to murmur. It was drowned out by the ringing of the bell and the announcement of the first race. The two friends watched as kids of all shapes and sizes raced in sacks, with legs tied in the three-legged race, or running backwards and forwards picking up potatoes. They cheered on Mary as she shuffled along cautiously watching her pot egg in a spoon. She was near the back when the two leaders dropped their eggs and were sent back to the beginning. One girl stepped in a cow pat and stopped to wipe her shoe. Another two bumped into each other and exchanged scowls as they trudged back to the start. Mary finished third and came running over to them waving her card. She didn't wait to be congratulated but turned towards Mr Finch to collect her prize money.

Bill surveyed the field.

"Where's Charlie Taylor?"

"Up on 'is lot." Tom pointed to the skyline to where a lone figure was jogging back towards the village, dragging a sack on a string. "Layin' a scent trail. 'Ave you smelled that stuff? It stinks."

The bell half rang and the two friends looked towards Norman Watterson who was fumbling on the ground for the ringer. Miss Taggart was flapping behind him. He stood up, waving the object and bawled out the start of the hound trail then finished off with, "Open Event."

The strangers and their dogs lined up at the start. The dogs sniffed the ground. Tongues lolled. Collars strained. The hounds bayed and pulled. Watterson's arm dropped, and they ran across the sports field to the wall in the far corner, over in a pack and round the back of the woods. The crowd fell silent as they waited for them to appear on the hillside, the clamour of cries and growls echoing through the trees. People rose from their seats as the first one was spotted, tearing across the long meadow, a streak of black and tan. Two more, one buff and one white, at least five lengths behind, gaining. Then the main pack and the stragglers as the leader bounded over and into the lane to the lot. It disappeared behind a thorn bush and appeared beyond the stream, dripping. The buff next, the white a yard behind. Men shouted, cheered. Eyes met and looked back to the skyline as dogs charged along the ridge, a weaving, snaking line of shadows. The first dog turned, still the black and tan. A man with a tin of meat stepped out of the gang by the line. The dog leapt from the heather onto the wall. It was back on green fields. Its pace quickened. The man with the tin was bent double bashing his forearms on his knees. Tom's eyes shone.

"This should be fun ... . Charlie's not back yet."

Bill's head jerked, his gaze focussed towards the end of the field. A heavy bloke burst through the hedge. Legs splaying. He splashed through the beck, dogs gaining. Voices were booming.

"Fleet! Fleet!"

"Buster! Buster!"

Kids screamed.

"CHAR-LEE! CHAR-LEE!"

Dogs tore down the hill, gaining. The man stumbled, got up, running, puffing, his forehead gleaming. Knees pumping, fists driving, the sack bouncing behind. His teeth gritted. He looked back, saw dogs, panicked. Dogs gaining. Dog men roared. Kids yelled. Youths laughed, howled. Twenty yards to go. Dogs exploding through the hedge, leaders almost on him. He ran, gasping, lead dog tugging at the sack. He yanked it away, dived for the line. Dogs piled in. Men cursed. Grabbed collars, hide, tails. The crowd cheered. Bill folded on the grass, laughing, shaking and clutching his guts but couldn't stop the pain.

"Oh God! Oh God!" and laughed till he was weak.

By the time Bill had regained his strength, most of the hounds had been led away, either into carts or the boots of cars. A group of men and dogs were heading towards the village and the station. Mr Finch and Norman Watterson were having a discussion about the cross-country race. Norman was waving his arms and pointing to two men wandering towards the lot. Mr Finch nodded and Miss Taggart, who was standing close by, rang the bell. It made a rapid tingling sound. Norman Watterson frowned at her and boomed out,

"After talking' it ower wi' Mr Finch we've decided ter delay fell race 'alf an hour an' brek fer tea. Yan o' them 'oonds is missin' an' we've given 'em chance ter gan an' find it."

Tom was grinning.

"Looks like y've got a reprieve fer a while. Are y' comin' fer some tea?" He headed towards the barn. Bill followed and joined him at the head of the queue.

"Just a tea, please." Tom took a mug from Annie Dobson and began spooning sugar into it. When Bill asked for tea, Tom handed him a plate and piled on sandwiches and pork pies. "Here. You're goin' t' need this."

Bill protested, but Tom continued stacking the plate with cakes. "Come on Bill. Lost yer appetite?"

Bill shook his head, and left the plate at the end of the table. He was making his way towards the benches by the finishing line when his father stopped him, handed him a parcel wrapped in brown paper.

"I've bin savin' these fer yer birthday, but y' might as well 'ave 'em now."

Bill put his mug down in the grass and folded back the paper. Stared at the shiny brown leather.

"Runnin' shoes!" Looked at his father. "Thanks, Dad." He carried them under his arm and sat on the end of the bench. Untied his bootlaces. Kicked his boots under the bench and slipped on the shoes. They felt light. He walked up and down. Tried to make the leather creak. It was soft.

"Yer'll need more than fancy shoes t' beat me." Tom's head was on one side, staring at the shoes. He looked up. There was no envy in his voice. "D' they feel all right?"

Bill nodded. "Grand."

"Stop pacin' about in 'em an' drink yer tea." Tom was watching the other young men who were beginning to gather near the starting line. "Usual crowd. We'll leave that lot standin' before we get to that first stile." He went silent for a moment. Then asked, "Who's that?"

A dark haired boy, about their own age was removing his trousers to reveal running shorts.

Bill watched him.

"That's the lad from Friar's Hall. Goes to grammar school. He could be good."

Tom was scornful.

"Nah! Legs like a sparrow. He'll be leadin' till we start climbin' an' he'll run out o' steam. He won't give us any trouble."

Bill nudged his shoulder.

"This one might tho'."

A tall young man was striding across towards the start. His tanned shoulders rippled as he walked. A sleeveless vest clung tight across his chest. He wore baggy trousers cuffed at the bottom, and his battered running shoes spoke of experience and triumph. He dropped his bag by the benches and turned his head towards the hill, looked at no one and strolled off towards the start.

Bill's voice dropped. "New shepherd at Leck. They say he won at Grasmere last year."

Tom was pulling at his sleeve.

"C'mon. Time t' find out how good he is."

They reached the start as the race was being announced.

Norman Watterson gave them a short talk about rules and the course of the race. He pointed to the postmaster, who was leaning on the bonnet of his car with a telescope.

"We'll be watchin' all of yer. We've got stewards at a' t' blind spots an' thu's a white paint mark on every stile. Are ye ready?"

They stepped up to the line, about twenty of them, mostly farm boys in shirts and trousers, one grammar school boy in white shorts and top.

"On your marks."

They tensed. The grammar school boy crouched like a sprinter.

"Get set."

They breathed in. The boy in shorts stuck his backside in the air.

"Go!" Watterson dropped his arm.

They ran. The toff in shorts took the lead. Bill tucked in behind Tom and the fell runner. The toff vaulted the first stile. Then the stranger, Tom and Bill. A steward directed them round the edge of the field. Half-way along the second wall, Bill glanced across. One of the lads from the chip shop was cutting the corner. He slowed as he sank knee deep in a bog. Bill followed in Tom's tracks as he raced along the narrow strip of dry ground. The toff was ten yards in front. The fell runner a few strides behind, climbing over the next stile and doubling back towards the lane. As Bill approached it, he saw black hair, bobbing along the other side of the wall. He pushed himself on. Almost stepped on Tom's heel. Followed him over the wall and back along to the lane towards the lot. He ran, shoulder to shoulder with Tom up the lane, and felt energy surge into his chest – his second wind. He increased his stride and gained on the shepherd, opened a gap between himself and Tom. They crashed through the beck and the gap in the wall. Running up through the heather. Gaining on the toff, pushing towards the

50

summit. The toff was cracking. Bill drove on, a stride behind the shepherd. They passed the toff, ten yards from the top. He was bent double, retching.

Bill pushed, picked his way along the sheep track, watching the fell runner's feet. He dodged stones, holes in the peat and turned by the marker post, down hill and into the wind. Tucked behind the leader. He didn't look back, waited for his chance, feeling the stones through his shoes, hearing the shouts from the sports field in the valley. He kept pushing himself. Leg muscles feeling hot. Over the wall and into the steep meadow, alongside the fell runner. Show him you're still there, still confident. It felt good. He was first to the hedge and over the stile. Leapt from the bank to the stream, heard a splash to his left, a hound in front of him, against his knees. He fell over it and hit his head on the bank as the fell runner dodged the dog and sprang back onto the bank towards the finish line. Bill shook his head, tried to get up. Stupid hound was licking his face. He swiped it across the muzzle and it ran back behind a thorn bush. He pushed against the bank but couldn't get up.

A fist grabbed his collar.

Tom's voice: "Come on. Don't let those buggers catch you."

Bill turned and saw runners approaching the hedge. Tom yanked him to his feet, not stopping, and dragged him from the stream, Bill stumbling up the bank. Tom running, still gripping his collar, hauled him to the finish line half a stride in front of the next runner, the crowd clapping them home.

"And second prize goes jointly to Mr Tom Waterford and Mr Bill Branthwaite!"

Bill slumped on a bench. Saw red blotches, felt sick. An arm reached out and shook his hand. The fell runner.

"Hard luck, mate. You gave me a good run. See you again sometime." He turned away, picked up his bag, took an envelope from Mr Finch's outstretched hand and headed towards the village and his train.

Bill breathed out and rubbed his head. Tom was walking towards him with two beakers of lemonade.

"Never mind. Could o' bin worse. They'll shoot that daft 'ound when they get it 'ome."

He looked back towards the stream and saw a boy in shorts clutching his side, a woman rushing to meet him.

✣

There was too much work to be done on the farm to allow Bill to brood. The memory of sports day soon faded when there were turnips and mangels to sow. The potatoes were growing through the tops of the ridges and his father set him off stitching up the rows. They hitched the horse to the stitching plough and Bill followed up the rows of green shoots. His arms began to ache from gripping the shafts as the plough pushed more soil up against the furrows. It was good training. He would do all the ploughing next year.

Jack returned after midday with a basket and a can of tea. They sat on the bank, resting their backs against a rail fence. Jack poured the tea. Handed his son a mug. Bill had noticed that his father was more at ease each spring when the rent had been paid but lately he seemed troubled.

"D' y' think y'll be up to a lot o' ploughin' next year?"

Bill looked at him. He already knew it would be his responsibility.

His father continued. "If this war comes, we'll have to plough a lot more."

"You think so?"

"I know so. We had to do it last time. I can't see this Hitler bloke lettin' grain come from Canada an' America if we're fightin' Germany."

"You think there will be a war?"

The older man looked at the ground, brushed off his cap and ran his fingers through his hair.

"I hope not. Can't see any other option tho'. It's all gloom in t' papers." He knocked back his tea and paced to the corner of the field, pointed to the bare soil. "Ridge this bit up when you've finished. We'll put veggies in on Saturday. Whatever happens in this world, we'll still need to eat."

Bill stood up and stretched. He looked at the rest of the potato field. It seemed bigger than the whole field had looked this morning. The worst thing about stopping for a rest was that it always seemed harder to start again. His boots felt heavy, his arms limp. He knew he would need to keep going to be finished in time for milking. The weariness in his limbs seemed to spread right through him. Thoughts of war and death began rising up from the trenched soil.

His father never spoke about the last war. The only time he'd asked him about it the answer had been short, blunt.

"They lied to us."

The old men at the club in the village hall spoke about the trenches; stinking and wet where men developed foot rot like sheep. Some would tell you everything. Some locked it away. Bobby Dobson had told him about how, at seventeen, he'd been sent to pick up bodies that had been lying in no man's land for three months. He and the corporal had gone to lift the first one into a cart. It was empty, light like a wicker basket, with just a covering of skin and uniform. And under the ribcage, a rat's nest, a whole family of them, huge bloated fat ones eating their way through the corpse. There'd been hundreds of bodies, all the same, thousands of rats in litters of ten and twelve. It was a far cry from the tales of glory in those books he'd won at Sunday school.

When he'd left the chip shop last Friday, Bill had heard Bruce talking to a group of girls in the street. He'd been saying that he hoped there would be a war. He wanted to join up and kill some Germans. Alice Taylor had shut him up.

"It's to be hoped they don't have hot chips and butter knives."

Bill thought about the people he knew who'd fought the Germans. There was the butcher with one arm, the man who came in the club and wheezed each time he laughed; blamed it on the gas. And there was the tramp who wandered around the market place chattering to everyone until they walked away. How would Bruce end up?

5

*The lamb, the calf, the colt, are far safer playmates than
the city urchin precociously wise in evil ways.*

Isaac Phillips Roberts. The Farmstead (1900)

The Barrow streets down towards the docks were lined with
uniform brick terraced houses. They all had a backyard,
outhouse and could boast being only five minutes walk from
the sea. They were dwarfed by shipyard cranes and the corn
warehouse on the dock. The people there were a whole
community dependent upon shipbuilding for their income.

Since the Great War they had known lean times. As many
as forty per cent of the shipyard workers had been unemployed.
Many had travelled to Coventry to find work, including Lucy's
father and her uncle. Her uncle had stayed, found a house and
settled there with his family, but when Lucy's mother became
ill her father had returned to care for her. He knew that job
prospects would be just as bad as when he left and that he
could probably have provided better for her in Coventry, but
it was as if he guessed right away that she was dying. He wanted
his wife to end her days surrounded by the people and places
she knew. He had even arranged for several trips in a motor
car up to Furness Abbey, where they spent their courting days.
He was a devoted father and, if it could be so, an even more
devoted husband, which meant that although she was
terminally ill they had spent many good times together in the
last years of her life.

A sympathetic foreman had found him work, probably at
the risk of his own job, but Barrow people were a community
and would look after each other as best they could, even and
especially when times were hard.

Alan's devotion meant that his own family had been split
up and Lucy hardly knew her cousin Mary whom she had

resembled so much as a small child. She had never seen Mary's brother William. He had been born in Coventry and knew nothing about life beside the shipyards. He would grow up a Coventry boy, with that funny accent that Lucy's dad used to imitate and make Lucy and her mother laugh.

They did laugh, many times, even during the hardest weeks towards the end. Alan only checked himself when laughter worsened the terrible pain his wife was going through. He loved her, loved her dearly like no one else would understand, and when she drew her last breath it broke his heart and the laughter stopped.

Lucy seemed lost after her mother's death. Staying in and caring for her meant that she had lost touch with people of her own age. She rarely ventured out of the house, leaving only to do the shopping or visit her mother's grave. Occasionally she would walk across the bridge to Walney Island and wander along the beach, a solitary figure blown by the wind and sprayed with salt water that tainted the grass on the shoreline. Her father became worried about her. It was this concern for Lucy that finally brought him out of his grief for his wife. He had been so buried in his own feelings that he had failed to notice the change in his daughter until it was commented on by one of his friends.

One day at the shipyard, Bob, Alan's work mate, had been telling him about his day's fishing on the island.

"Was that your Lucy I saw on the beach on Walney?"

"Er, I don't know. When?"

"Sunday. She must've been up early, looked like she was walking right round the island. I just said, 'Hello, is it Lucy?' an' she turned an' ran like a frightened rabbit. Poor lass still missin' her mum?"

"I guess so."

"I hope you don't mind me sayin' Alan, but she needs a change. It's not good for a young un' like that bein' all on her own. Fetch 'er round to our house one Sunday. My missus is good at talkin' to folk. She'll bring 'er out a bit."

"You think so?"

"It can't do any harm, Alan. She needs a motherly type. Someone she can talk to."

Alan knew that Bob was right. He had been focussed for so long on the suffering of one woman who was no longer in pain that his dulled senses had omitted to tell him that there might be a more immediate problem, one that was still here.

Realising that Alan would not suggest a time to come round, would not want to impose, Bob's simple, practical solution was drawn from generations of families who had read nothing of psychology but could sense the direction of someone else's thoughts by the hunch of their shoulders or a certain outlet of breath. The remedies too, were simple: a well timed joke in a pub; a hand on a shoulder in the workshop; or an offer to help move furniture, accompanied by cheerful whistling or questions about how the vegetables were growing. The knowledge came not from books or lectures but was learned by mimicry and unconscious absorption until it became woven into the fabric of shipyard workers and their families as tightly as the history of the town itself. They breathed it in the same way as they breathed the salty air off the Irish Sea.

"Send her round tonight. I've got some fish you can have fer tea."

✣

Lucy went along to Bob's house, picking her way through the streets like a mouse that had found itself far away from its own safe domain. She had lost the habit of talking to people, did not know what she was going to say. She knocked on the door, too softly at first, not wanting to disturb anyone when the whole object of knocking was to attract someone's attention. There was no reply, so she knocked a little louder and was about to knock a third time when Ruth opened the door, to be greeted by the knuckles of Lucy's raised hand. Lucy lowered her hand quickly and cradled it in the other as if she was trying to hide it.

"Sorry."

"You must be Lucy."

"I've come for the fish."

"Come on in. I've just put the kettle on." Ruth knew that Lucy would not refuse, even though the thought of sitting talking to anyone would be daunting to a girl who had turned inward and was attempting to shut out the outside world. She guided Lucy towards the sitting room and pointed to the settee.

Lucy sat, gazing towards the fire, with her hands clasped between her knees. Her face was drained grey and her eyes, although open, seemed to be focussed on something that was inside her head and not in the room. Ruth turned towards the kitchen, noticed how Lucy jumped at the sudden movement, and took a deep breath before returning with a tray of scones and fruitcake.

"Here we are. You look cold, dear. I'll just stoke this fire a bit." She prodded at the coals with a poker, disappeared into the kitchen and came back carrying a teapot and some cups.

When the tea was poured, Lucy drank politely and took a slice of cake, still staring at the fire, avoiding meeting Ruth's eyes. The girl was afraid to speak, only uttering "Thank you," each time she was handed something, and chewing the cake slowly, almost disinterestedly, which less patient women might have taken for bad manners.

"I've been looking through some drawers in the sideboard. Perhaps you would like to have a look at these." Ruth brought out three boxes, each filled with tissue paper. "My father brought these things back from his time at sea." She parted the tissue paper and lifted out a piece of bright red rock, which Lucy only glanced at without moving her head. "This is coral.

It grows in the sea in Australia." Ruth placed it in Lucy's hand and Lucy's gaze scarcely moved, but her fingers absently began to explore the texture as she passed it from one hand to the other.

"This is another piece." This one was white and branched like twigs. She placed it in Lucy's empty hand, and the girl turned to look at it and then to the piece in her other hand, her eyes widening as if she had just noticed the colour of the thing she had been turning over with her fingers. Something behind that vacant stare was beginning to unlock.

Ruth placed her hand into the bottom of the box. "Have you ever seen a boomerang before?" she asked, producing the dark wooden object. Lucy placed the coral on the table and ran her fingers over the boomerang's carved surface, noticing the fine cut marks.

"Does it really come back?"

"I've never dared to throw it in case it broke." Lucy stiffened slightly and quickly handed it back.

"Let's have a look in this one," said Ruth, distracting Lucy once again. She lifted the next box onto her knee and brought out a large, olive green egg.

"What's that?" asked Lucy in amazement.

"That's an emu's egg."

"It's very light."

"That's because it's had the insides blown out through that hole. This one's heavier." The next egg was larger and almost round. It was completely white and felt like porcelain. "This is an ostrich egg from Africa."

"Did you see all those places?"

"No. But my father told me all about them."

She noticed something in the bottom of the box. "Oh, I'd forgotten about this. It's made of ivory from the tusk of an elephant." She held out a tiny white angel. It had a loop attached and was fastened to a leather bootlace. "You can have this if you like."

"Really?" asked Lucy.

"Yes, keep it. My boys won't want it." She placed it round Lucy's neck and fastened the clip at the back. "It's supposed to bring you luck. I'm not superstitious myself, but it is nice."

"Thank you very much. It's beautiful."

Ruth picked up the third box. The contents of this one seemed more ordinary to Lucy. It contained a horseshoe and some brightly coloured pebbles.

"Where did you get these?" Lucy asked.

"I collected them when I worked on a farm. I went to the hirings in Ulverston when I was fifteen. I liked the life but most of them didn't. It all depended on what type of family you ended up with. Some were kind, and some were cruel. I worked there for one term, and came back when the war started and there was plenty of work in Barrow."

"Why did you come back?"

"It was home. You only stayed if you married a farm lad. I came back here and met Bob. We got married during the war, and when he came back he got a job at the shipyard and here we stayed."

Lucy looked at the clock on the mantelpiece and breathed in sharply. "I've got to go. I need to get Dad's tea ready." Ruth brought her the two fish that she had come to collect and followed her to the door.

"Come and see me again next week. You can help me stitch up a rug I've been making."

"Er, okay." She was fumbling with the door handle, opening the door just wide enough for her to squeeze through. She glanced up at Ruth and gave her a smile that was more like a grimace. "Bye."

During the following weeks her visits to see Ruth became a regular occurrence. They completed the rug, baked cakes and planted sweet peas in a trough in the back yard. Lucy began asking more questions. How did Ruth make the swirling patterns on the walls in the house? Where did she get the porcelain figure on the mantelpiece? But the one topic that crept into their conversations more and more was about life outside Barrow. Had Ruth been to London, Paris or America? Each answer, though negative, was carefully presented so that Lucy's interest was fuelled rather than quelled. London, with its palaces, parks and museums was just a train ride away. Paris was a place of beauty, and Mrs Roberts who ran the haberdashery shop had two sons in America, both with families and their own businesses. It was becoming evident that the emptiness inside Lucy was being replaced by an appetite for learning and travel. Ruth knew that, in the same way as it could be harmful to present a starving man with a banquet, Lucy's fledgling curiosity would not be best served by sending her on a tour of Europe or to stay with strangers across the Atlantic.

6

Such is the weight of the lower classes in the great scale of national importance, that a traveller can never give too much attention to every circumstance that concerns them; their welfare forms the broad basis of public prosperity; it is they that feed, cloath, enrich and fight the battles of all the other ranks of a community

Arthur Young. A Tour in Ireland (1780)

The sun was already high in the sky as Peter Smith the postman cycled past the garage. Although it was still only May he was stripped to his shirt sleeves, and sweat had soaked a long dark stain down the centre of his back. His hair was sticking to his forehead under the peak of his cap, and his hands were blackened, revealing that he had been handling more than the morning's invoices, parcels and correspondence. He heard a loud metallic thump from a barrel standing beside the wooden workshop.

"It's warmin' up." The voice came from the shadows inside the garage.

Peter brought the bike to a stop and squinted into the shed.

"I said it's warmin' up. That barrel alus meks that noise when t' sun warms it." Vince the mechanic appeared in the doorway wiping oil from his hands and arms. "Yer must be late."

The postman drew his arm across his brow.

"I had a puncture about two miles back. I wanted to be finished before it got too hot but I've no chance now. I'm too late to be early so I'm not going to try." He leaned his bike against the barrel and handed the mechanic a letter. "They say Mr Churchill wants us to sign a treaty with the Russians."

"Better them than the bloody krauts. Sooner or later some bugger's gonna have to stop 'em." The mechanic took a cigarette from a smeared packet in his pocket and lit one.

"You think so?"

"It was just t' same last time. I wouldn't trust 'em wi' nowt. Chamberlin should've wiped 'is arse wi' that bit o' paper they gave 'im."

The postman blushed.

"I think it's time I was getting on." He stepped onto one pedal of his bike and freewheeled round the corner to the post office. The door was open and Mrs Finch was sweeping the step.

"We thought you'd got lost. I'll go and put kettle on. Looks like you're roasting. A puncture, did I hear you say?" She missed nothing. "I've got some of your favourite cake. Come into the kitchen. He's gone into town for some new glasses." She hurried past the counter, checked herself in the mirror and pulled out a chair. Peter sat down and dropped his bag by his feet. He winced as she handed him a cup and saucer, leaning a bit closer to him than he would have liked. He handed her the mail and held out an envelope for her to read the address.

"It says Friar's Farm, but the name on it says Robinson."

"There's no Robinsons at Friar's farm. I've been here for nine years and Branthwaites have been there as long as I can remember. Is there anyone staying with them?"

"I don't think so." The postman guessed that if Mrs Finch didn't know then there probably wasn't. He drank his tea, stuffed down his cake and retreated to the safety of the street. He would stay a bit longer tomorrow when Mr Finch was at home.

It was almost noon when he handed the letter to Agnes Branthwaite and paused on the step expecting an explanation. She took it, thanked him and closed the door.

When Jack came in for lunch the envelope was on the table, unopened.

"Someone's out o' touch. It's nineteen years since Robinsons left an' Mrs Robinson's been dead for five years." He picked up the letter, turned it over and put it back down.

"Have they any family?"

"Not that I know of. Postmark says Barrow in Furness. I bet it's from some lad who worked here. They used to hire at Ulverston. What d' you think we should do with it?"

She picked it up and tore at the seal.

"Hey! Y' can't do that. It's not addressed to you."

"I just did." She was unfolding the letter, scanning down the page and holding it out for him to read. Jack gripped it with both hands and read:

> 29 Michaelson Street
> Barrow in Furness
> Lancashire

> Dear Mrs Robinson,

> I hope you are keeping well. This letter may come as a surprise to you as I have not been in touch for such a long time. I recently found your address in the bottom of a drawer and it reminded me of the happy times I spent as a maid in your household. I am writing to ask if you require anyone to work for you. I know a young girl who is eighteen and would benefit from some time away from home. She is a quiet, hard-working girl who has recently lost her mother. Her name is Lucy Rogan. I would be very grateful if you were able to offer her a position.

> Yours Sincerely
> Ruth Matterson (Hawthorn)

Jack scratched his head.

"What d' you think o' that?"

Agnes's reply was swift. "I think it's time we got a maid. You always had one before Mabel died. I can't go on as I am.

What would happen if I was ill?"

"But she'll know you've opened the letter."

"That letter was sent to the woman of the house at Friar's Farm and that's me. I'll explain that Mrs Robinson has passed away and we now live here. If I say that we're able to take the girl, I'm sure that this Ruth Mackieson or whatever she's called will see that we're doing her a favour."

Two weeks after Agnes had written her reply, a girl stepped cautiously onto the platform at Sandholme station. Her woollen coat was too thick and hot for July and the case handle was growing sticky in her hand. She had ridden all the way from Barrow with the case on her knees, keeping an eye on the sea whenever it appeared and searching for it as it hid behind a hill or clump of trees. It was as if the bay was a friend she was leaving behind, or a last thread that connected her to home. She hadn't seen a glimpse of it since before she changed trains at Carnforth station and here nothing was familiar.

The village station was built into a cutting, which widened out to form the station yard. On the far side of the track the land was higher than the station house, so Lucy could see nothing of the surrounding area. She guessed it was all countryside, similar to that she'd seen from the train, but she'd seen so few houses since the train stopped at Borwick Station that she wondered where anyone could live. Everything was strange. After the train disappeared on its way to Leeds it seemed so quiet. There were no engine sounds or distant pounding of steam hammers; no cars and vans pulling in and out of the station. There weren't even any gulls in the sky. The place smelled different to Barrow. She was beginning to feel a long way from home. The only people around were the stationmaster and a porter who was wheeling a trolley with a wicker basket full of hens.

She walked through the alleyway to the station yard and looked around. The letter had said someone would be there to meet her, but no one was in sight. She sat on a bench and waited with her case by her feet.

Since her mother died, Lucy had felt empty, as if she did not belong in Barrow, but now, sitting in this strange place, she began to wonder whether leaving home had been the right thing to do.

Above and to her right she heard the clatter of a horses hooves trotting over the bridge and saw a man's head appear above the wall as he steered the horse and trap along the road and down into the station yard. He came to a stop in front of her and looked her up and down.

"You must be Lucy."

She nodded.

"Stick yer case in t' back an' climb up. I've left t' missus at post office. We'll pick 'er up on t' way back."

She climbed up and tried not to sit too close. The farmer flicked the reins and the horse set off at a trot away from the station and back over the bridge. The village was closer than she'd expected, just a couple of hundred yards away. There was a crossroads with a school, a pub and a long stone building with a tin roof. She guessed it was the village hall. Opposite this was a garage and post office. A stern looking woman in a grey dress was waiting with a basket over her arm. The farmer stopped the trap and the woman stared at her.

"Move over girl and let me get up." The woman pushed the basket at her and squeezed up beside her, pushing her against the farmer. She noticed a strong smell of animals – not horses; it must be cows. The woman talked across her to the farmer. She was telling him about a Mrs Finch and what an interfering busybody she was.

Lucy sat silently, watching the houses as they headed away from the village and up the hill to the farm. She let her mind drift as the woman prattled to her husband.

"I'm talking to you girl! Have you no manners?"

Lucy turned. "Sorry."

"I said, have you worked in service before?"

"No."

"Then what have you done?"

"I looked after my mother until she died."

"Then at least you'll know how to cook and clean. You do know how to cook and clean I take it?"

"Yes. I did all the ... ."

"Yes Ma'm. You call me Ma'm."

Lucy shrank into her seat. A knot had developed in the pit of her stomach and she felt her hands beginning to shake.

"You know we're doing you a great favour, taking you on at this time of year. We'll keep you until Michaelmas, and if you're suitable you'll be allowed to stay for a full term. We'll expect you to work hard and mind your manners."

"Yes, Ma'm. Thank you, Ma'm."

The farmer turned the trap through the farm gate and round the back of the house. The woman climbed down and headed for the house. She turned as she reached the door.

"Bring that basket, girl. I haven't got all day."

Lucy climbed down and the farmer handed her case from the back of the trap.

"Don't mind Agnes. She's not as bad as she seems."

She managed a smile and followed the woman through the back door. The maid's room was at the back of the house, overlooking the farmyard. Agnes had told her to put her things in there and come back to make tea. She opened the blackout curtains and looked round the room. The walls were lime-washed, coloured with blue distemper. She would have preferred white but it could have been worse. She hated orange. The floor was covered with brown lino. They had the same in the kitchen at home. She placed her case and coat on the bed and ran her hand along the brass bed head. It needed a polish. A sound in the yard made her look up and she saw two young men around eighteen or nineteen sending cows into one of the buildings in the yard. One of them was tall, dark and dashing backwards and forwards. It made him look nervous. The other was slightly shorter, had light brown hair and looked like someone she'd seen in a film. He had a kind face.

"Girl!" The shout came from the kitchen.

She hurried across the landing and down the stairs. Mrs Branthwaite was hunting through cupboards. The kettle was on the range. Lucy was about to ask her what to do when she turned, pointed and snapped, "Set the table, three plates, three cups and three knives." As Lucy was finishing, the woman pointed down the passageway. "Milk. In the pantry."

The pantry was long and narrow, cold and not much wider than the passage. Stone slabs against one wall had vegetables stacked on them. Two sides of bacon hung from the ceiling. She couldn't find any milk bottles so she lifted the lid of a large enamel jug. Yes, milk straight from the cows. She hurried back to the kitchen where the woman was standing, thrusting out a smaller jug to pour the milk in. The back door rattled and the men came in for tea.

Over the next few days Lucy began to understand the running of the house. Unlike at home, the men didn't do any of the housework. They didn't even pour their own tea. She was expected to be on hand at mealtimes with the teapot ready as soon as they sat down.

Agnes seemed to delight in scolding her, as if she was there to be punished for something. She decided that the woman was not going to bully her, so she began getting up at six o'clock with Jack and Bill. She brewed their tea then began cleaning the house before breakfast. Her commitment was not going unnoticed.

✠

Jack and Bill were drinking their tea before morning milking. Bill had felt uneasy around the new girl in the house. His only conversation with her had been a muted 'Thank you' when she poured his tea. His father looked across at him and inclined his head as Lucy disappeared outside to beat a carpet.

"She's a good worker, that lass."

Bill nodded. He was never sure whether a comment like that had another meaning to it. Did it mean that he wasn't? Was it a suggestion that he should be working harder?

"I think I'll let her look after t' hens. She can feed 'em an' collect eggs. We'll 'ave enough to do when harvest comes."

Bill raised his eyebrows. At least his dad had taken to Lucy. He'd noticed the way his stepmother ordered her around. Either she was too slow at doing jobs or she didn't do them well enough for her. She'd scolded Lucy for ruining the cake she'd baked on Tuesday. It was no worse than any of Agnes's cakes and miles better than the one she had presented him with for his birthday the first year she'd been at the farm.

He was still thinking about Lucy when he went for the cows. He hadn't noticed it before but she was quite good looking. She was a bit pale, probably from spending her time in a dingy place like Barrow. But she had a kind, gentle face. She stood out against Agnes with her cold stares and tight lips. He wanted to find a way of talking to her, but decided to make sure Agnes wasn't around. She'd only shout at Lucy for not getting on with her work.

He found himself hanging around the farmyard when he expected to see Lucy crossing towards the garden with a pile of washing. He would take extra care in cleaning up the yard after the cows if he thought she was on her way to feed the hens. He didn't know what to say to her. He wasn't good at starting a conversation, and on the few times that their eyes had met he felt colour burning in his cheeks. It was easier with girls outside the chip shop or at a village dance. He'd chatted to Alice Taylor lots of times, and often the other girls came to talk to him. Whenever he came into the house for meals he found himself blushing, then blurting out an embarrassed "Mornin" or just muttering "Thank you" when she passed him his breakfast.

Lucy had been at the farm nearly three weeks when he had his first real conversation with her. He was following the cows up for afternoon milking when she came walking up the paddock with a bucket hanging from her elbow. She met him at the gate.

"Are t' hens doin' OK?" It seemed like the right thing to ask.

"These hens are lazy."

He was shocked by her straightforward answer. They were light Sussex. They'd always had Sussex hens.

"My granddad used to keep white Leghorns on his allotment. They laid twice as many eggs as these. You've got over thirty hens in that hut, and I'm only collecting between twelve and fifteen eggs a day. Granddad would kill them all and get some new ones if only half his were laying."

To his surprise, she seemed to know what she was talking about.

"He used to keep twenty-eight hens. He had an order for two dozen eggs a day at the grocer's shop and he always had some left for himself. He said he would've starved or gone bankrupt if he hadn't changed from Sussex to Leghorns."

"Are you goin' to tell Dad?"

She paused and twisted the side of her face.

"I think, maybe you should … . But not in front of your mother." She looked back towards the house.

"She's not my mother. My mother died."

Lucy turned to him. For the first time since she arrived she felt as if she was no longer alone. Someone else knew the loss, the grief, the utter sadness and unfairness of losing someone so close who you thought would be there for ever. It wasn't just his words that struck her. It was a certain tone in his voice, the way it dropped when he said it out loud,and when she saw his face she could see in his downcast eyes that he still suffered the pain. For a moment she was unable to speak, but she saw something creep into his expression – embarrassment, shame almost – and felt as if she was leaving him hanging by his words. He'd voiced his situation and exposed his innermost feelings to her, and she was in danger of leaving him to choke on what he had just said.

"So did mine." She looked away again, feeling that the moment had become too intimate. This was their first conversation and each of them had shared a common event in their histories that had left them isolated and grieving. She became aware that she was twisting the strap of her apron between her fingers. She moved her hands to the bucket handle, which had been hooked over her elbow. She hoped he hadn't noticed. "I'd better go. I've got to get the tea ready." She hurried off towards the house.

Bill watched her go.

When he went in for tea, Agnes was hovering. She was watching Lucy's every move as if she was trying to catch her doing something wrong. Lucy poured the tea and went to get the washing off the line. She hardly ever spoke when Agnes was around.

Agnes was pacing the kitchen, doing half jobs, putting things in the sink, getting things out of cupboards and putting them back.

"I don't know what that girl is doing to those hens. She's only bringing in a dozen and a half eggs each day. How can I make any money out of one and half dozen eggs?"

Bill sat quiet and his father looked up at Agnes.

"Don't be so hard on t' girl. They were only layin' that amount when I was feedin' 'em. They'll be moultin' soon. Then they'll stop layin' altogether."

Agnes looked like she was going to say something, then grabbed a plate and headed for the pantry.

Bill remembered how he'd persuaded his father to buy a binder the year before. The old corn reaper was worn out and Tom Waterford had told him how much easier harvesting was with a binder. It made sheaves without needing a man to tie them. Jack had been against it at first, but when he'd seen one working he'd been convinced. He'd bought one and used it for the first time last year. Bill had heard him explaining in the auction café about what a marvellous machine it was. Most of the men listening had binders already.

He took a gulp of tea and spoke, not looking at his dad, trying to sound casual.

"Some of t' lads at chip shop were talkin' about hens last week. A lass told me her granddad kept white Leghorns. She said he got 'em from a bloke in Kendal. He told her he'd've gone bust or starved if he'd kept on keepin' Sussex."

Jack looked up from his plate.

"Who's her granddad?"

"Don't know." He hadn't told him any lies.

"Charlie Taylor's brother farms up that way. He keeps white Leghorns; sells eggs on a stall at Kendal market. I'll 'ave a word wi' Charlie when I take t' milk to t' station tomorrow."

Bill tried to hide a smile, bit the inside of his cheek and looked down at the mat by the stove.

The first Monday in August, Bill and Dennis were taking the cart down the paddock. In the back were two empty poultry crates and four crates filled with white pullets fresh from the station. Propped at the back were a bag of sawdust from the joiner's shop, half a bucket of lime and two shovels.

They stopped the cart by the cabin, carried the empty crates inside and began catching the old hens and stuffing them in the crates. Bill lifted one up and put his hand under its breastbone.

"This one's as fat as a pig." He shoved it in with the others. They carried them outside and began cleaning out the hut, spreading the muck across the paddock. Bill took the lime and spread it around the floor. Dennis followed with the sawdust. Bill lifted one of the perches and ran his finger round the socket on the wall.

Dennis stopped.

"What're y' doin'?"

"Checkin' for mites." Bill held out his finger. "It's clean, thank God. Those little buggers can suck 'em dry when they're asleep."

They went outside and carried in the crates full of pullets. The birds flew to the perches and against the windows. Dennis stood back.

"They're a bit flighty."

"They'll calm down."

Dennis reached into the last crate where one pullet was cowering in the corner.

"They're a bit skinny."

Bill smiled at him

"They're workers, Dennis. Like you. Those other fat things are like Joe Moss."

Dennis gave him a sideways glance.

"I thought he was more like a turkey." He dragged the empty crates outside and lifted them into the cart.

Lucy was coming from the yard with a bucket of grain. Bill leaned across the cart to Dennis.

"Take the cart back to t' yard. I'll just wait till these birds are settled."

Dennis nodded and left Bill peering into the hut. Lucy

arrived swinging the bucket. She was smiling and her eyes seemed to sparkle.

"How do they look?"

"A bit nervous, but they'll settle down. Leave 'em fastened in for a couple of days till they realise it's home."

"I think Agnes would like to do that to me."

"How are you coping? It's five weeks on Friday."

"If I keep one step ahead of her it's okay. I'm in trouble if I'm too slow, and in trouble if I do any jobs faster than she does. I'm learning though. She thinks she's going to break me but she won't."

"We had a maid when I was little. She'd been there since before my mother died. Agnes drove her out. She couldn't get another one after that. Everyone round here had heard what she was like."

Lucy poured out the grain for the hens and looked towards the house.

"I'd better get back. I left her talking to a travelling salesman."

"We've got to kill and pluck those old hens by dinner time. Dad wants to take 'em to t' butchers this afternoon." He walked back to the yard with her, and as she headed towards the house he called after her, "Do you want to come down to t' village wi' me an' Dennis on Friday?"

She turned, swinging the bucket with her, tilted her head on one side and said,

"Yeah. Why not?"

✣

Friday night would be his chance. Dennis was going to see his mother, so Bill knew that he would be walking home with Lucy. He wasn't sure about asking her out. Would it cause a scandal? The only cases he knew of where one of the family had become involved with someone working on the farm had ended in disaster. That maid who worked for Charlie Taylor, or that case in the papers where a farmer had almost killed the farm lad when he caught him in bed with his daughter. He felt strange about being attracted to Lucy; almost guilty. She was a nice girl. They could be friends, but he knew he wanted more. He also knew that just being friends with her would not be acceptable to Agnes. It would not be seemly to be fraternising with one of the workers, even though she never had any objections to the way he was with Dennis.

On Friday evening Bill and Lucy set off to the village, with Dennis bobbing behind them from one side to the other, talking to each of them in turn.

"Are you having fish?"

"Yes Dennis."

"Do you like fish Lucy?"

"Yes Dennis." Lucy treated Dennis with a kind of understanding, as if he was the same as anyone else. The girls in the village avoided him as if they were afraid or as if they thought he was somehow beneath them. Bill would find himself torn between turning away from his odd work-mate, ignoring him in order to chat with the girls, and including him in the conversation. The second option was met with squirms, which usually resulted in them whispering and walking away, leaving him thinking that he and Dennis had been tarred with the same brush. Lucy was different. She treated Dennis with a kind of respect and almost affection that he'd only seen in Annie Dobson.

Halfway down the hill Dennis stopped by a rabbit burrow, looked up and down the road. He knelt down, thrusting his arm into the hole. A look of concentration came over his face as he pushed his shoulder hard against the bank. Bill watched his face turn to a smile and leaned to Lucy's ear.

"Watch this."

Dennis drew back from the hole holding a rabbit by its

back legs. He grabbed the rabbit's head and wrung its neck like a chicken.

"I'll tek it home to mother. Rabbit stew tomorrow."

Lucy stared at him in amazement.

"How did you do that?"

Bill whispered in her ear.

"He can tell how deep the hole is by the pile of soil. He gets a rabbit one out of every three attempts."

Dennis was taking out his penknife. He made a hole through the rabbit's hind leg, just behind the heel and pushed the other foot through so that he could carry it, using the legs as a handle. When they reached the chip shop he nipped round the side and hung the rabbit in the hedge out of sight.

"I'll pick it up on me way home." He followed Bill and Lucy into the shop.

Bill introduced Lucy to Alice Taylor and Phyllis Laycock. Alice pulled out a chair and asked Lucy to sit with them. Phyllis looked her up and down, wrinkled her nose as if she'd been exposed to an unpleasant smell.

"A serving girl." She turned away towards the next table so that Lucy was left looking at her back and dark hair. Bill and Dennis went to sit across the aisle.

Alice shrugged, pulled her chair closer and began asking Lucy about her family and life in Barrow. Lucy seemed unfazed by the other girl's rejection, gave her a sideways glance and was soon in deep conversation with Alice. She told her about the street party they'd had for the coronation, about watching the Hindenburg fly over, was surprised to hear that Alice had seen it too. Lucy thought for a moment and said,

"My dad said they were up to no good. One of his mates at the shipyard saw them taking photographs."

"Do you miss your dad?"

She glanced towards Phyllis who was still talking to the other girl, looked back to Alice.

"I miss him a lot, but I'm getting used to it."

"How do you get on with Mrs Branthwaite?"

Lucy breathed out slowly and tried to think of a polite answer.

Alice leaned towards her; continued.

"She doesn't talk to my mum. She seems to think she's above all the other farmer's wives." She stretched across the table; whispered. "She only talks to Phyllis's mother. They own a big farm in the next village. The Laycocks think they're better than all the tenant farmers, but the Branthwaites are tenants too." She sat back as she heard Phyllis and the other girl stop talking.

Phyllis shifted towards Alice, so that she didn't have to look at Lucy.

"If you're going to talk to her all night we're going back to the vicarage." She pushed her chair back and she and the other girl marched out of the shop.

Alice didn't answer her. She watched them go and shrugged.

"The other girl's Clarissa, the Vicar's daughter. She's training to be a teacher. It's the first time I've seen her in here. I don't think she'll be back. She didn't eat her fish."

Lucy watched Dennis get up and leave. Bill was watching too as Dennis turned back towards the farm. A few moments later he passed the chip shop window and open doorway. He was looking straight ahead and using his elbow to grip something that bulged under his jacket. Lucy smiled and looked towards Bill. He winked at her and looked away.

By nine-thirty the chip shop was almost empty. Annie Dobson was wiping tables and talking to Bill, who'd been joined by Tom Waterford. Tom had arrived late and was telling Annie that he'd been helping his dad with a heifer that was struggling to calve.

"It had a leg back so we had to push t' head back inside to

get hold of its foot."

Annie had stopped wiping and was sitting at the next table listening.

"Was it all right?"

"Aye. It wasn't breathin' at first but we got it goin'." He was talking between mouthfuls of chips. "It was a big bull calf an' all. Heifer's a bit wonky, but she was up on her feet lettin' it suck when I came away."

Alice was getting up to leave.

"It's time I was going. I'm helping to milk in the morning." She touched Lucy on the shoulder. "You can walk back with me as far as my gate if you want."

Bill saw she was leaving and jumped up to follow them. He looked back towards Tom.

"I've got to go. I'm walkin' Lucy back to t' farm."

Tom looked up towards the door, back towards Annie Dobson, his mouth open and a forkful of chips in his hand. Annie returned his gaze and raised her eyebrows.

"Looks like you're left on your own tonight."

✣

Bill caught up with the girls at Alice's front gate, Lucy just turning back towards the road as Alice disappeared round the corner of the barn.

"Thanks for introducing me to her. She's nice."

"I thought you'd like her. We've known each other since we were little. She's a year older than me. She was the one who showed me round when I first started school."

Lucy was watching him closely as he said it. He caught her eye briefly then looked away. As they walked back towards home, Lucy pulled her cardigan around her and crossed her arms. Bill found himself struggling with what to say, stumbling in the dark like a man on unknown territory. He groped for something familiar, a recognisable path towards his destiny.

"Did you see Dennis leaving with that rabbit?"

She laughed and he could see her eyes shining in the moonlight.

"Is he always that furtive? He looked like he'd stolen the crown jewels."

"You want to see him when he's got a salmon."

"He poaches fish, too?"

Bill shrugged. "It's not real poaching. He never takes more than enough for his tea, and he'd never take pheasants. No one minds him catching rabbits. Some of them would probably pay him to do it. But that's not Dennis. If he's caught a meal he's happy."

"Has he ever had a girlfriend?"

"Dennis? No, he has enough trouble copin' with everybody else, let alone a girlfriend. I worry about him sometimes."

"Why?"

"He's always been a bit odd but he seems to be gettin' worse; more twitchy, more nervous."

"You like him a lot, don't you."

"He's t' nearest thing I have to a brother. A lot of folk think he's simple, but he's really bright. He's just clever in a different way to most people."

Lucy reached out and squeezed his shoulder.

"Don't worry about Dennis. He's happy."

Bill wasn't used to the physical contact, but she did it so gently that he hardly noticed. They'd walked a few more steps before he realised that she had her arm round him. He wanted to hold her but wasn't sure whether he should. A shiver crept through him that wasn't the cold. He put his arm round her waist and they walked back to the farm.

As they reached the front gate, Lucy was surprised when Bill pulled his arm away and walked in front of her. He pushed open the garden gate and followed the path round to the back door. She glanced up to Jack and Agnes's bedroom. The window was open. When she got to the door Bill was taking off his jacket and hanging it on a peg. As she bolted the door he sat on the stairs to take off his shoes. He glanced towards her, said a quick 'G'd night' and went up to bed. She opened her mouth to speak, but he was gone. Lucy checked the stove in the kitchen and went to her room.

✥

The next morning Bill was awakened by a knocking on his bedroom door.

"Bill. Bill." It was Lucy's voice. "You forgot to set your alarm."

He dived out of bed.

"What time is it?"

She opened the door slightly. She was dressed.

"It's only quarter past six, but your dad's not up so I thought I'd better call you before it got late."

"Right. Thanks. I'll be down in a minute."

When he got downstairs she was holding out his tea.

"I'll come and give you a hand."

He wondered how she could help, but when they got outside most of the cows were waiting by the gate so they got them inside and Bill rolled the churn into the shippen as Lucy carried two buckets from the dairy. He hung one bucket on a nail and carried the other to the first cow.

"There's still five missing. Can you go and get them? I'll start milking." He took the stool and sat by the first cow. He was pouring the milk from the second cow into the churn when she arrived back.

"They're waiting by the gate."

They brought them in and Lucy stepped forward to tie one up. It darted back and wandered up the passageway behind the other milkers.

"Don't move so fast. It scares them." He brought it back,

tied it up and reached for his stool. Lucy took the other and went to start milking one of the heifers.

"Not that one. She'll kick. Try the next. She'll let anyone milk her."

She placed her stool and began pulling at the cow's teats. No milk came and the old cow lifted her foot then put it down.

"Don't pull. Squeeze." He was leaning round from the next cow. "Top first then gradually down with your fingers. Don't move your hands."

She giggled as the milk began to flow, slowly at first but then faster as she got the rhythm. She was beginning to feel proud of herself when her fingers and wrists began to ache. Her forearms felt as if she'd got cramp. She persevered until the milk stopped flowing, then changed to the other two teats. Bill had milked four of the other cows by the time she stood up. Her back was aching. She stretched and carried the bucket across to the churn. Bill was smiling at her.

"Not bad for a beginner."

She rubbed her forearms, put down the bucket.

"I'd better go and start breakfast. Agnes will be up soon."

She ran to the house to wash and change.

7

Pastoral life has always, been regarded as one of tranquil enjoyment; and poets, both ancient and modern, sacred and profane, have sung its praises, and extolled its pleasures in the most glowing terms.

Duncan MacDonald. Cattle, Sheep and Deer
(1872)

The heifers were due to start calving from the fifteenth of August onwards. On the Friday before, Bill and his father had picked out five that looked close to calving. They walked them down from the lot and tied them in the shippen. They were jumpy. Heifers always were. Jack frowned.

"They're worse than usual. Bloody flies."

Bill watched a fly settle on a heifer's swelling udder. The heifer kicked at it and shivered, rippling the hide across its shoulders. "We'll have to tar 'em."

Bill went to the granary and searched on a shelf. Dennis stuck his head round the door.

"What're you lookin' for?"

"A tin of tar."

"There's a big drum in that corner. It's half full. I found it when I was chasin' a rat."

Bill looked at the drum.

"That's roofing tar." He found a tin behind some bags, prised off the lid and held it out to Dennis. "Stockholm tar, for t' heifers. Smell it."

"Pine resin."

"That's what it is."

He took the tin and began smearing its contents on the heifers' udders. One lashed out with its hind leg and caught him hard on the thigh.

"Jesus. Shit." He tried to rub away the pain before the muscle started to go numb.

Dennis was watching.

"I bet that hurts. You'll be a bit more careful next time."

"Bloody hell, Dennis." Bill glared at him.

"I didn't kick you." His mouth was turned down but his eyes were laughing. He turned to walk away. "I bloody would if you tried tarrin' my bag."

Bill's leg throbbed. He couldn't help laughing. He leaned against the wall to steady himself. Jack was releasing the first heifer, looking away and shaking his head.

By the time Bill came back from putting the heifers in the front meadow, the pain in his leg had eased. Lucy was carrying a bucket of eggs from the paddock.

"Twenty three eggs today."

Bill nodded.

"Looks like you're doin' a good job."

"I'm doing my best."

Agnes was cutting some roses by the back door.

"Stop making such a noise girl. They're only doing well because Jack bought those new ones."

"Yes Mrs Branthwaite. Of course." She glanced back to Bill, raised her eyebrows and took the eggs inside.

Agnes stood and watched her go into the house. Bill felt her eyes burning into his back. She was looming by the rose bed, trying to cut him down, crush him. He lifted his head, stared right back at her. Made his voice cheerful.

"It's a grand day. I bet your washing's nearly dry."

Her face was like a rock. She turned back to the trellis and tore the head off another rose.

✤

Jack was sitting at the breakfast table, brandishing his knife and smearing butter onto slabs of bread, tearing each slice as he attempted to grease it with the yellow, then bending it in two with his rough fingers and squashing them onto the side of his plate. When Mary came to show him her doll in a summer dress he stopped buttering and snapped at her like a dog interrupted from its scraps.

"Tek it away and come an' get your breakfast."

She shrank back into the living room and Jack turned his attention to Bill. "I want you to take a scythe after breakfast and mow all those thistles along t'riverbank. If you get stuck into t' job you'll be finished in time for milking. Tek your dinner with you an' don't come back till you've finished. I'm sendin' Dennis to mow some up on t' lot."

He didn't usually split them up, not unless one or both of them were being punished for something.

Bill thought about how many thistles there were. It would take him all morning and half the afternoon if he worked really hard. He finished his breakfast and got up to leave. Jack stopped him.

"You'd better take a sickle as well. It'll make it easier knockin' those nettles off on that high bank under t' hedge."

Bill went out to the shed, took the best scythe and a sickle. He slipped a whetstone into his pocket, remembered his grandfather's voice: A blunt knife and a blunt scythe are no good to anyone.

Lucy met him in the yard. She was carrying a basket and a tea can. Cold tea and sandwiches for dinner. He hated cold tea.

"Your dad told me to give you these."

"Thanks." He didn't feel like talking, looked down at the cobbles as she handed him the basket. She squeezed his hand.

"Cheer up. The sun's shining."

He left her standing in the yard and set off down the lane.

By the time Bill began to feel thirsty he'd cleared a large bed of thistles and knocked off most of the single ones scattered across the field. He made his way back to the hedge where he'd left the basket in the shade and the tea can in the sun. He sat on the bank and reached into the basket for an Eccles cake. Lucy must have made them. She'd put sugar on top. His mother used to do that. There was a mug in the bottom of the basket. He left it where it was and poured tea into the can lid. It was still warm. He drank his tea and laid back listening to the sounds of grasshoppers. A shrew squeaked in the grass near his head. He was almost falling asleep when he felt a sting in his arm.

"Bastard." He slapped at the horsefly, killed it and looked at the bite, knew it would swell into a lump. He picked up the scythe and trudged across to the next clump of thistles, swinging at them as his arm throbbed. When he'd finished those he tackled a huge bed half way up the slope, working with his head down. The stems were strong and woody. The clump stretched from the river almost to the hedge. He stopped to sharpen the scythe; heard the swish of feet in the dry grass behind him. It was Lucy. She'd changed into slacks and a white blouse.

"I thought I'd come and see how you were getting on. Agnes gave me the day off, so I walked down to the village to buy stamps and post a letter. I only just caught the post office. It was closing."

"Hi." It was all he could manage.

"Is there anything I can do to help?"

"Not unless you fancy going round that hedge side with the sickle."

"Okay. Where is it?"

"By the basket." He pointed to the corner of the field. "Are you sure you want to?"

"Yes. First, it helps you; and second, I'm sure Agnes only gave me the day off because you were busy. I heard her having a go at your dad last night."

Bill put the stone back in his pocket.

"What was she saying?"

"She thinks I'm a bad influence on you. She told him we should be kept apart."

"Who the hell does she think she is? We're not kids."

She shrugged and went to find the sickle.

Bill turned his anger to his work and felt the strength in his arms as he sliced through the hollow stalks. He thought about all the times his father had given him the worst jobs to do after he'd stood up to Agnes. He went from clump to clump, not noticing where he was or how he was progressing.

As the clumps of thistles became more spread out he realised he was getting to the end of the field. Lucy was only a few yards away, finishing off the nettles under the hedge. He cut off the last few stalks and looked round to see where she was. She'd taken the basket and can to the riverbank, sat dangling her bare feet over the edge.

He went to sit beside her and she poured him some cold tea. He gulped at it and handed back the mug, took off his boots and socks and let the air blow between his toes.

"What time do you think it is?"

"About half past two. I heard the church clock across the valley."

He was surprised. They'd finished with time to spare. Lucy was looking at the water. She stood up suddenly.

"Fancy a swim?"

Before he had chance to speak, she dived in and swam under water to the centre of the river. She bobbed to the surface, shook her hair from her eyes and turned.

"Come on. Dive in. It's great."

He shook his head, suddenly felt embarrassed. She was watching him. Her face changed and she swam back. He didn't want to look at her. She swam round to where he was looking.

"What's up?"

"I don't know how to swim. I don't think anyone in the village does."

"Nobody?"

"You're the first person I've seen swimming in the river."
She looked up at him.

"Really?"

"Yes."

"There's one thing for certain." She was pulling herself up.
"You won't learn by sitting up there." She grabbed his feet and
dragged him off the edge of the bank. He tried to grab hold of
something. All her weight was pulling him. He hit the water
and felt it close in above him. His arms lashed out. Water was
up his nose, in his mouth, his lungs. His feet were scrambling
for something to stand on. They touched the sandy bottom
and he stood up, choking, coughing and rubbing the water
from his eyes. Fear turning to anger.

"What the hell did you do that for?"

She was standing close to him, trying not to laugh.

"I could have drowned."

She was laughing, looking at the water. It was just above
his waist. He felt something in his stomach, rising. He laughed
out loud and tried to poke water from his ear. Flung his arm
out and splashed water at her. His shirt was clinging and cold.
He realised he felt refreshed, ran his fingers through his hair
and thought for a moment.

"Okay. How do you do it? How do you swim?"

She walked him to where the water was a bit deeper,
almost up to his chest,

"Hold out your hands. Keep your feet still." Took a step
away from him, still holding his hands.

"You're pulling me over."

"Stop panicking." She took another half step. "Now
breathe right in. Hold your breath." She seemed to know what
she was doing. As she stepped back and moved quickly his feet
came off the bottom. When he felt his face sinking he
protested and she pulled harder.

"Right. Now breathe in and out but don't empty your lungs." She kept dragging him round. It seemed like hours. "Now start kicking your legs."

He felt himself pushing forwards and she kept moving away, just fast enough to keep away from him. He noticed the colour of her skin through her blouse, the line of her underwear. He glanced away in case she caught him looking.

"Concentrate. Keep your arms out straight." She stepped to one side and let go of his hands. "Keep kicking."

He kept going until he felt the sand scrape against his chest. He stood up.

"I did it."

"That's enough for one day. Next time I'll get you using your arms."

They climbed out onto the grass and laid down in the sun, first staring at the sky and then rolling over to let their backs dry. Bill breathed in. The seductive smell of meadow-sweet hit the back of his nose and throat. He heard a sound in the distance, the whistle of a train through the cutting before it burst out onto the viaduct. He looked up the valley to see it steaming across the bridge. It disappeared into the trees leaving only a plume of smoke and a distant echo.

"I'd better go. It's half past three."

Lucy sat up, straightened her blouse and brushed grass from her slacks. They were crumpled and creased. Her blouse had a dull grey look to it. Bill picked up the tools and they walked together to the bottom of the lane. Lucy stopped, handed him the basket and can. He took them, looked at her, puzzled.

"Are you not coming back with me?"

"No. If Agnes knows we've seen each other today she'll only find another way of keeping us apart. I'm going to call in and see Alice Taylor. I might even help her to milk. It'll give me an explanation for being dirty."

She pecked him on the cheek, climbed the gate into the next meadow and set off across the field.

✤

On Sunday Jack and Agnes were going to see Jack's brother Harry. He farmed seven miles away at the other side of Hutton Roof Crag. They would go straight after church. When Bill said he was not going, he was sitting at the breakfast table. Agnes stood over him, hands on her hips.

"You should go and see your Uncle Harry. He's your godfather."

"I saw him last week when he came to look at t' binder. I'll see him again next week at t' show."

"That's not the same. You'll only be hanging around the farm up to no good."

Bill felt the anger boiling up inside him but decided to let it go.

Agnes persisted.

"What are you going to do all day?"

Jack had been sitting silently. When he heard this he looked up.

"One o' those heifers is looking like calving. He can keep an eye on it."

She glared at him. She wasn't going to get her own way. Bill glanced after her as she went to get ready for church.

After breakfast he sat and read for half an hour. The daily papers were full of Mr Churchill's speeches about troop numbers in Germany and Russia. There were millions of them. The local paper had a photo on the front page of air raid shelters being dug in Lancaster. He picked up the *Farmer's Guardian*. The headline said *Grain Shortage Feared As War Looms*.

He turned to the back pages and studied the show reports. When he'd finished reading he put on his boots and went across the road to the vegetable patch. The water barrel was almost empty, so he poured the last of the water into the watering can and watered the first row of winter cabbages. The latest crop of lettuces were growing really fast and beginning to wilt, so he went over to the edge of the field and clambered down into the ditch.

He dipped the watering can into a deep hole his father had dug in the bed of the stream. The stream had reduced to a trickle but by the time he'd emptied the can, the hole would be full again. He finished watering the cabbages and went back to refill the can, careful not to disturb the silt in the stream. He didn't want to block the spout.

As he climbed out of the ditch he saw Lucy walking towards the vegetable patch. She was carrying a basket and an empty flour sack.

"I've come to pick some peas and beans. Agnes wants some for tomorrow."

"When I've finished watering I'll give you a hand."

He held down the wire netting for her to climb over. She laughed as she almost overbalanced, put her hand on his shoulder to steady herself. She smelled of perfumed soap.

"Thank you."

He noticed the softness of her voice. Watched as she disappeared behind the rows of runner beans. When he'd finished watering he took the sack and went to help her, working along the opposite side of the row. Caught glimpses of her through the leaves and orange blossom. He watched as she stooped to pick the lower pods, noticed the smallness of her hands, the way her hair lifted in the breeze.

When she reached the end of the row she stepped round and began picking from the plants that brushed his back. As she worked closer he heard the rustle of her clothes, the sound each pod made as she pulled it from the stem. She reached behind him and her arm stroked his back. He saw a ladybird that had landed on her blouse and was climbing between her shoulders.

"Stand still." He lifted his hand to let it crawl onto his thumb. Held it out for her to see and raised it into the sunlight.

"Watch this."

The ladybird opened its wings, hovered and flew away towards the trees. They watched it shrink against the oak leaves, soar over the treetops until it was just a dark speck against the sky. Then it was gone. Lucy looked into his eyes, raised her face towards his. He put his arms around her and kissed her. He felt the slenderness of her back, the glide of the fabric against her soft skin.

A heifer bawled loudly from behind the hedge and he felt her whole body move suddenly.

"Sounds like that heifer's starting to calve."

She drew away from him.

"Had you better go and look at it?"

"I'll leave it a few minutes to settle down."

"Can I watch?"

"I don't see why not."

They finished picking the beans, and Lucy emptied the basket into the sack. They quickly picked the peas, working at opposite sides of the row. Each time Bill's hands were full of pods he reached over and dropped them into Lucy's basket. As they climbed back over the wire netting Bill split a pod and poured the peas into his mouth. He tossed the empty shell into the hedge and crept quietly round the corner.

The heifer was lying on its side about ten yards away. Each time she pushed, the nose and feet of a calf appeared. She carried on pushing and the head popped out. She bawled again and gave another push. Bill and Lucy leaned on the gate and watched as the calf's chest emerged. The heifer stood up and turned round, sniffing the ground. As she turned the calf's fore legs swung and its head lolled. Lucy turned to Bill.

"Is it okay?"

"Yeah. The weight of t' calf's front end'll pull its back end out."

The heifer arched her back and gave another push. Bill noted two small jerks as first one then the other of the calf's hipbones freed themselves from the heifer's pelvis. The calf dropped onto the grass with a sloppy thud. The heifer wheeled round and stared at it, bawling and spraying it with saliva. She stepped back, lunged forwards and bawled again. Lucy looked worried.

"What's the matter with the heifer?"

He gave a slight laugh.

"She's just a bit shocked. She's never seen a newborn calf before. No one bothered to tell her what was going to happen. She'll calm down in a minute."

The heifer sniffed the calf, made a muffled mooing sound. The calf shook its head, clearing the mucus from its ears. She licked it. Bawled and carried on licking. The calf pushed with its back legs and tried to get up. It fell forwards on its face and tried again, stumbled, then got to its feet. It stood, quivering, with its legs apart, as the heifer continued licking. The calf tottered and turned towards its mother, trying to suckle. She bounced away and bawled again. When it found the teat she stood quietly, letting it suck and nuzzling its tail.

Lucy looked up at Bill.

"Thank you."

"What for?"

"For letting me watch. I've never seen a calf being born before."

"You can't easy miss it, living here."

"Will they be all right now?"

"They'll be fine. I'll leave 'em outside till this afternoon, an' bring t' heifer in for milking. Calf can go in a pen. I'll leave t' heifer inside tonight an' let her out tomorrow."

"Don't you need to bring them in now?"

"No. Dad wouldn't. If she'd calved later this afternoon he'd leave her out all night."

They went back to the house and Lucy made some sandwiches. She was pouring the tea when Bill had an idea.

"Do you fancy goin' swimmin' again this afternoon? If we just go for an hour we'll have plenty o' time to get the heifer an' calf in."

"You're keen." She thought for a moment. "If you're sure it's okay we can go. Have you any swimming trunks?"

He shook his head, looked at her. It was a silly question.

"I've got some shorts I used to play football in at school. They'll be a bit small but I reckon I'll still get into 'em." He went upstairs and searched through the bottom drawer of his wardrobe. Brought them back. Laughed. "They'll be a bit tight."

She raised her eyebrows.

"They'll do. Go and put them on under your trousers." She followed him upstairs went to her room and met him on the landing. "I'll get some towels." She searched through the airing cupboard and found two old towels. They were badly worn with holes in. "Agnes won't miss these. They were right at the bottom. I'll wash them when she goes to market with your dad on Wednesday. They'll be dry and back in the cupboard before she gets back."

"I hope it doesn't rain." He looked at the towels. "I've never seen those before." They left the house and headed for the river. This time Bill led her down onto the shingle and left the towels on a patch of short grass. They waded into the water and within half an hour Bill and Lucy were swimming out together through a deep fishing pool. She kept looking across at him, commenting on his breaststroke. Bill was surprised how soon his arms and legs got tired. Lucy was swimming effortlessly. He headed for the towels. She followed him and laid beside him on the grass. He kept asking questions about swimming, why people in films swam differently and why his arms were aching so soon.

Lucy was still thinking about the calf.

"Why is it such a different colour to its mother? The calf."

He reached across to the shingle, began selecting pebbles. He made two piles. A pile of white ones and a pile of dark orange ones. Pointed to the piles.

"That's a white bull. That's a red cow." He took half the pebbles from each pile, mixed them together and put them in another pile. "That's a roan calf."

"Like the heifer." She was looking at the third pile.

"That's right." He picked up the remaining red pebbles. Placed them beside the mixed pile. "We have a red bull."

Lucy was studying the two piles. She seemed to be working it out.

"So the roan heifers will have either red or roan calves." She paused. "And all the red heifers will have red calves."

"That's right. You've got it."

"Why don't you keep any white ones?"

"They're weak. Some of 'em are really sickly."

"There's a field up the road with lots of white ones in."

Bill's expression changed.

"Joe Moss'll buy anything if it's cheap." He stood up and grabbed his towel. "We'd better be gettin' back."

When they got back to the house Lucy went inside to hide the towels and put the kettle on. Bill went round the front of the house towards the road. As he rounded the corner he knew something was wrong. The calf was bawling somewhere in the front meadow. He increased his pace, sprinted across the road. Put his hand on a post and vaulted the fence. The calf was pacing around, a few yards from where it had been born. Its mother was lying beside it, bloated, still.

He raced across the meadow. The heifer hadn't moved. He

reached it, put his hand on its belly, still warm but no sign of life. He dashed round to her head. Her eyes were glazed. Something was hanging from her mouth. The heifer was dead. She'd choked on her own afterbirth.

Something stuck in his throat. His eyes were filling. He kneeled beside the heifer, put his arm across his eyes, slumped against the dead animal. How was he going to tell his dad?

✛

The next morning Bill hesitated before going in for breakfast.

Jack had seen the heifer from the road late in the afternoon as he came home in the trap. He knew Bill would be milking. He'd raced across to it and seen what must've happened. The calf wasn't there so he guessed that Bill already knew. When he walked into the shippen he saw that his son was upset.

"It's just one o' those things, lad. You can't do nothing about it. I'll get hold of t' knacker man tonight an' we'll get it out o' sight. Worry about t' live 'uns Bill. It's too late to go bothering yersel' about a dead 'un." He pointed to a splash on the floor by the churn. "Spilt milk, Bill. That's what it is. Spilt milk." He patted him on the shoulder and went to change his clothes.

Bill pushed the back door open. He could smell the bacon. When he'd finished milking the night before he'd gone for a walk on the lot. He'd arrived back late and gone straight to bed. He hadn't seen Lucy. Hadn't spoken to Agnes.

When he sat at the breakfast table Agnes was waiting.

"What have you got to say for yourself?"

Jack reached up and touched her arm.

"Leave him, Agnes. He feels bad enough about it as it is."

She wouldn't be placated.

"What were you doing when you should have been working? Out cavorting with that girl?"

"Agnes." Jack sounded sterner. "If you'd 'ad your way he'd've been with us." He held out his hands as if he were holding a box. Placed them on the table. Lowered his voice. "It's like this. Hundreds o' cows'll eat their cleansin' like that heifer did. I bet less than one in ten thousand'll choke on it. You can't do nothing unless you're there when it 'as it in it's mouth. After it calves, y' never know whether it's goin' to take five minutes or 'alf a day to part with it. How can you be there to see whether t' animal eats it?"

She waved her hand at him. Bill could see she wasn't listening. She leaned towards him.

"So, where were you when it calved?"

"Watchin' it. I'd been waterin' t' veggies an' pickin' peas."

She reeled to look at Lucy. Turned back to Bill.

"You obviously weren't watching it when it choked. Do you realise how much that cow was worth?"

Bill had had enough. He burst to his feet. Sent the chair crashing to the floor.

"What the hell do you know about cows? You've been here ten years an' I 'aven't seen you in t' shippen once."

Everyone else was silent. Mary's lip was quivering. She looked at Bill and Agnes then turned to her father.

"Daddy. Why's everybody shouting?"

Bill shrank back, felt his cheeks burn.

Agnes took Mary's hand and led her away as the girl burst into floods of tears. Bill gave a deep sigh, picked up the chair and slumped in his seat.

⁂

On Monday evening Bill was surprised to see Tom Waterford cycling into the yard.

"I can't stop. I've got to get back. I just called to ask if you wanted to come beatin' on Saturday."

"Beating?"

"It's up at High Gill so it's grouse, not pheasants. They're wantin' t' make it a big day. They reckon there might not be any more this year if t' war comes so it could be t' best shoot for a while. It pays well."

Bill dashed across to the house. Jack was taking off his boots. When Bill asked him the reply was swift.

"Aye. Earn it while y' can. There'll be a good feed too. Trewin estate always puts on a good spread."

Bill went back outside and told Tom.

Tom nodded.

"Great. We'll pick you up at half past eight. Ted's takin' us in 'is car."

He jumped back on his bike and sped off round the back of the house.

✣

The car journey was a novelty to Bill. He'd been in cars before, but not for a while. He squeezed in the back with Tom and another young bloke whom he'd never met. In the front passenger seat was a boy of about thirteen. Bill guessed it was Ted's son. Ted didn't speak. Bill knew he lived near Tom and had some connection with the estate but he'd never found out what he did. He earned enough money to own a car when the only two cars in Bill's village belonged to Charlie Taylor and Sir Charles Seabrooke.

They drove up to the moor and turned off the road onto a rough track that led to a stone-built shooting hut about half a mile away. When they reached it Bill could see the shooters standing around chatting. Most of them were dressed in tweeds and knee-breeches. One was passing round a flask and laughing. Ted glanced across at them and made a snorting sound through his nose.

"Here they all are, dressed up to t' nines. Be polite lads. You'll get better tips."

Bill listened to his advice. He would be polite anyway. There was something in Ted's tone that he didn't like.

The shooters turned to look at them as they climbed out of the car. Bill recognised his landlord, Sir Charles Seabrooke, and Colonel Trewin who owned the estate where Tom and his dad were tenants. They were standing with two other men. One Bill knew as last year's president of the Westmorland Show. The other was a tall, slim, city-looking guy with a thoughtful expression. He had dark hair, going silver at the edges. Bill felt a bit self-conscious. They seemed to be talking about him. He looked round towards the others from the car and realised he stood out against them. Before he left home, Bill had put on his best jacket that he wore for beating pheasants. He'd polished his boots and leggings. Tom looked fairly smart, but Ted and the other two looked to be wearing the same clothes they'd been working in all week.

Bill heard footsteps behind him.

"I say. Bill Branthwaite."

He turned. It was Sir Charles.

"We're short of someone to load. I believe you've done some loading for guns on my estate."

Bill nodded.

"Yes, sir."

"You'd better come with us."

Bill looked back towards the others. Tom winked at him and went to tell Ted, who was talking to one of the keepers. Bill walked across to the shooters and glanced back to the car. Ted gave him a cold stare as he bobbed down into the driver's seat.

Sir Charles was talking.

"Young Bill here's quite a runner. He ran my boy off at the knees in the village sports."

"Did you win?" It was the city bloke. Bill noticed his accent was different, more southern; London maybe.

Sir Charles answered for him.

"No. Poor bugger got tripped up by one of the hounds. Damned near knocked himself out. Clambered out of the stream half drowned, poor chap. Damned bad luck, if you ask me. Some young wag from up country steamed past him and took the cup."

The other shooters shook their heads in sympathy. Sir Charles put his arm across Bill's shoulders, walked him away a couple of paces.

"We're putting you with John here." He nodded towards the city bloke, lowered his voice. "He's a surgeon from London. He's married to my cousin, so look after him. I doubt whether the fellow's much of a shot. You'll probably not have much trouble keeping up with him. Sorry, I'd better introduce you." He turned back to the surgeon. "John Pettifer, Bill Branthwaite."

Bill shook his hand politely. The man had a firm grip.

The shooters drew lots for the hides, and the Colonel cursed under his breath as he realised he'd been put on the end. Bill and the surgeon were right in the middle. They took up position behind the wall. It had been built in a half circle, with soil piled back on the outside. Heather and grass grew on the soil bank so that the hide could not be seen by the birds as they fled.

As Bill loaded the guns the surgeon made a confession.

"It's the first time I've shot grouse so it might take me a while to get used to it."

The first grouse flew over and the surgeon fired, missed. He missed the second too, but Bill noticed he made no comment. He was concentrating. Bill could hear shots up and down the line. He handed over the loaded gun and reloaded the other. Two birds flew over in quick succession. The surgeon hit them both, reached for the other gun. Bill realised he'd been slow, worked hard to keep up. It continued, Bill loading and the surgeon firing. He never missed another shot. The grouse were falling thick and fast. The man seemed to shoot every bird cleanly. He was no novice. When the whistle blew and the birds stopped Bill looked at him.

"I thought you said you hadn't shot before."

The man gave a wry smile.

"I said I hadn't shot grouse. I've shot pheasants. I learned to shoot in the army. My father was a doctor and I soon decided that I'd rather help save men than kill them, so I started my professional life as an army surgeon. I'm doing research into brain surgery."

They walked out through the heather towards the shooting hut where a group of women had laid the tables for lunch. The surgeon made a space for Bill and beckoned him to sit beside him. Bill wanted a word with Tom, but he was sitting with his back to him at the other table with the beaters.

The chauffeur walked across to Sir Charles and leaned to his ear to say something. Sir Charles pointed towards the Colonel, and the driver walked round the table towards him.

"Excuse me sir. We've received a message from the house. Sir Charles asked me to pass it on." He stooped beside him and spoke in a whisper. Bill was sitting so close that he heard the message clearly. "Germany have invaded Poland."

The Colonel clenched his teeth, his face reddened and he banged his fist on the table. The cutlery rattled.

"Damn Chamberlain. The man's a bloody postman, not a leader." He banged his fist on the table again, and Bill grabbed for his cup. The table fell silent.

After lunch the Colonel was first to his feet.

"Come on. We might as well enjoy it while we can."

Everyone returned to the shoot. Bill noticed that John Pettifer missed quite a few shots, and guessed his mind was elsewhere. They returned to the hut for tea, and just as Bill was about to get up and say goodbye to the surgeon Sir Charles came across.

"I say, John. The Colonel says we can go now. It's only a few minutes drive away, so we'll go and see the guy then drive straight home." He placed a hand on Bill's shoulder. "Thank you, young man." He paused. "Oh. You keep sheep, don't you?"

"Yes."

"Come with us. You may want to see this. We'll drop you off at the farm on the way home." He led them towards his car.

Bill was passing the other table when Tom grabbed him by the cuff.

"Where y' goin'?"

Bill shrugged.

"Don't know. They didn't say. They're takin' me home tho'." He followed them to the Rolls Royce and climbed in the front with the driver.

The chauffeur drove back onto the road and along for a couple of miles then turned down a narrow lane. Bill heard Sir Charles in the back.

"I really want to see this."

They crossed an old bridge and the chauffeur put his foot down as the car climbed a steep hill. He turned into a farmyard and the car came gently to a halt. The three men got out of the back, and Bill followed them across the yard. He noticed how tidy the place was and saw the farmer in the tool shed, working on an axe handle with a drawknife. The farmer came out and shook them all by the hand. The Colonel introduced them all to the man, who must have been one of his tenants, then he scanned the yard.

"Okay Hector. Where's this animal you're going to show us?"

The farmer looked slightly embarrassed.

"There isn't a lot to see." He led them round to a small croft where a forlorn looking ewe was grazing. She had a bandage tied round her head.

John Pettifer stepped forwards. He seemed to be the reason why they had come. He asked the farmer to tell him everything from start to finish.

The farmer was looking at him, almost ignoring his landlord and Sir Charles.

"This ewe had sturdy."

"Sturdy?" The surgeon looked puzzled.

"If a sheep gets dog tapeworms, the worm lays its eggs in a sack in the sheep's head, between the brain and the skull."

"How do you know where they are?"

"The sheep walks in a circle. The sack's allus on the inside of the circle."

The surgeon nodded and let him continue.

"The sack's under a soft spot on that side of the skull. All I do is take it out. If you don't, the sheep dies."

"You take it out?"

The farmer nodded.

"From inside the skull?"

"Yes."

The surgeon ran his hand through his hair.

"How do you stop the blood?"

"With this. Blacksmith made it." The farmer reached into his pocket and brought out a short iron tube with a handle across one end. "I heat it up in a fire and press it onto the skull. It seals round where I'm goin' to cut."

"And how do you cut through the skull?"

"With my knife." He showed him his penknife.

Bill noticed it was one with three extra blades for bleeding cows and horses.

The doctor smiled, shook his head.

"And then what do you do?"

"I take out the sack. I use a quill for that. Then I put back the piece of bone and bandage it up."

The surgeon's eyes were wide. He looked from the farmer

to the ewe and back again.

"Do you realise it's taken me twenty years to find a way of doing what you've just told me. Where did you learn to do it?"

"My father taught me. He learned it from his father."

"Can I have a look?" He gestured towards the ewe.

"No." The farmer stood firm. "That ewe's been through a lot. She wants leavin' quiet."

The Colonel blustered forwards as if an order had been disobeyed.

"Come now, Hector. Let the surgeon see the ewe."

The surgeon held up his hand, spoke quietly.

"It looks like Mr Beck knows what he's doing. I think I've seen all I can." He shook the farmer's hand and turned back towards the car.

As they drove away, Bill sat in the front and listened to the talk in the back. He heard the Colonel's voice.

"Interesting chap, old Hector. Parents left a small farm in the Dales and emigrated to Australia. The father got malaria, so they came back when Hector was eight. Bloody man's seen more of the world than the rest of us put together."

8

To emerge from desperate situations, desperate measures
have to be employed, and it is beyond dispute that our
position at the beginning of the last war was desperate.

R. G. Kendal. Land Drainage (1950)

When Bill arrived home his father wanted to know how the shoot went and why he had arrived home in the Rolls Royce. Bill told him about the visit to the farm and Jack nodded, rubbed his chin.

"I've heard about that kind of operation before, but I've never seen it done. I wouldn't know anyone who could do it."

When Bill said he'd heard that Germany had invaded Poland, Jack froze. He hadn't heard the news. The radio batteries were flat.

He dashed outside to the shed, disconnected the batteries from the radio and put them in the trap. Went to get the pony. Bill met him back in the house as he fumbled for his wallet.

"Where are you going?"

"To t' garage to swap t' batteries."

"It's nearly eight o'clock. It'll be closed."

Jack stopped. As if he hadn't realised the time.

"He'll be around somewhere. I'll get some." He shot out of the house, leaving the back door flapping. He returned half an hour later and carried the heavy batteries to the shed, ran towards the house and looked back across the yard. He put the pony back in the stable and went to turn on the radio.

Bill saw him reach into the top cupboard and pour himself a glass of whisky. He had that look on his face, the one he got when someone asked him about his time in the trenches. Bill thought it would be best to leave him alone.

Following the declaration of war, Bill noticed his father settle down a little. It was as if the reality of war was less of a burden to him than the threat of it. Nevertheless, he wasn't the same as he used to be. It started with small changes; things that Jack had been meticulous about were let slip. The grain bin was left open one night and was swarming with rats the next morning. Bill found a lame ewe untreated on the lot. A gate had been left unfastened and the bullocks had escaped from the riverbank and trampled some of the ripening oats. These misdemeanours were usually blamed on Dennis in his absence, with a snapped retort to Bill.

"That bloody lad'll be the ruin of us." Or when Dennis was in earshot. "How many times have I told you lads to fasten gates. Even Mary remembers to do that." Each of these chastisements was delivered hurriedly, with no time for objections, and usually just before Jack hurried off to do something else. He never looked his son in the face.

As a result, Bill began to feel the resentment boiling up inside him. Dennis had not been the last to take grain from the bin before the rats got in. Jack had been the one to close the gate the last time they had been working on the riverbank. And he had been checking the stock on the lot the week before Bill found the lame ewe. Jack Branthwaite was setting himself apart, above reproach, and because of this, Bill found it impossible to see his point of view. He could not confide in him any more. It had never been easy before, always under the shadow of Agnes's influence. But now that his father came across as both dishonest and cowardly in his inability to admit the slightest mistake, the son found that not only did he no longer trust his father's opinion, he was rapidly losing respect for it too.

Harvest started the first week in September so Bill was kept busy from dawn until dusk for two weeks. He saw Lucy in the mornings and at mealtimes, but they were never alone together and never got time to chat. When he finished work each night he flopped into bed, aching from forking sheaves and leading the horse.

Lucy was kept busy making meals for the three men and the labourers who came to help. She was taught how to stack the corn in the stack yard, catching the sheaves as they were thrown from the cart and making a round stack ready for sheeting or thatching.

Bill had asked her to keep an eye on the heifers across the road, so when Agnes sent her to take his supper down to the cornfield she said, "I'd better check those heifers first. Bill says that roan one's going to calve."

Agnes waved a hand at her.

"I checked them earlier when you were helping Mr Branthwaite to milk. They're all fine. The roan heifer's calved, a red one. It was up and suckling when I left it."

"Are any of the others looking like calving?"

"No. Now hurry up. Dennis and Bill will be hungry. Go and take them their supper. Come straight back. They can bring the basket back with them when they come back to the yard with the next load."

Lucy set off with the basket and tea can. She thought what a waste of time it was. Bill and Dennis were loading the cart and the four-wheeled wagon, then bringing them back to the yard. Why not have their supper up at the stack instead of Agnes sending her down to the fields with the food? Bill could even check the heifers himself whilst he was eating his tea. Agnes seemed to be running the show and wanted Bill and Dennis out of the yard for as long as possible.

Lucy reached the field just as they were finishing the second load. The horses stood patiently. Jack was stooking the last sheaves at the far end of the field. She handed the basket and tea can to Bill.

"Agnes wants me to go straight back."

"Don't be daft. You can ride back with us."

They sat in the stubble, the two men leaning their backs against the cartwheels. Lucy propped herself against Bill's shoulder, passed a mug of tea to Dennis.

"Thank you, Mrs Bill."

"Dennis." Bill was staring at him.

Lucy felt herself blushing.

Dennis gave a sly grin, shrugged and bit into his sandwich.

Lucy took a deep breath.

"Dennis ... ." She paused. "You won't make comments like that in front of Agnes, will you?"

He took a gulp of tea. Spoke without looking at her. Stared straight ahead.

"A lot o' folks thinks Dennis is daft. Lucy should know he's not stupid." He turned to look at her. "Besides, I knows to keep my mouth shut when she's around. Sometimes I thinks I'm t' only one bright enough to do that."

They all laughed. They finished eating and climbed up to take the loads back to the yard. Lucy sat beside Bill on the wagon and Dennis waited for Jack to join him and followed with the cart.

It was getting late when they finished stacking the two loads. There were almost two full loads left in the field, so Lucy went back with the three men to finish the field. When they got back it was dark. Bill backed the wagon into the barn and Jack threw a stack sheet over the cart. They put the horses in the stable and went to bed.

Lucy was helping with the milking every morning now, so that the men could start harvesting earlier. She could milk almost as fast as Bill. Jack told them that another heifer had calved, then went with Dennis to bring them in. They put the calves in a pen and tied the heifers in the shippen. Jack rubbed the two heifer's udders.

"Both calves were suckin' t' roan heifer. T'other needs milkin'."

Lucy stood and held its tail while Bill milked out the thick yellow colostrum. He handed her the bucket.

"Take half o' this an' feed both those caves. Chances are, they haven't had enough. Give t' rest to Agnes. She can make a custard."

Lucy fed the calves and went into the house with the men for breakfast. When she was pouring Bill's tea she looked at him, puzzled.

"I thought you told me all those red heifers would have red calves."

"Aye. They will. Calves are all by a red bull."

"That other calf's a roan one." She looked towards Agnes. "Didn't you say that the roan heifer had a red one?"

"Yes." Her words were sharp. "I know a roan heifer and a red calf when I see them."

Lucy continued.

"So that red heifer must've had the roan calf."

Agnes was stabbing at the bacon in the pan. "Red calves, roan calves. I don't see what all the fuss is about." She slammed a plate in front of Dennis.

Bill turned to his father.

"I was readin' an article in t' paper a few weeks back. Some professor was explainin' it."

Jack put down his fork.

"Aye. I saw it. I didn't tek a lot o' notice. I don't allus 'ave a lot o' time fer professors talkin' about cows, but this time I think he's right. I don't remember any red cows ever havin' a roan calf to a red bull."

Agnes crashed some dishes into the sink.

"That red calf was definitely sucking that roan heifer. What difference does it make? They're all alive aren't they?" She wiped her hands on a tea towel.

Bill ploughed in with the next question.

"Did it look like it'd calved when you checked 'em?"

"Look. I saw it from the bedroom window. All right?" She grabbed Mary's arm, yanked her from her seat. "Come on child. It's time you were setting off for school."

Jack turned to Bill.

"Bloody hell, there's a war on. Haven't we more things t' worry about than t' colour o' calves?" He left the table and went to switch on the wireless.

As the weeks went by, the war seemed a long way from Lancashire. The wireless and newspapers reported that Russia had invaded Poland. Bill heard of people being called up into the army, but nobody he knew had received their papers. All his friends worked on farms and were exempt.

The most pressing matters were jobs on the farm. When harvest was finished they started lifting the potatoes. Two weeks of wet weather meant that the last few rows were still in the ground in October. The potato digger was left standing in the field, and water stood in pools between the rows.

As soon as the sun began to dry out the furrows Jack sent Bill to hitch the horse to the potato digger. The soil was barely dry enough and the potatoes rolled out with clods stuck to them. Dennis, Jack and Lucy arrived with the other horse and the cart. Mary had stayed off school and came running across to help.

Jack looked at the soil, picked up a lump and broke it in two.

"We'd better get on wi' it. This weather might not last. Sooner we get finished an' we can start pullin' turnips."

They set about picking up the potatoes spun out of the first row. Jack looked at his daughter.

"Use both hands. You'll pick 'em a lot faster."

She scowled up at him and carried on, using her left hand to help keep her balance as she reached for the next one.

As they reached the end of the row the soil was drying a little, and Bill took the horse back to spin out the next furrow.

They finished the job by the end of the day, and as Bill and Dennis finished emptying the sacks into the barn Jack came back from the house. His face looked pale.

"Germans have sunk the *Royal Oak*. Agnes's cousin was on that. News says over eight hundred men lost."

When Sergeant Jackson rode into the yard on his bike a week later, Bill wondered what he'd come for. When he asked to see Agnes, Bill guessed it was about her cousin. The sergeant leaned his bike near the back door and knocked. Agnes invited him in, and Bill watched from the cartload of turnips as the door closed behind him. Jack left Bill and Dennis to throw off the turnips, and went into the house. It was over an hour before the policeman left, and as Bill passed the kitchen window he heard his father's raised voice coming from inside.

"Why didn't you tell me?"

Agnes was shouting too.

"There's nothing to tell. I was born in Plymouth and my father was a captain in the navy in the last war. I'm a British citizen. That's all there is to it."

"Sergeant Jackson didn't seem to think so."

Bill listened from the granary doorway. Agnes's voice was higher, agitated.

"You heard him. He said it was only a formality. He had to check because he'd received information. I've never been there and I never met my grandparents. I don't know any of that side of the family. God knows, my mother answered enough questions last time. Will they never learn?"

Bill peered round the corner of the granary. The kitchen was gloomy. He couldn't see Agnes but his father was sitting at the kitchen table with his head in his hands. He looked up to his left. Agnes must be standing by the stove.

"You do realise they're locking 'em up all over the country? What are folk going to say when they find out?"

Agnes appeared, her back to the window.

"Well they're not going to find out. Are they?"

Jack's reply was muffled.

"For God's sake don't let Bill find out. Things are tense enough round here as it is."

When Bill finished work he went into the house to look for Lucy. She was busy helping Agnes, so after supper he followed her outside when she went to shut the hens in.

"What was all that about this afternoon?"

"I don't know. Agnes sent me down to the shop."

"Agnes and Dad were havin' a hell of a row about summat."

Lucy stopped him.

"Oh. Mrs Finch was gossiping as usual. She said she has it on good authority that Sergeant Jackson has been going round questioning anybody with German connections. Would you believe it? There's someone in the village who's half German."

Bill told her what he'd heard.

Lucy put her hand to her mouth and sucked in breath.

"You don't think she's a spy?"

Bill laughed.

"I shouldn't think so. Her dad was a naval man in the last war. Besides, what's she goin' to report? Heifers calving at Sandholme? The latest news from Mrs Finch?"

Lucy hit him on the shoulder.

"Stop mocking me."

He put his arm round her, kissed her, and they walked back to the yard. As they reached the gate, a fox barked in the woods by the river. Bill looked back.

"You do right to shut the hens in every night. I'll have a word with Tom. He does a bit o' shootin'."

❖

As the weeks rolled on, the nights began to draw in and Lucy started shutting the hens in before milking. The cows came in for the winter; the rest of the heifers were brought off the lot and housed in the shippens surrounding the out-barn. Lucy helped with the milking while Dennis was kept busy mucking out. As the weather worsened, Mary found it more difficult to dry the washing, so each night she set up a clothesmaid by the fire and another in front of the stove in the kitchen.

By the end of October most of the trees were bare. Only the huge oaks that sheltered the farmyard still kept their leaves. The threshing team came and set up the huge machine in the yard. Bill, Dennis and Jack worked furiously, loading the thresher, moving the sacks of grain and forking straw into the barn. A violent wind blew chaff onto the building roofs and into drifts against the back door of the house. Each time the door was opened, chaff blew into the passage and lodged in the coconut matting.

Agnes bawled at Lucy to sweep it up. Lucy was cooking for ten men; she kept her head down, continued working and promised to clean up when she'd finished.

Bill noticed how the men in the threshing gang poked fun at Dennis. They treated him like an idiot, tried to hit him in the face with a sheaf or a handful of chaff.

He tightened his grip on the pitchfork. Kept working. There wasn't time for an argument. Upsetting the threshers might mean being put lower down on the list next year. He threw straw into the barn as the steam engine pounded and the huge belts spun. They'd be gone tomorrow.

Leading up to bonfire night the weather stayed fine. Dennis looked over the yard wall towards the heap of thorns and sticks at the bottom of the paddock.

"Looks like we'll have a proper fire tomorrow. Them slashin's'll 'ave dried out a bit by now."

Bill nodded.

"Lucy's bakin' and Mary's helpin' her make treacle toffee."

"I've sorted out some big taties t' bake. I'll tek 'em in to Mrs Branthwaite at teatime. Do y' think t' Germans'll see t' fire?"

"I wouldn't worry about it Dennis if I were you. I don't think they're interested in our bonfire."

Dennis watched as Lucy appeared from the hen cabin.

"I thought Tom would've shot that fox by now."

They were finishing milking, when Tom walked into the shippen.

"I've come to 'ave another go at that fox."

Bill glanced towards the door and saw that he'd brought someone with him. He thought he recognised the pointed features and bushy eyebrows. Tom reminded him where he'd seen him before.

"Ted's goin' t' give me a hand. He can call a fox."

Ted sucked in his bottom lip and sucked air through his teeth. It made a sound like an injured rabbit. All the time, Ted's eyes flicked around, scanning the buildings and yard as if he was looking for something. He gave Tom a nudge and they walked out into the darkness carrying their shotguns and carbide lamps.

At around nine o' clock there was a knock on the back door. Bill put down the newspaper and went to answer it. It was Tom. He was holding a big dog fox by its tail.

"I told you I'd get it. Ted called it an' I shot it."

Ted stepped into the lantern light.

"Looks like you owe us one." He climbed into the car and started the engine.

Tom seemed a bit embarrassed. He ran to the boot of the car and threw in the fox, reached in and pulled out a pheasant, held it out towards Bill. When Bill's expression changed he blurted out,

"It's all right. We didn't shoot it here." He glanced back at Ted. "Our gamekeeper's lad's 'ave been called up. There's only t' old man left. Ted says 'e doesn't know 'is arse from 'is elbow."

Bill pushed the pheasant away. Shook his head. Went inside. He'd not seen Tom at the chip shop for months. When he thought about it he hadn't really had a conversation with him since that first time he took Lucy home. He'd seen him briefly each time he'd come to try and shoot the fox, but he hadn't had time to stop and talk. The one thing he couldn't understand was what the hell Tom was doing, hanging around with Ted. No one seemed to know what Ted did for a living. He was often beating at shoots. Bill had seen him coming out of a pub in Bentham one afternoon when Bill had been to the auction, but he wasn't connected with farming, and Jack had said that he didn't work for the estate. There was a dance coming up in the village hall next week. Bill hoped he'd see Tom there.

When they went to light the bonfire the following night Agnes said it didn't seem right, having it on a Sunday. She went along, and Bill thought for a minute that it was the first time he'd seen her beyond the farm gate since last bonfire night. He corrected himself when he remembered seeing her rolling eggs with Mary on Easter Monday. They lit the bonfire, and when it was roaring Agnes handed Bill the baked potatoes to finish off at the edge of the fire. Lucy passed round some gingerbread, and Dennis kept commenting that it was the best he'd ever tasted. Mary gave him some treacle toffee, and Bill saw him slipping it into his jacket pocket for later.

Bill had brought a pitchfork and went round the fire pushing in any branches at the edge that hadn't caught light. He stopped and gazed into the flames at the opposite side of the pile to everyone else. Lucy wandered round to join him and he stood there with one arm resting on the fork and the other round Lucy's waist. He looked up to see Agnes marching towards them. Just before she reached them, Jack grabbed her arm.

"Leave 'em Agnes. They're not doin' any harm."

She looked back at him and started to protest, but he led her away. Bill didn't hear what she'd said.

Mary came running round and pointed to the sky as a rocket flew up from the garden at Friar's Hall. She pointed round the valley to where bonfires had been lit at all the surrounding farms, burning like beacons from one end of the country to the other.

When all the baked potatoes had been eaten or thrown back on the fire Agnes led the way back to the house. Bill forked the embers over one last time and followed them back inside.

✤

On the night of the dance, Jack took Bill and Lucy down in the trap. They'd been going to cycle down but Jack said he'd take them and pick them up at half past ten. It was Agnes's idea.

As Jack disappeared back up the road, Lucy grabbed Bill's arm.

"Come on. Let's go for a drink first."

Bill hesitated. He'd never been in the pub before.

"Don't worry. I'm not going to get you drunk."

He followed her inside and up to the bar. Lucy ordered him a pint of mild and a bottle of stout for herself. They sat at a table near the fire and Bill looked round at the men in the pub.

"How're y' doin' Bill?" It was Vince, the mechanic. "First time I've seen you in here."

Bill blushed.

"We're havin' a night out."

"An' how's Lucy?"

Bill was surprised that he knew her.

"I'm doing fine thanks. Did you get that cultivator fixed?"

"Aye. I did." He turned to Bill. "I was cursin' it when Lucy

walked by t'other week. These bloody farmers who've bought tractors; they're wreckin' all their machinery. They don't realise that a tractor won't stop when they hit a rock, like a horse does. It keeps me in a job, but some of 'em tek some mendin'."
He turned to the man sitting next to him and started complaining about the Laycocks. "They're allus bustin' summat. They're not right obligin' either. They want it fixed right away, whether I've other jobs lined up or not. They're bad payers an' all."

Bill leaned across to Lucy.

"They're Agnes's friends. They claim to be better than everyone else."

Lucy nodded

"Alice told me."

They finished their drinks and crossed the road to the village hall. Inside, the dance had started. The hall was lined with chairs, and couples from the surrounding villages were seated waiting for the next dance to be announced. On the stage at the far end a four-piece band were playing background music between the dances. The billiard room had been taken over for the night and the table was covered with plates of sandwiches and cakes. A stove in the corner was glowing hot and Annie Dobson's head was visible through the hatch into the kitchen.

Bill and Lucy found seats near Alice and a young man whom Bill didn't know. He tried to get him in conversation but the guy was so shy he only answered yes or no. When the next dance started, Lucy dragged Bill to his feet.

"But I don't know how to do it."

"You didn't know how to swim either."

He laughed as she guided him round the floor, and tried not to think of how he looked to the people sitting at the side. When the music stopped he returned to his seat. They watched as Alice and her partner stayed on the dance floor.

The shy bloke knew all the steps and seemed to dance better than anyone else in the room. When the dance was over Alice brought him back and sat next to Lucy. Bill heard her whispering.

"He's a bit of a bore, but his mother taught him to dance. I came with Tom last time, but I went home with sore toes."

Bill looked across.

"Where is Tom?"

"I was going to ask you the same thing. Haven't you seen him?"

Bill shook his head.

At about ten o'clock Bill was heading out for the toilets. He stopped to talk to Mr Finch and Norman Watterson who were on the door. The doorknob rattled and Tom walked in.

"All right, Bill?" There was something different about him. A kind of tone that made Bill uneasy.

"All right, Tom? Where've you been?"

"Out and about. You know how it is." Ted was behind him. Mr Finch held up two tickets.

"Two shillings please."

Tom put his hand in his pocket but Ted stepped forward, started to protest.

"You can't charge that at this time o' night. Dance is nearly over. T'other folks have had their supper here. It shouldn't be any more than half price to us."

Mr Finch shrank back. He looked from Bill to Norman Watterson.

Norman stepped forwards.

"I'll tell you what I'll do. If thee an' thi mate buys a couple o' books o' yon raffle tickets, I'll let thee in fer hafe price."

Ted looked down at him, triumphant.

"Sounds all right t' me."

Norman tore out the raffle tickets, handed them over with the dance tickets.

"That's two shillin'."

They handed over the money, strode into the hall and across to the kitchen where Ted started hassling Mrs Taylor to give him some supper.

Mr Finch stared at them, looked at Norman Watterson.

"You can't do that. They only come in late 'cos they've been to the pub and we've got a late bar. You've let 'em in for half price and now they've got their supper."

"Can't I?" Norman took the stubs of the raffle ticket books, tore them in half and tossed them in the stove. He gave Bill a disapproving frown. "That mate o' yorn's keepin' some queer company."

Bill walked back into the hall just as the raffle was being drawn. Norman Watterson nudged him in the ribs and nodded towards Ted who was looking at his raffle tickets. Norman's growl had humour in it.

"A pund sez yon bugger doesn't win a prize."

Bill had the last dance with Lucy. A slow waltz. He managed without standing on her feet. They clapped the band and walked towards the door. Jack was already waiting.

9

*All weeds as such are pernicious, but some much more
than others; some do more injury, and are more easily
destroyed; some do less injury, and are harder to kill;
others there are, which have both these bad qualities.*

Jethro Tull. The Horse Hoeing Husbandry (1733)

Since the fox had been around, the geese had started sleeping
in the yard. Agnes had been complaining constantly about the
mess around the back door. Each morning, after milking, Lucy
would sweep the muck from the flagstones and shovel it into
the wheelbarrow. She took a bucket of water from the horse
trough and swilled away the green smears left by the brush. Bill
knew the geese wouldn't go back to sleeping in the stack yard
even though the fox had been shot. They felt safer within sight
of the dog kennels.

The morning after the dance, Bill was cleaning out a small
loosebox in the corner of the yard. It was piled high with
hessian sacks, too big for potatoes. Against the wall were old
fencing rails, half-rotten and worm-eaten. Some of them
crumbled to dust when he lifted them out and piled them in
the wheelbarrow.

Dennis walked past with an armful of hay for the bull.

"You should've done that before t' bonfire."

"Yes Dennis." He snapped them into short lengths and
threw them in the coal shed. Returned to the loosebox and
started carrying out some old pieces of iron.

Jack hurried across to him.

"Don't throw them away. They might come in handy fer
summat." He pointed to several of them. "Them's t' ends off
an old flail fer threshin' corn an' that's a coulter off an old
plough. Save them sacks. Tinkers'll give us a couple o' bob for
'em in t' spring."

Bill groaned to himself, dumped the iron in the corner of the cart shed and went back for the sacks. When he lifted the first bundle mice ran in all directions, between his feet, out of the door, across the floor to a hole in the corner. Some hid under the next bundle.

Bill shouted across the yard.

"They're full of holes. Mice've been at 'em."

His father shouted back.

"Tinkers'll sort through 'em. Chuck 'em over a beam."

Bill carried the sacks round and tossed them up onto the beam above his head. Something small and rubbery bounced off his cheek. Another one slipped inside his collar. He could feel it moving under his shirt. He wrenched his shirt tail out of his trousers and let the thing fall onto the floor. It was a tiny mouse, pink, hairless and blind, squirming between the cobbles.

One of the farm cats that had been rubbing itself against the cart shafts leapt forward and grabbed it. It stopped for the one that had hit Bill's face, picked it up with the other and disappeared round the corner, growling. Bill shuddered and went back for the rest of the sacks. There was a trail of pink twitching mice all the way from the loosebox to the cart shed. Some of them had been squashed to pink splodges where they'd fallen under his boots. The others were dying on the cold stones. He made sure that he shook all the mice from the other bundles before he carried them out.

He was finishing sweeping up the rubbish and dead mice when Lucy appeared from the garden with the washing. She put down the basket and walked over to him.

"What are you doing?"

"I'm cleanin' out this loosebox. I'm goin' to bed it down for t' geese. If we shut 'em in here every night it'll save you a job in t' mornin'. We're goin' t' start fattenin' 'em up." He picked up a wooden trough that was leaning against the wall, carried it inside and placed it in the middle of the floor. "We'll give 'em some barley meal in this."

"I can feed them, if you like. I'll do it when I've fed the hens in the afternoon."

"Okay." He smiled. "I was goin' to ask you anyway."

The geese were wary the first night. Bill had told Lucy to leave them until after milking, so he, Jack and Dennis could help her put them inside. He hung a lantern in the loose box, and all four of them walked slowly round the geese driving them towards the light. They huddled together, flicking their heads from side to side and letting out little honks as if they were asking each other what was going on. As they reached the doorway one of the two old geese stuck her neck out and strode in. She went straight across to the trough and started guzzling the wet meal. The other old goose followed and the gander gave a honk and raced after them. The young geese crowded round the door and followed. At the last minute one of them made a dive for the yard and Dennis trapped it against the wall with his knee. He picked it up as it honked and flapped and tried to bite his hands. He threw it inside, and Bill slammed the door.

"They'll be easier to get in tomorrow." Then to Lucy, "By next weekend they'll be followin' you in with t' bucket."

By Christmas week they had orders for eighteen of the nineteen young geese. Miss Taggart the schoolteacher called in on Wednesday asking for one, but Jack sent her down to Charlie Taylor's. When she'd gone he said he wasn't giving up his Christmas dinner for anyone, least of all a flappy school mistress who hadn't the good sense to put her order in early.

He was glad it was frosty weather. Christmas day was on Monday and he would have been worried if the dressed birds had been hanging around all weekend in mild weather. He remembered the time when Mrs Finch's sister had bought one and complained the following week that it had gone off. What did she expect? She'd picked it up two days early and left it in the cupboard by the fire.

They wanted all the geese killed and plucked before milking time. They would dress them on Friday. Most customers would pick them up on Saturday; especially the Methodists who wouldn't want to do business on a Sunday. Dennis and Bill held each goose under their arms as Jack held out its head and stuck the knife through its neck just below its beak. They gripped them tightly until the blood stopped flowing as the struggling and flapping grew weak. Then they carried them, heads swinging, to the wash house, and hung them by the legs from the drying rack and nails in the wall.

They'd carried half of them across the yard when Lucy came out with three mugs of coffee. Dennis was holding out another goose to Jack and he grabbed its beak, raised the knife mechanically. He was just about to cut its throat when he stopped and said "Whoa. Not that one, Dennis. That's Bertie."

Lucy put the cups on the pigsty wall.

"Bertie?"

"He's t' gander. We need 'im for next year."

"Why do you call him Bertie?"

Jack laughed.

"We named him after a bloke who used t' be t' postman."

Bill finished the story.

"Because he had two women on the go."

She went back to the house, shaking her head.

By milking time all the young geese had been killed and rough plucked. The gander and the two mothers stood in the stack yard, honking for their family.

After milking, the men ate a quick supper and returned to the wash house to finish plucking the geese. They started by removing all the down, then pinching out any short pens with a blunt knife held against their thumbs. When he'd finished the first bird, Jack placed a flat pan on an old card table and poured methylated spirit into it. He struck a match and the meths burned with a blue flame. He held each goose by its head and feet, turning it over the flame to singe away any coarse hairs that hadn't come away with the feathers. They worked in the cold to keep the birds fresh.

At nine o'clock Lucy came out with cups of tea and stayed to help finish penning the last few geese. Jack went inside to hear the news and didn't come back.

After about half an hour the latch lifted and the door opened. Bill expected to see his father but was surprised to see Tom. As Tom stepped into the lantern light, Bill's surprise turned to shock. His friend had a black eye and a big lump on his forehead. His lip was swollen and crusted with blackening scabs. His jacket was torn and missing a couple of buttons. The cocky aloofness had been ripped from him, pulled apart at the seams, leaving nothing but the old Tom – no front, no air of superiority that made him sound more like one of Luther Barrett's sons than a boy from a farm.

Bill looked into Tom's eyes and saw his friend, the one who'd dragged him from the stream, the one who'd stuck up for him at school and asked him round to play the day after Bill's mother died.

"What the hell's happened to you?"

Lucy looked across at him, took Dennis's arm and stepped past Tom towards the door.

"Come on Dennis. We'll leave Bill and Tom to finish off. I'll make you a hot drink before you go to bed."

Dennis got up, handed his goose to Tom and left with Lucy. Tom slumped on a chair and began ripping down from the goose's wing. It was a few moments before he spoke.

"I got caught poachin'."

Bill had already guessed, but he let him continue.

"We were lampin' some pheasants up in t' top wood. The one y' can see from your lot. Me an' Ted. We thought it were all right 'cos t' gamekeeper's sons were away in t' army. We'd had a good night, shot about ten. Ted had 'em in a sack an' I was carryin' t' gun an' lamp. It was a good night fer it, cloudy an' right dark."

Bill was letting him ramble. Let him get it off his chest.

"We were followin' that stream down towards our lot. It's right easy to get lost in there. You remember when we were kids?"

Bill nodded and said "Hmm" when he saw that Tom was looking away.

"We were about half way down, about where we med that dam. Remember? That big un that Bruce Crabtree wrecked when we were away fishin'. It turns out that keeper's lads were both home on leave after basic trainin'. They were hidin' in those rhododendrons where we made a den."

Bill remembered the narrow path between the bushes and the stream.

"We heard a twig crack an' made a run fer it. They were right behind us but I reckoned I could lose 'em once we were in t' open. Clouds were clearin' a bit an' we were runnin' wi' t' lamps out. Ted got to t' wall first an' he was half way o'er when I got there. He looked right back at me. Oh he's a bad bastard, Bill. I never saw it before. He swung that bag o' pheasants an' hit me right in t' face, knocked me over so I fell against t' wall. That's how I got this." He lifted his fringe and pointed to the lump on his forehead. "He dropped t' bag next to me an' next thing t' keeper's lads were givin' me a right kickin'. I spent last night in t' cell at Hornby."

Bill was plucking idly at the goose's neck.

"What're they goin' to do to you?"

Tom had put his bird down. He reached into his pocket for a cigarette. Bill saw his hands shaking as he lit it.

He sucked in, long and hard, blew smoke towards the geese hanging on the wall.

"Sergeant Jackson was all right, considerin'. He knew who I'd been wi' even tho' I never let on. Asked me what I was playin' at, hangin' around wi' Ted. I told him I'd known Ted since I was a kid. He said if I had any sense, I'd stay away from him. He let me go, reckoned I'd had my punishment."

"Is Colonel Trewin goin' to press charges?"

"No, Bill." He was leaning with his elbows on his knees, staring straight ahead. His lip was moving. He turned towards Bill. His eyes were red, full of tears. "He's turnin' us off t' farm."

"Oh, Tom."

Tom stood up. Paced. He was chattering.

"Dad pleaded wi' him. Said I'd never bin in trouble afore. But he was havin' none of it. He said if he heard tell that dad were involved, we'd be gone before rent day."

"So he's given you till April?"

Tom was crying now.

"Three generations we've bin at that farm, an' I've gone an' buggered it up."

Bill said nothing. Didn't think there was anything he could say.

✢

When Bill told him next morning, Jack just gazed at the stove.

"Well. They're not the first." He cradled his mug in his hands and stared into it. "I bet Brian Waterford's cut up about it though. He's as straight as they come. You know, it's a pity they didn't get turned off a few years ago."

"Why?"

"Farms are bein' snapped up now. If this war lasts long there'll be a food shortage. A lot o' folk are seein' it as an opportunity t' mek money. Remember what a struggle it was for us before your mother died?"

Bill nodded.

"Year of t' crash, yows were mekin' half t' price they cost t'

125

year before. Same wi' cows. Depression carried on for years. It got as landlords couldn't let a farm for love nor money. Down south there was land goin' idle." He got up from his chair, put on his jacket. "Things are different now. Trade's up at Bentham already. Farms are easy to let, an' landlords are gettin' fussy. Tom an' his dad might not find it easy t' get another farm."

Bill followed him to the back door.

"People are sayin' this war won't last long."

"They said that last time, an' look how long that took. Just remember what they said in September. 'It'll all be over by Christmas'. It's Christmas t' day after tomorrow, an' it's hardly started yet." He stopped as he unbolted the door. "Anyway. Don't go wishin' fer hard times, Bill. That won't help nobody." He took the lantern and walked out into the dark.

During the night it had frozen hard. An east wind had blown under the doors and frozen the water in the dairy. When Bill rolled the churn into the shippen and lifted the lid he noticed that some of the milk in the bottom had frozen to the sides. The wind kept up, and last night's clear skies had been hidden by a thin blanket of grey.

As he finished milking, Bill looked up from the shippen doorway. There would be no thaw today. Dennis was shovelling muck from the pigsty. He was complaining that it was like stones. Some of it was frozen to the ground.

Lucy was coming across the yard, struggling with a bucket of warm meal and another full of water. She stopped by the door.

"The hens have nearly stopped laying. There were only five eggs yesterday. Water's frozen every morning now. The stream's frozen over too."

Bill's mind was elsewhere.

"I hope Tom got back all right last night. It's a long walk over t' lot."

"He'll be fine. He knows those hills and woods as well as

anyone else."

Bill thought about last night.

"Right now, he's probably wishing he didn't." He watched her trudge off down the paddock.

The air was still freezing when Bill lifted down the first goose to dress it. He turned it over to check for any pens or down. It was completely plucked and singed apart from its head and wing ends.

"Just a minute." Jack came in with a pair of clippers, cut off the ends of the bird's wings and stuffed them into a sack. He continued along the line of hanging geese until the sack was full.

Lucy was coming in with the coffee. Jack handed her the sack.

"Here. Put these to dry by t'fire."

She looked into the sack.

"Oh good. I need a new one for sweeping the hearth. I'll put the rest in the cellar when they're dry." She left the mugs and took the sack of wings into the house. Jack went round the row of geese cutting off their legs at the joint and dropping them in a bucket.

Bill cut into the first goose. He felt the crunch of ice as he pushed his hand in to remove the guts. He cut off the gizzard, put it on the table and dropped the guts in a bucket. Then he put his hand back inside, pulled out first the liver then the heart and lungs. He cut the gall bladder from the liver and let it drop onto the pile of guts. The liver went on the plate along with the heart. He threw away the lungs. Next he cut off the goose's neck, peeled back the skin and cut again, discarding the skin and head. He placed the neck with the other giblets.

As Bill continued gutting the geese, Jack took a knife and began splitting the gizzards, scraping away the grit, peeling off the leathery yellow skin and washing the fleshy part in water before placing it on the plate.

When he cut into the third gizzard he laughed, held up a marble.

"Is this Mary's or did you lose it a long time ago?" He rinsed it in the water and handed it to Bill.

Bill dried it on his sleeve. It was a deep blue colour with flecks of gold and purple swirls.

"Never seen one like that before." He tossed it back to his dad.

"Haven't you?" He rolled it in his palm. "Our Harry had some like that when he was a kid." He shrugged and put it in his pocket.

By the time Bill had finished all the geese his fingers were numb with cold. He washed his hands and wiped every bird down with a cloth then carried each one with its plate of giblets into the house. He laid them out in a row on the slab in the pantry.

Agnes was tipping the giblets into cellophane bags. She weighed each goose and put a label on it with its weight and the name of the customer. Bill noticed how many customers were Agnes's friends. She must have sold at least twelve of the nineteen geese. The Laycocks had bought three.

Lucy was crouching by the cupboard and lifting the lid off the nearest of three large pots.

"Agnes needs some eggs for baking." She lifted them out of the water and put them in a bowl. Each egg was crusted with white crystals. She was putting back the lid when she said, "Ah – Christmas pudding." She picked out another four and replaced the lid. She stood up, pecked him on the cheek and returned to the kitchen.

Saturday was a busy day in the farmhouse. People were coming and going all morning, picking up their geese. Bill couldn't help noticing what a good saleswoman Agnes was. She offered all her customers tea and mince pies. Each time he nipped into the house Lucy was boiling the kettle for someone who was sitting in the front room. At dinnertime he heard Agnes talking to his father.

"You shouldn't have given Miss Taggart such short shrift. Charlie Taylor's charging threepence a pound less than we are. We could have made two shillings on her goose if we'd bought it off him."

"Be careful Agnes. We don't want t' price ourselves out of t' market."

"Charlie hasn't sold all his. He's still got half of them running around his paddock. Everyone says ours are better."

"Are they better?"

"I don't know. But if they believe it, I'm not going to change their opinion."

Jack was protesting. He said he'd been neighbours with Charlie for a long time and didn't want to upset him. Agnes told him that even Lucy had heard Charlie say he'd had enough of keeping geese. They were too much work around Christmas, and the fox had taken his old gander along with three young geese. She came into the kitchen.

"Bill, can you take Sergeant Jackson his goose this afternoon? Your father and I usually deliver it but he's got to look the sheep, and I need to stay here until the rest of these birds have gone."

"All right." He turned to his dad. "Do you mind if I call and see how Tom is? I'll be back for milking."

"You go ahead. Both Tom an' his father'll be glad t' see a friendly face. Mind how you go. It'll be icy today."

As soon as he'd finished his dinner, Bill took the goose in a shopping bag and put it in the basket on Agnes's bike. He hooked the basket on the handlebars of his own bike and rode out up the road and past Moss's farm. A wagon was tipping a load of turnips in Moss's yard. Bill remembered Jack telling him that Joe Moss was too lazy to grow his own.

He turned off down the lane towards Hornby. As the

bike gathered speed, the wind hit him and he felt the chill bite into his chest. He couldn't remember cycling on a day as cold as this before. He rounded a corner and skidded where water running across the road had frozen and left a sheet of ice like glass. The bike slid from under him and he found himself sliding across the ice on his side. The shopping bag had fallen out of the basket and had landed by the verge. He picked up his bike and put the bag back in the basket, checked to see that the policeman's goose was still there. He knew it was by the weight. The handlebars had gone a bit askew so he stood with the front wheel between his knees and straightened them. He set off again and wished he'd listened to his dad.

When he reached the police house there was no answer at the front door. An old lady was walking up the next path with her shopping.

"He'll be out the back, love."

He thanked her and went round the end of the house. His feet crunched the frozen mud on the path as he carried the shopping bag round the back of the police house. Passed the frosted cabbages. The garden was a huddle of wooden huts and pigeon lofts. One door was ajar. Croaks, growls and screeches echoed from its shadows.

He whistled and Sergeant Jackson emerged, holding a gamecock by its legs. Its dubbed, combless head dripped blood onto the stone by the door. He looked at the bag.

"Put it down on that crate. Come in, lad. I'm busy." He stepped back into the creosote-reeking hut.

Bill followed. Watched him dip the bird's head in a bowl of bloodied brine. It croaked, coughed and shook its hackles. The sergeant threw the bird back in its pen. It crowed, beat its wings. Splashed red on the boards. Rushed to the front and attacked the wire with its beak. The policeman pulled his fingers back quickly as he fastened the gate.

"This one's got promise. Look at the fire in him."

There were four pens at the back of the hut, wired from waist height, boarded below. Each had a perch at the back, about the height of Bill's chest. Near the perch the boards dividing the pens extended to the roof. Jackson noticed Bill studying the layout.

"They can only see t' next cock when one bird is on t' perch and t'other is on t' ground. They spend all day flyin' up an' down, tryin' t' get at each other. It keeps 'em 'ard."

Bill glanced round the hut. Saw iron spurs hanging from a nail.

The officer took him outside. Showed him the pigeon lofts. Lit a cigarette and stood leaning against the shed, puffing out plumes.

"Sounds like that mate o' yours is gettin' punished 'ard for 'is crime."

"You've heard then?"

"It was all round t' pub last night. I'd like to get my hands on t' real villain."

"You mean Ted?"

"Aye. He'll probably lie low for a bit. I doubt whether poachin's his only income. I can't understand why t' Colonel's let him go beatin' for so long, unless he has somethin' on him. I'll catch him sooner or later." He winked. "One way or another."

Next door's latch clacked and Bill heard the old woman calling.

"Puss, puss, puss. Ch, ch, ch."

The sergeant's eyes shifted.

"She'll be shouting a long time. Pussy isn't coming home tonight." He stretched out an arm to the water butt by the pigeon loft. The lid tilted. A hinge. The ice in the water butt had been smashed with a rock. The sergeant parted the broken chunks.

Bill leaned over. Saw tortoiseshell fur, soaked, green, and floating.

The sergeant paid him for the goose, handed back the bag and headed for the back door. He turned as he opened it. "Have a good Christmas, Bill."

✣

Tom and his dad weren't around when Bill cycled into the yard. He went to the house and Tom's mum invited him in for a cup of tea. She broke down when she told him that they'd gone to look at another farm. She rubbed her eyes with her handkerchief and apologised.

"We've always been happy here. The place they've gone to see is miles away, over near Settle. The old man who farmed it died three weeks ago. Brian's brother's driven them there. I hope they get it. Even tho' it is smaller than ... our farm." As soon as she said the words she burst into tears again.

Bill thanked her for the tea and told her he'd better be getting back.

Much of Christmas eve was spent making things easier for Christmas day. Dennis was having Christmas dinner with his mother so he pulped extra turnips for the cows and heifers to save himself time the next day. He piled hay in the gangway in front of the cows so he only needed to lift it over to feed them next morning. Bill took enough hay for the sheep to last until Wednesday and Jack bedded the calves down with extra straw. Bill knew that Dennis would be up first in the morning and would be tearing round the yard like a man possessed.

✣

Christmas day came with the usual rush in the morning, getting everything finished in time for dinner. Mary was up before her father and Bill. She waited until she saw the flickering light from the landing, then ran downstairs after her father and brother. Jack lit two candles on the mantelpiece so she could see the presents under the tree. He'd cut it off the top of a spruce in the far wood when he'd been to look the sheep, struggled back with it over his shoulder, and some sprigs of berried holly in his hand.

He stood smiling down at Mary as she found a new paint box and some gloves knitted by her aunt. He didn't tell her about the school desk and chair that he'd hidden in the sitting room. He'd let her find that at breakfast time.

After milking, when they were sitting at the breakfast table, Mary came running into the kitchen.

"Look. It's gone." She was holding a plate with some pastry crumbs on it and the sherry glass she'd left out the night before. She peered into the bottom of the glass and saw a dark smudge in the bottom.

Dennis watched and tried to add to the fantasy.

"Something had been chewing at that pile o' turnips I left out last night."

Mary didn't get it. Bill suggested that it might have been a reindeer.

After breakfast they went to feed the heifers. Dennis finished with the wheelbarrow and was loitering as the heifers drank. He helped them get the heifers back inside and Jack let him go back to the farm whilst he and Bill finished the feeding.

When Bill and Jack got back to the house Dennis was cycling into the yard.

"I forgot to change." He dashed back to his room above the granary.

After Christmas dinner, Bill and Lucy played ludo with Mary. Bill won. Lucy could have, but she held back two of her counters that could have gone home and moved out one at the back. Mary took Lucy's leading counters and sent them back to the start. When she threw the dice and sent her last one home, she jumped up and down.

"Did I win?"

Bill was about to say, "No," when Lucy stopped him.

"You beat me."

Mary got up from the kitchen table and ran through to the front room.

"Daddy. I beat Lucy at ludo."

Jack was getting up from his chair. He stretched, rubbed his hand through his daughter's hair.

"Well done, lass." He went to get his jacket. "Come on Bill. Cows are waiting."

Lucy put on her coat and went to feed the hens.

10

*Strait let the vig'rous steer
Turn the rich furrow in the New-born Year,
And Summer's Heat with rip'ning Suns pursue
The sluggish Glebe, and all the Clod subdue.*

Jethro Tull. The Horse Hoeing Husbandry (1733)
(From Virgil's First Georgic)

The New Year was always a time of optimism for Bill. He felt as if he'd closed the door on last year's troubles, and any problems not yet resolved were just waiting to be sorted, like Agnes' spring-cleaning. A kind of truce seemed to be settling over the household.

Agnes seemed to be accepting Lucy more than she had and Bill himself was noticing more of Agnes's good qualities. He'd recognised her skill as a saleswoman and, although she wasn't practically minded like Tom's mother or Mrs Taylor, she had a kind of foresight as if she was always planning ahead.

One evening at the beginning of January the whole family were sitting in the front room. The wind was blowing so hard it was lifting the doorknocker. The air sucked up the chimney till the fire roared. Lucy had found Mabel's old pegging frame under the stairs and had suggested that they made a rug. To Bill's surprise, Agnes agreed.

Lucy brought in a clean sack from the granary and was stitching it to the frame. The sack had FLAKED MAIZE stamped across the middle. Mary was looking at it.

"We don't want a rug with writing on it. People will laugh."

Lucy stopped stitching.

"Don't worry, Mary. When we've finished nobody will be able to see the writing."

Jack glanced up. He was leaning his elbows on his knees with some old newspaper between his feet. He'd cut two short lengths from an old brush shaft, had shaped and pointed them with his penknife. Lucy had told him they were too rough for pushing through the strips of cloth, "They'll catch and pull." So he was sanding them down smooth.

Agnes had an eye for colour. She'd cut up a heap of old coats, jackets and the thickest parts from some worn-out trousers. The greys, tweeds and checks had been cut into strips about four inches long and slightly less than an inch wide. She'd folded out the dining table and piled the strips in the middle, all blended to make a uniform mix. The blacks and navy blues were in a bag at her feet. She was working on an old red coat that was too small for Mary.

"I need some orange." She got to her feet and went upstairs, came back carrying the two orange towels from the bottom of the airing cupboard.

Bill gave Lucy a sly glance. Lucy looked away, reached over and rubbed the material between her finger and thumb.

"What's the matter?" Agnes breathed in half a breath and Bill guessed that she'd sounded sharper than she meant to.

Lucy twitched.

"The fabric's worn it'll fray."

Agnes peered at her over her reading glasses.

"Are you sure?"

Lucy nodded.

"Wool would be better."

"Never mind. I've got something else." Agnes took the towels back upstairs and came back with an old jacket that Bill had never seen her wear.

When Lucy had stretched the sacking tightly over the frame she took a tape measure from the sowing basket and marked a border round the sides and ends, using Jack's wooden straight edge and one of Mary's crayons. She found the centre of the rug and made a dot. Then she took a piece of string, tied a loop in both ends and used it as a compass to make a circle in the centre of the rug. Bill watched as she shortened the string, checked to see that the drawing pin in the centre hadn't moved, and marked another circle inside the other one, about two inches smaller than the first.

"Here." She handed Bill one of the pegs and showed him how to push the strips through the sacking. "Push one end through, then push it back." She showed him how to end up with the two ends the same length. "We'll trim it up when we've finished."

Bill watched his father start at the other end of the frame. He seemed to be an expert, taking the strips and securing them firmly. He shook his head, and looked up.

"This teks me back. My mother used to 'ave us mekkin' one every year."

Lucy went into the kitchen to put the kettle on and Agnes looked up from her cutting.

"I've been thinking about the geese. Why don't you go down to Charlie Taylor's place and see if you can buy those young one's he has left over."

"Why? Christmas is over. No-one eats goose after Christmas."

"If you could buy four young geese and two ganders we could have more young ones to sell in December. Those old ones have been here longer than I have. They won't last forever. Jack says we'll be growing more barley and potatoes this year. We haven't enough room to keep any more pigs, so we'll need something to eat up the waste potatoes."

Jack was listening, nodding slowly.

"It meks sense." He looked at Agnes. "Are you sure y'can sell 'em?"

"I think we'll be able to sell anything next year. And we've got money left over from this year's geese to pay for them."

Jack agreed.

"I'll talk to Charlie tomorrow on me way back from station. Our Harry's kept some young 'uns on this time. I'll 'ave a word wi' 'im too an' see if we can swap ganders."

The next morning Jack arrived back saying that he'd bought the geese. Agnes said he'd paid too much for them, but Jack insisted he'd only been fair. Bill said he'd walk them back with the dogs but Jack said no.

"Y' know what geese are like. If they've walked here they might tek it on th' selves t' walk back again. Charlie sez y' can pick 'em up this afternoon."

Bill was glad of half an hour's break after dinner to pick up the geese. He'd spent most of the morning emptying the midden with Dennis, forking and shovelling muck into the wagon and taking it out into the meadows where they dragged it out into heaps for scaling.

When Bill arrived back from Charlie Taylor's, Dennis peered into the cart. There were six sacks tied with string. Each one was rustling. The geese muttered to each other in the bottom of the cart. Bill put them in the loosebox for the night and went back to work emptying the midden.

It took nearly two weeks to empty both middens. Bill and Dennis stank of cow muck all the time. Their hands became rough, with cracks in them that they couldn't get clean. Dennis never tried at this time of year. The dark half moon between his thumb and forefinger, where he gripped the shovel, stayed there from October until May. His knuckles were covered with cracks that opened up the skin like mouths when he closed his hands. The edges healed into crusty scabs like the lips of a toad, but the cuts remained open and sore. Lucy found him some hand cream to put on them but he only used it once.

"It smelled funny."

When they'd finished the midden, Bill's next job was to help Jack hedge laying. Dennis had tried his hand at it last year but he'd chopped into his thumb with the axe. Agnes had bandaged it up but insisted he needed the doctor to stitch it. Jack hadn't trusted Dennis with an axe after that, and he was given other jobs.

Dennis' answer had been short and cheerful.

"That's grand. I'd rather go muck scalin' anyway."

Bill was sorry Dennis had never learned how to hedge. Dennis was left handed, which meant he could work on the opposite side to Bill. It made the job easier, quicker with one man cutting with his left hand and laying the thorns down with his right. Two men could work all day without either of them having to climb over the bank to cut out or lay stems that they couldn't reach.

Bill and his father had to work several yards apart, both on the same side, always laying the stems up the slope. Each worked until he reached where the other had started and then moved lower down to start again. The hedge they were laying was high, over ten feet, with long stems and all the bush and thorns at the top. Sheep had been pushing through the bottom last year and getting into the meadow, so Jack had woven dead branches and rails into the gaps to stop them. By the time they'd finished it would be a yard high and a yard wide, with all the stems cut through half way so they could be folded down and left at an angle. The ewes would be confronted with a thorny barrier which last year was above their heads.

Bill liked hedging. Once you'd burned up all the rubbish, all the spare or dead thorns, you were left with a neat job, if you knew how to do it.

Jack was walking towards him with the tea can and basket. "Dinner time."

Bill took off his leather mittens and loosened the straps on his knee pads, sat down on some dead leaves on the bank. Jack sat beside him

"Look at that hedge o' Joe Moss's. He's too bloody lazy t' bend o'er his belly an' lay it properly. If he kept a lot o' sheep on his side we'd never be rid of 'em."

Bill looked at the gaps in the bottom of Moss's hedge. His

father continued.

"If y' go further north they all lay hedges like that. Down south they do it different again. They don't knock stakes in on either side like we do. They put 'em in a row down t' middle an' weave hazels along t' top."

"Why do they do that?"

"Don't know. It's just their way. It meks a good hedge though." He was opening and closing his hand, rubbing his fingers.

"What's up with your hand, Dad?"

"Pins an' needles. Started yesterday when you were still cartin' muck." He turned to Bill and laughed. "Do y' reckon it's old age creepin' up? Just usin' different muscles, that's all. I'll be right by t' time we've finished." He looked back at the long line of discarded branches. "We'll bring Dennis tomorrow an' let him start burnin' that lot up. I think it could snow by weekend."

They finished the hedge on Friday afternoon and helped Dennis to scrape up the last of the twigs. Jack looked across at the hedge along the end of the field.

"We'll do that 'un next year."

They jumped on the cart and rode back to the farm.

The last day of January the skies stayed dark all day. Jack looked up at the clouds.

"They look full o' snow t' me."

When Bill went to bed he looked out into the dark. Flakes of snow were beginning to fall.

Bill woke at around five thirty. The world outside was silent and the air in his room was chilled. He pushed back one curtain to see a silver grey landscape of moonlight reflected against the night's snow. The blizzard had blown itself out and left an eerie silence, a kind of blanketed cocoon that almost whispered, beckoning him outside. He found his socks and trousers, pulled them on and reached for his shirt and jumper at the end of the bed.

He met his father, rushing along the landing. His arms were flaying as he struggled with his shirt.

"Come on, lad. It's drifted. God knows where t' sheep'll be." As he grabbed the candle from the table at the top of the stairs, Bill could see his eyes were still red. He stank of whisky. Downstairs they grabbed wellingtons and coats. There was no time for tea this morning. Jack dashed outside with the lantern.

"I'll get the dogs. You get Dennis and three shovels."

Dennis was tying his jacket with string. As Bill reached him he looked up, wide eyed and spoke.

"It's drifted. I was gonna come an' get you. I've 'ardly slept." He already had a lantern lit and three shovels had been leaned against the granary door. Bill saw the footprints across the yard. Dennis had been pacing. They followed Jack across the yard and out into the hill pasture. Milking would have to wait. If the sun thawed the surface of a snowdrift with sheep underneath, the ewes were finished. The deep snow would refreeze the water and the flock would suffocate.

The dogs were off, Fly leading the way, bounding across bare wind-blown ground, then struggling belly deep through drifted snow. The men raced after them; three clumsy silhouettes, following the two fleeting shadows. Time was short. Under the snow, the pregnant ewes were beginning to die.

Fly had the scent in her nostrils. Her ageing milky eyes were no hindrance in the dark and the snow. She tore across the hill and raced up a deep drift where only yesterday there had been a wall and dry ditch. She sniffed around and as the men reached her she was already digging frantically, up to her haunches in snow. This dog knew her business and the urgency of the task.

Dennis reached her first, dragged her out by the collar and began flinging snow away with the shovel. She shook snow from her pelt, sniffed the ground about a yard away, began digging and barking where Bill took over with the shovel.

Flash was behind his mother, running in circles, barking, confused. He dived into the hole with Dennis as the farmhand pulled out the first ewe, dazed and caked with snow.

Jack reached the drift, panting.

"Jesus bloody Christ! They're all under here." He followed Fly to where she'd found another scent and started hurling first powdery snow and then shovelfuls of compacted chunks. Dennis was widening his hole. Another sheep had been trapped beside the first. He reached its head and stopped digging.

"This one's had it." He climbed out and bundled through the snow drift to where Flash was sniffing. "Good dog! Good dog!" The pup was learning. Dennis shovelled back snow as the pup barked.

Bill's arms were aching. Sweat was running down his face. His back felt cold and wet. He glanced up at his father who'd dropped his cap. His head was steaming in the cold air. They dug and dug, dragged out sheep, moved on to the next, dug again. Flash was searching and digging as fast as his mother. Each time one of the men hauled out a ewe he moved on to where the dogs were searching, and started shovelling again. The work was too hard and too urgent to talk. The only sounds were the swish and crunch of snow being moved and then the bark of a dog when another ewe was sniffed out; the bleat of another ewe as she was saved from suffocation.

Dennis pulled two from the same hole and stood up, arching his back and rubbing away an ache. Jack turned and snapped,

"Keep diggin', lad! There's still thirty of 'em under here!"

Dennis shrank and followed the dogs. He'd pulled out as many as Jack and Bill together. Bill looked up, bit his lip and returned to his task.

The sun was rising by the time the last ewe was freed and

Jack was peering over the wall into the park.

"I 'aven't seen t' shearlings yet."

Bill pointed to a dark mass under the trees. The shearlings were safe. They were stirring from their sleeping place, oblivious to the plight of the rest of the flock.

Jack walked along the wall side through the disturbed snow.

"Bloody hell! Three dead! Bloody hell!"

Bill looked at the ewes they'd saved. There were over fifty of them, weary but beginning to graze on the crown of the hill. He glanced at Dennis but Dennis was looking at the ground avoiding eye contact.

Jack's voice bawled out again.

"Jump to it lads! Yer'll have to milk bloody quick if we're goin' t' catch that train. Dennis, leave muckin' out till later. You'll 'ave t' milk as well."

They hurried back to the yard, grabbed buckets and stools and started milking, three hours late. Breakfast should have been an hour ago. They had two hours work in front of them.

The cows' udders were full, and some were running milk. Bill and Dennis started in the long shippen and Jack went to milk the two cows across the yard. After an hour Lucy came in with a can of tea and bacon sandwiches. They stopped milking and ate quickly with dirty hands and hollow stomachs, swilling tea into mouths full of bread.

Lucy poured them each another mug, looked pityingly at their reddened hands and trousers soaked by melted snow.

"Get some dry clothes on as soon as you can. You'll catch your deaths walkin' around all day frozen like that." She was passing Dennis his second mug when Jack burst through the door.

"What're y' doin', holdin' these lads up? They've got milkin' t' finish."

Dennis handed back his mug and headed towards to the

next cow. Lucy glared at Jack. She'd just left him in the farmhouse finishing his bacon and eggs. He tried to stare her down. He wasn't having a housemaid getting the upper hand. But Lucy had seen men like him before and didn't blink until he'd averted his eyes and gone out into the cold. She placed Dennis's mug on a churn and took the empty basket back to the house. Jack was leading the horse from the stable. He kept his head down as Lucy crossed the yard, her skirts leaving a wide wake through deep snow. She would never cow to him. He was her employer, not her master; and she had stood up to bigger bullies than Jack Branthwaite.

That afternoon Bill was milking with Jack. He sensed his father felt guilty about the sheep. Perhaps he felt sorry for the way he'd shouted at Dennis. He'd been quiet all day. Sometimes Bill guessed he was deep in thought.

Jack got up from beside the next cow to Bill. As he passed him he stopped, put down the bucket of milk and rubbed his left shoulder. He moved it round in a circular motion.

"I'm a bit stiff today, lad."

Bill hated it when he called him lad.

Jack bent and straightened his elbow a couple of times, rubbed his upper arm.

"I reckon it's all that shovellin'." He picked up the bucket and continued towards the churn.

Bill continued to milk the cow and glanced towards his father.

Jack faltered, stumbled and fell. Hit his head on the heelstone behind the cows' feet. The milk tipped beside him and flowed around his head.

Bill sprang to his feet, tore down the passageway. Turned him over away from the cows feet and shit. His shirt was dripping milk and cow piss.

"Dad?"

He wasn't moving. He looked grey.

Bill raced to the house, flung open the back door.

"*Agnes!*" She was in the kitchen. "Dad's collapsed in t' shippen."

She ran along the passage, grabbed her coat and ran after him across the yard. She pushed past him into the shippen, rolling up her sleeves. Knelt beside Jack, ignoring the cow that stepped on her coat.

Bill stood over them

"He just fell."

Agnes lifted Jack's hand, placed two fingers on the side of his neck. She put down his arm, put her finger in his mouth and hooked out cow dung. Wiped milk and piss from his face and put her mouth to his lips. She blew, and Bill felt sudden relief as he saw his father's chest rise. Agnes turned her head and spat. Made the seal again and blew.

Bill watched his father's chest rise and fall. Agnes kept blowing.

Bill was twisting his fingers. Agnes straightened up, put two fingers on Jack's breastbone, made a fist with her other hand, placed it beside them, gripped it and pressed down with both hands.

Bill noticed the deep cut on his father's forehead. There was no blood.

Agnes kept pumping Jack's chest, bent over again and began to blow. His chest rose and fell. When she straightened up again Bill looked into her face.

"Is he going to be all right?"

She shook her head.

"He's gone."

Dennis and Lucy were in the doorway, Dennis gnawing at his fingers, Lucy, her hands clasped at her waist.

Agnes beckoned them inside, got them all to crouch beside Jack.

"We'll carry him into the house."

They struggled across the yard, two at each side of him, gripping each other's forearms. They were wet and covered with muck.

He was heavy. They squeezed along the passageway and his head hung backwards. They laid him on the table. Agnes poured water from the kettle into a bowl, took a cloth and wiped his face.

"Lucy. Go and get him some clean clothes. No one's going to see him like this."

She waved them out of the kitchen.

"You'd better go and finish work." She closed the door and started to unbutton his shirt.

Next day Agnes sent for the undertaker. Bill waited with her in the front room. He'd put on his good clothes. Agnes looked up from her cup and saucer.

"I never expected him to go like this."

Bill thought about his grandparents. They were old when he was born. He'd hardly known them. He'd thought his father would be there for ever.

Sergeant Jackson arrived before the undertaker.

"I'm sorry. I have to ask you a few questions. It's because he hasn't been seen by a doctor."

Bill felt suddenly responsible.

"Should we have got the doctor first?"

"No. I would still have to come. Because the doctor never saw him before he died. There'll have to be a post-mortem. Your father was still a young man. Can you show me where he died?"

Bill took him outside. A lot of the snow had been trampled to ice in widening tracks between the buildings, the midden and house. Sergeant Jackson glanced across at a patch of deep snow with a cluster of egg shaped melt patches in it, behind each one, a frozen pile of goose droppings.

Bill pushed open the shippen door and the policeman

followed him along the alleyway behind the cows.

"It's a bit warmer in here."

Bill pointed to the spot where his father had fallen.

"He hit his head about there."

The sergeant looked down and saw a slight mark on the stone and what could have been hair and skin. It might have come from the cows.

"Whereabouts were you at the time?"

Bill walked along till he came to the cow near the end where he'd been sitting.

"Milkin' this 'un."

When the Sergeant leaned over to check the line of vision, Bill suddenly felt something hot inside him, rising to his cheeks. Up to now he'd been giving the details, to be recorded somewhere, maybe on the death certificate. Suddenly he felt under suspicion.

"It's all right, Bill. I just need to check these things." The sergeant stepped back from between the cows and looked back towards the door. "What was he doing at the time?"

"He was carryin' a bucket o' milk. That's why it smells funny down there." He pointed to the place where his father had died. "It's goin' sour."

The policeman was taking notes.

"Thanks Bill. I've seen enough here." He walked back along the shippen and glanced down at the milk stain between the cobbles, wrote something down and put his pad away.

Back in the house, the policeman asked if he could see 'the body'. Bill led him into the pantry. They'd laid Jack out on the slab.

"Why's he in his good clothes?"

"He was all mucky. Agnes didn't want to leave him like that."

The policeman nodded.

"He was a good man. I wouldn't want him left like that if

he was my family." He walked over to stand beside Jack's head, casually leaned over and looked at the gash in the dead man's temple. "A nasty fall. That's enough to kill a man." The policeman placed his hands under Jack's head and gently turned it so he could see the wound better. Bill thought he saw his fingers searching through the scalp for bumps.

The sergeant lowered Jack's head and went with Bill back into the front room. The undertaker had arrived. The old man walked over to Bill and shook his hand.

"I really am very sorry. I'd known your father a long time."

The policeman said goodbye and left. The undertaker and his assistant carried two trestles into the pantry, went back to the car and returned with a coffin. Bill watched from the kitchen as they set the coffin on the trestles, lifted off the lid and placed Jack Branthwaite in the coffin. He held the front door open as they took his father out to the hearse. Agnes watched. Her face remained still.

Jack's body was released two days later and the funeral was arranged for Friday. Bill had left Agnes with the responsibility of organising the funeral and informing Jack's friends. She'd put a notice in the paper.

Bill found himself working almost unconsciously. He milked and fed the cows, sometimes without remembering having done it. Sometimes he felt his emotions overwhelm and swallow him.

He was taking some hay for the sheep when he noticed that one of them was lame. He called Fly to his side and whistled; two short bursts. She ran out wide to the left, followed the line of the hedge, running fast and low, until she was beyond the furthest ewe. She continued round in an arc as the ewes bunched together. Bill whistled, one drawn-out note. The dog dropped to the ground with the flock directly between her and Bill. He gave two short whistles, two-toned, rising at the end. Fly stalked forwards, bringing the ewes towards him. Each time they tried to break he whistled her right or left to bring them together and herded them to a dry corner of the field.

He stood beside his dog with the sheep in the corner and scanned the heads for the face of the lame ewe, gave the dog a low command to bunch them up tighter. At the last moment he dived into the centre of the flock and caught the lame ewe round the neck. He turned it on its rump and checked all four feet with his fingers. There was foot rot in its right front hoof. He could smell it. He took out his penknife and cleaned away the soil, pared the hoof back to healthy tissue. He reached in his pocket for a flat tin and flicked off the lid with his thumb, balanced the ewe against his knees and dug brown paste from the tin with his knife. He pressed it into the ewe's foot with his knife and fingers, put her back on her feet and let her run towards the rest. He put the tin and knife back in his pocket. He gave a deep sigh and put his hand to his face as he listened to his first thought, wiped his eyes and face as the words sank in.

"I must remember to tell Dad when I get back."

✣

The hearse arrived on Friday at one o'clock with the body of Jack Branthwaite. Bill and Dennis were in black suits. Bill had been into town to buy one and Dennis was wearing an old suit of Jack's. It was almost a good fit. Bill's two cousins and his Uncle Harry were in the front room. Bill noticed how much his uncle looked like Jack, the same nose and jaw line, but Harry was stockier with a grey beard and moustache.

At quarter past one the procession set off towards the village. Agnes, Bill and Mary rode in Uncle Harry's car behind the hearse. Dennis, Lucy and Bill's cousins were in Charlie Taylor's car. They drove slowly down the village and towards the church. Mary clung to Agnes's arm. Bill sat motionless, staring at the car in front.

As they approached the church, the road was lined with horses, traps and several cars, one of them a Rolls Royce. Bill noticed the ponies' manes blowing in the wind. Most of them were black. The cars stopped at the church gates and the undertakers in the front of the car got out. They opened the back of the hearse and slid the coffin out. Everyone else in the cars began to get out. Bill, Dennis and the two cousins shuffled forwards towards the coffin.

They lifted the coffin on their shoulders, Bill and Dennis in front, the two cousins behind. They held the coffin handle and clasped arms across each other's backs. They followed the Vicar into the church. Bill listened to the words as he bore his father's weight.

I am the resurrection and the life, saith the Lord: he that believeth in me, though he were dead, yet shall he live: and whosoever believeth in me shall never die. The words rang and echoed as they entered the porch. Bill felt Dennis shaking as they carried Jack into the church.

The church was full. People were standing at the back. Bill saw suits, coats, hands and feet, but no faces. They placed the coffin at the front of the church and Bill stroked it with his hand as he stepped away. He heard sobs beside him and behind him. Agnes stared. Her eyes were dry.

There were hymns and prayers. Later when Bill thought back, he couldn't remember what the order was or what the prayers were.

Uncle Harry walked to the front and spoke about Jack's life. One line stuck in Bill's mind.

"Jack Branthwaite was my brother."

He spoke about their time as boys, growing up on the farm. He mentioned Jack's time in the war and held up two medals. Bill looked at them for the first and last time.

When they sang the last hymn, Bill felt a vibration in his

voice that he had never felt before, a kind of strength. He wondered where it came from.

They buried Jack Branthwaite in a plot on the south side of the church. It was protected from the east wind by huge oaks and sycamores clinging to the hillside that fell away towards the river. The Branthwaite family huddled around the graveside as the rest of the village stood back, further up the slope towards the church.

Norman Watterson stood with Charlie Taylor and Mr and Mrs Finch a few yards from the church wall.

"It's a bad day fer a fun'ral." Norman was looking towards the ageing relatives, great aunts and uncles left over from Bill's grandparents' generation. They were wrapped in thick coats and clinging to arms and elbows as they shuffled through the mossy grass towards the grave. "Yon owd folk shouldn't be stood out on a day like this."

As the local gravedigger, he'd studied the headstones in the village and those of the two neighbouring churches. He'd noticed how often a funeral in winter was followed by that of an old member of the same family less than a month later. He'd dug graves for old men and women he'd seen shivering in the churchyard only weeks before. He shuddered as he remembered his spade smashing through the rotted lid of a coffin that had moved downhill through the earth into what he'd thought was an empty plot.

Bill took one last look at his father's coffin and stepped away from the grave. He hugged his mother's Auntie Maisie when she held up her hands to him. Her face was cold. He picked his way between the gravestones towards the path where his neighbours were talking in groups. Some of the villagers were walking away towards the gate. He spoke to Norman and Mr Finch, shook their hands and listened as Charlie Taylor told him what a good neighbour Jack had been.

"If you ever need anything, don't be afraid to ask."

Bill shook his hand.

"Thank you."

Mr and Mrs Laycock were in the church porch, sheltering from the wind. As Bill walked past, Mrs Laycock stepped forwards.

"Hello, Bill. We're so sorry about your father. You must come round to dinner sometime."

He remembered how they'd looked down on Jack, Mr Laycock's comments that Phyllis had repeated in front of Bill's friends. The Laycocks were here for Agnes.

Lucy hurried through the mourners to reach Bill. Mrs Laycock looked away and pushed her husband out of the porch. They went to meet Agnes who was walking towards them with Mary, Bill's Uncle Harry and Auntie Doris.

After the funeral the family and friends went back to the village hall. Annie Dobson was serving tea and sandwiches from the serving hatch in the kitchen. Bill wandered from table to table, talking to distant relations he hadn't seen since the last family funeral.

Tom was sitting at a table in the corner with Lucy and Alice Taylor. Dennis was sitting behind them with a plate on his knee. Alice beckoned him over. As he squeezed between tables and chairs Annie Dobson stopped him and refilled his cup from a large teapot.

Bill pulled up a chair and sat with his friends.

"All right, Bill?" Tom had been watching him. "How are you bearing up?"

"Better than I expected. I haven't had time to think today?"

Alice leaned across to him.

"Have you seen Mrs Finch talking to your Uncle Harry?"

Bill looked across and saw the postmistress chatting up his uncle. He was looking round the room in panic, desperately searching for his wife and safety. Alice giggled and the rest of them looked away trying not to laugh. Bill swallowed hard and changed the subject.

"Tom, I haven't spoken to you for ages. Did you get that farm?"

Tom shook his head and tried to sound cheerful.

"No. It wasn't big enough anyway. I reckon we'll find somethin' come spring."

Bill said nothing. It was less than three months until rent day. He thought time was running out for Tom and his dad.

Dennis was getting up. He looked round for somewhere to put his plate. Lucy took it from him and put it on the table. He nodded at the others and headed for the door. Bill knew that he would have finished cleaning out the cows by the time everyone left the village hall.

Soon everyone began to disperse. Most of the families in the village hall had cows to milk. Many of them would be working late tonight. Uncle Harry came across to Bill.

"Are you ready fer goin'? I'll give you a lift back to t' farm. My lads are keen t' be getting' home."

"Okay." He went with Lucy to get his sister and stepmother. They were standing with Mr and Mrs Laycock. Mrs Laycock stepped across in front of Lucy, caught Bill's arm.

"Bill, dear."

He cringed.

"We've invited Agnes and Mary to stay the night. We'll bring them home in the morning." She drew him closer and whispered loud enough for Lucy to hear. "Agnes is going to be a bit sensitive for a while. Don't go letting that servant girl upset her."

Bill bit his lip and headed for the door.

His anger didn't give way through milking. One of the cows kicked at him as he wrung at its teats. It knocked the bucket of milk over and he stood up and punched it hard in the ribs. It gave a startled bawl and he punched it again. He was bringing his fist back when he looked up, saw Lucy staring at him. He looked away, stooped to pick up the bucket and the tears came. He cried out of anger, shame and for the loss of his dad. He felt small, like a little boy who'd lost sight of his parents. He slumped on the stool and wiped his face with his jacket sleeve.

Lucy came over to him, put her hand on his shoulder and when he looked up she kissed him. His arms were weak and his chest felt so heavy that breathing seemed like a chore. He couldn't look at her. He looked towards the floor and she held his head close to her.

"I know. I know." She drew away from him and he gave a deep sigh. He looked up at her and she said, "Come on. We're nearly finished now."

He turned back to the cow and drew out the last few drops of milk.

When he went inside Lucy had changed her clothes. The fire was crackling and she'd placed the bath on the hearthrug. She was carrying the kettle from the kitchen.

"I've boiled the water. Take off your boots and I'll fill the bath." She went into the front room and filled the bath with water from the boiler, topped it up with the kettle. She handed him a glass of his father's whisky. "Drink this, and when you've had your bath we can talk."

Lucy had left a towel, soap and a flannel by the bath. Bill's dressing gown was folded neatly by the fire. He pulled off his jumper. One cuff was still soaked with milk. He unbuttoned his shirt and dropped it by his jumper, unbuckled his belt and began to remove his trousers. He glanced round quickly to see that the door was properly closed then chided himself for not trusting Lucy. He took off his underpants and socks and stepped into the bath. It was a bit too hot but he sat down in it and watched his skin darken beneath the water line.

He'd left the whisky on the hearth so he picked it up and

took a gulp.

"Urggh!" He'd forgotten how much he hated the taste. He wondered how his dad had got into the habit of drinking so much. Perhaps it was the warm glow it gave you inside. It seemed to fill the emptiness in his chest. He thought about the farm. The responsibility was his now. He'd be the one making the mistakes and having to choose when to plough and when to cut the grass for hay. Only last week he'd been following his father. Now he was on his own. How would they get through the work without Jack? How would Agnes react? A thought flashed through his mind. What if she wanted to sell and move back to Plymouth? He had some money in the bank but not enough to start farming. If he left the farm he'd probably get called up to fight. He imagined himself standing in a trench in France, dead bodies around him and an officer with the whistle to his lips.

He reached for the jug and poured water over his hair, rubbed it with the bar of soap and rinsed it with the jug. He scrambled for the towel, rubbed his head and wiped soap and water from his eye. It stung. He soaped the flannel and rubbed his arms and legs, dipped the cloth in the water and washed himself down.

When he stood up to dry himself he felt cold. He stood on the hearth and put on his dressing gown. He picked up his clothes. They smelled of cows. He took them down the passage and went to the kitchen to find Lucy. She was making two cups of tea. She carried them back into the front room and Bill followed her. He drank his tea but didn't speak. They sat cradling their mugs, thinking.

Bill opened his mouth to speak at the same time as Lucy and they both fell silent again. Lucy laughed.

"You first."

"I don't know where to start." He was thinking about everything at once. The work, the farm, how he expected his dad to come back.

Lucy turned her mug in her hands.

"When my mum died it was like a relief. She'd been in a lot of pain and she didn't even look like my mum any more. I'd been looking after her for a long time and suddenly it felt like I didn't matter any more. It felt as if my usefulness had come to an end."

Bill stopped her.

"This isn't like that. I just don't know where to start. Whenever I had a problem I couldn't solve he'd allus have an answer."

"What do you think he'd say now?"

Bill thought for a moment.

"Take one day at a time an' look after yourself."

Lucy raised her eyebrows and Bill smiled. His face went serious again.

"Did you get angry when your mum died?"

"Not after she died. I was very bitter when I found out she was dying."

"That bloody woman got my back up today. They used t' look down their noses at Dad. Agnes invited 'em round for Sunday dinner once. They were just leavin' when she looks round the yard an' says, 'You can always tell a rented farm because the place looks like it's not cared for.' Cheeky bitch."

"I think she quite likes you; 'Bill, dear'."

Bill tensed, saw she was teasing him and laughed. Lucy could always make him laugh. He noticed how close he felt to her. She was watching him.

He put down his empty mug and stepped over to her. She stood up to meet him and flung her arms round his neck. He pressed his lips to hers, hard and passionately. She pushed him against the sideboard. His hands were round her waist, pulling her forwards. She was pushing herself against him. Her elbow caught a brass candlestick and it fell with a crash. They both jumped, turned to look at it and Lucy stepped back. She picked up the candlestick and replaced it on the sideboard, took the lamp and led him upstairs. She pulled him into her room, put the lamp on the dressing table and pushed him onto the bed. She was throwing off her clothes. She looked at his dressing gown.

"Take it off."

He stood up, dropped it by the bed and she pushed him back down, climbed on top of him. He rolled her over, kissed her neck, her shoulders, her breasts.

He was clumsy at first. She had to help him. He pushed into her, felt her arms loosen around him. She held him closer, kissed him harder. He couldn't hold back any more. The wind groaned through a crack in the window frame and he opened his eyes. This room used to be his.

Suddenly he was nine again. He could hear his father's grunts and heavy breathing, Agnes's moans and cries, the rhythmic squeak of the bed. He felt that same hot prickle spreading across his face. He shouldn't be hearing this. Agnes was in bed with his father. His mother's coffin was downstairs. He remembered screwing up his eyes, pushing his palms into his ears.

He rolled over and stared at the ceiling.

11

Very often seemingly insoluble problems that confront the breeders of one particular kind of animal are not really problems at all: they have been solved over and over again in very similar instances in other animals, and often in plants.

Arend Lourens Hagedoorn. Animal Breeding
(1880)

Lucy noticed a change in Agnes as soon as she came back from the Laycocks'. She'd dropped Mary off at school on her way home. Lucy had helped Bill to milk and was sweeping the hearth ready to light the fire. A few months ago Agnes would have shouted at her for being late lighting the fires. Since Christmas this had subsided to a stern "Don't let your work in the house slip, Lucy."

As Agnes closed the front door she glanced across at the empty grate, looked at the carpet and went upstairs. Lucy loaded the grate with newspaper and kindling and struck a match. She watched the fire take hold of the split sticks then begin to lick at the remnants of last night's logs.

Before milking she'd emptied the cold bath water down the drain and rinsed out the bath. She hadn't known what time Agnes would be home. She'd found a scratch mark on the sideboard so she'd rubbed it with a stub of wax crayon from Mary's box. All visible signs of last night had been removed.

She couldn't understand Bill. He'd acted as if he didn't want her and when she'd asked him what was wrong he'd just said, "It's not right," and had gone back to his room. She'd tried to talk to him this morning but he'd been sullen as if he was ashamed. She felt angry because he wouldn't talk, and now even Agnes was different.

She took the ashes outside and went to the granary to mix some mash for the hens. The hens were clamouring to get out when she opened the door. They tussled round her feet as she poured the mash into the trough. She looked into the nest boxes. They needed more straw. Something white was sticking out from under the nest boxes. It was a hen's wing. She pulled out the dead bird and carried it back to the yard by its leg, found a spade in the corner of the cart shed and went to the far end of the garden to bury it. The soil was still frozen. The spade slid along the ground. She tried to dig deep using her foot but only managed to chip off a sliver of turf. She took the dead hen back into the yard and tossed it on the midden.

✣

After Jack died, Bill found himself working harder and longer. He started getting up earlier so that he could finish milking in time to catch the train. He had to take it to the village himself now, which meant another hour of his day was used up. It was an easy job but he couldn't give it to Lucy because she wouldn't be able to lift the full churns off at the station. She was doing enough anyway. She was feeding the dogs and calves now as well as helping with the cows.

He unloaded the churns and rolled them on their edges to the platform. They felt heavier this morning and his throat felt sore. He sneezed a couple of times on his way back to the farm so he nipped into the house and took a handkerchief from the drawer. By lunchtime his nose was running constantly and his head was beginning to pound. He dropped the sodden handkerchief in the washing and took another from the sideboard. His mouth felt dry.

When he went to feed the sheep, the hay made him cough. It was a bit brown but not dusty. He finished work late and went inside. Lucy asked him if he was all right and he told her he was starting with a cold. He ate his supper and went straight to bed.

Bill woke up coughing. He didn't know what time it was.

When he stepped out of bed his pyjamas clung to his back and he felt the chill as sweat turned cold. He crept downstairs and into the kitchen, found the lamp and lit it. The kettle was warm on the stove and when he lifted it, it was half full. He pushed it into the centre and found a jar of honey. The teaspoon crunched as he scraped the bottom of the jar then dropped it in a mug.

The kettle was slow to boil. He poured water into the mug and found he could drink it almost right away. He licked the undissolved honey from the spoon, turned on the lamp and set off back to bed. He felt so weak he could hardly walk up the stairs.

Next morning he felt worse. The smell of the cows made him feel sick, and by breakfast time Lucy had milked twice as many as him. The first churn tilted back at him as he struggled with it into the cart and Dennis rushed to help him. At the station Charlie Taylor had to move the churns for him.

"Looks like you've got the flu. There's a lot of it about. I'd send one of our lads to help you but Bert's in bed wi' it an' Alice is trailin' about half dead."

Bill followed him back as far as the village where Charlie turned off towards the shop. He rode back to the farm and sat on the cart for a few minutes before he felt ready to move.

In the afternoon he was supposed to be helping Dennis sort some potatoes. He sat on the cold pile dropping the biggest ones into a sack. Dennis had filled three. Bill couldn't lift the sack. He got up and went outside for some air. He was leaning with one hand against the barn wall when he heard a sound behind him. He looked up. It was Tom.

"Postman said you were bad wi' t' flu. Get y'self t' bed. I've come to give you a hand."

Bill made his way to the house and went to bed. He laid awake thinking about the work he had to do. Tom was helping him now, but soon he too would be busy with his spring work, wherever that was. The chances were that Tom would be living a long way off. He wouldn't be able to pop round whenever he was free.

Shearing was going to be difficult without Tom and his dad. Last year there had been four of them shearing, first Tom's sheep then the Branthwaite's, with Dennis wrapping the fleeces at both farms. This year Bill would be on his own. He was isolated. He was losing his father and best friend within a matter of months. He doubted whether he could afford to employ someone else. The worst thing of all was he didn't know how much anything cost or even how much the rent was. His father had never told him. How could he run a farm without any idea of the finances? Agnes would know. He knew that, but Agnes was lost in her own grief and wasn't talking to anyone. He couldn't even get the information from her. His head was spinning and his body felt useless. He closed his eyes and wished for … he didn't even know what to wish for.

He slept until daylight and awoke wondering why Lucy hadn't woken him. His body felt strange, alien, with limbs that had neither the strength nor the sensation he could identify as his own. He stumbled out onto the landing and into the nursery to get a view of the back yard. Dennis was wheeling the barrow from the shippen, his head almost obscured by the steaming pile he was pushing. He turned towards the midden and took the shovel from where it had been wedged down the side of his load.

Bill steadied himself against the window ledge, scanned the rest of the yard. He wondered how he'd missed it. Tom's bike was leaning against the wall by the shippen door. Relief was like stepping out of a storm, throwing off the heavy sodden coat of worry that had been dragging him down by the shoulders. His head had cleared since last night. He found some clothes and went downstairs. The sun was peering over the cart shed roof and was poking through the window in the back door, edging its way round the corner of the passage like a friend wondering whether to come in.

He made himself a cup of tea. Agnes was reviving the fire, prodding at last night's embers and sneaking pages from yesterday's paper between them until they smouldered and caught light. She turned when his shadow cast across the hearth.

"Feeling better?"

"Yes thanks. I was wonderin' how I was goin' to manage today." He sat in his father's chair. "I've been worried how we're goin' to cope without Dad."

Agnes got up from the hearth, propped herself on a chair by the window.

"I've been thinking too. These last couple of weeks I haven't been thinking at all. You, Dennis and Lucy have been working yourselves into the ground and I ... well I've come to the idea that we've just got to carry on." She took an envelope from her apron pocket and passed it to Bill. It was a letter from the solicitor. "He wants to see us, to read the will."

Bill went to get the coal as Agnes made the breakfast. As he carried the brass bucket back to the house he knew that he wouldn't be working for the rest of the day. He stopped by the back door trying to catch his breath.

Agnes ordered him back to bed and he didn't see Tom or Dennis till lunchtime. Tom came bursting into the kitchen and perched himself on the end of the bench where he usually sat at shearing time. He reached for the teapot and poured himself a cup.

"You're lookin' rough, old lad. I think you've been working too hard."

"Thanks for comin'."

"I was glad to get away. Mum's upset again 'cos t' new tenant sent his horseman to start ploughin'. Our John's helpin' Dad t' milk before he goes t' school." He heaped sugar into his tea. "Those heifers are a nuisance. It took us ages t' get 'em back inside. It's time you had water bowls down there and for t' cows. It 'ud save you half a mornin' every day if y' didn't have to let 'em all out to water."

"How can we afford it, Tom? Besides, t' firm's stopped advertisin'. I doubt whether we could get 'em if we tried."

"Dad ordered some in November. Dennison's rang t' say they've come an' they can fit 'em next week but we won't be needin' 'em now. Dad's goin' t' look at a farm near Preston on Saturday. It's got all mod cons. Big tidy place, it is. All square, flat fields too. Good soil."

Agnes was listening.

"We've enough money for the rent, Tom, but we haven't any to spare."

Tom was in full swing.

"It's simple. You've got a cow to calve next week an' there's two o' them heifers at t'out barn goin' t' calve."

"What?" Bill sat up. He'd missed something. "Those heifers aren't in calf."

"Two o' them heifers down there are goin' t' calve. They're a bit small, but the two of 'em will give as much milk as that cow, so sell her an' get water laid on to all yer stock."

A light struck in Bill's head.

"Moss's bull!" He stood up and ran his finger over Agnes's Mothers' Union calendar. The dates tallied.

Agnes said she'd think the idea over.

Bill wanted to see the heifers himself. He couldn't understand how he'd missed spotting them.

Tom was determined.

"I'll tell Dad tonight that you might be interested. He can ring Dennisons an' tell 'em to hang on to 'em for you."

Lucy was bringing a jar from the pantry. She had a bunch of snowdrops in her hand. When Bill's look turned a bit too questioning she turned back at him, casual.

"Tom picked them for me. He found them when he was getting a ewe out of the bottom wood."

Bill hadn't felt jealousy around Lucy before and he guessed it must be showing on his face when Tom started justifying himself.

"Well somebody had to cheer her up. You didn't get her a card."

The date had slipped his mind. His finger was still resting on the calendar, the fourteenth of February.

✧

As rent day approached, Bill was beginning to feel more confident about the running of the farm. He'd been to the solicitor's office in Lancaster with Agnes. It was in one of those tall fronted terraced houses up by the castle. They were all up there. Brass plaques on every door with long names that made Bill think they'd never been farmers. Their families had probably been up in the law since the castle was built, at least since it had been used as a prison. The Brocklehursts, Barringtons and Hasslingtons had been representing the town and rural communities since the days when they branded you with an 'M' meaning 'malefactor' for stealing to feed your children. Bill had heard that the branding iron was still there, bolted to the dock as a warning to the accused that the law could be changed. It was a reminder that harsh punishments had been meted out by the courts in the past.

As he'd walked up the cobbled hill he'd glanced across at the huge oak doors of the prison and wondered what it must be like as they held you down, waiting for the iron to get hot. The glow of the wrought iron letter as it got closer to your palm, the searing pain and smell of burning flesh as the red hot metal was forced onto skin.

He'd wondered what it would be like trying to get a job when employers only needed to ask to see your palms to find out whether you'd been in trouble.

Since Tom had been caught poaching, his dad had been round seven farms as far apart as Liverpool and Carlisle. They'd been turned down every time, once in favour of an ex-docker who wanted to be away from the crowds. Word had got round the landed gentry of Tom's misdemeanours, and no landlord was going to let them a farm as long as there was someone else willing to rent. Things hadn't changed that much.

The Waterford's sale was booked for the week before rent day. Brian had managed to get grazing rights on some salt marsh north of the river Keer. This meant he had somewhere to graze his heifers and sheep for the summer, but the cows and pigs would have to go. The old iron workers' cottage they'd got at Mill Head didn't have a garden. They couldn't even keep hens. Brian's dog would have to sleep in the house.

Tom had applied for a job at the brick works. If he got it he'd start the morning after the sale.

Bill's trip to the solicitors had been less intimidating than he'd expected. The old bloke was frail, short-sighted and quite a friendly sort of man. He'd read the will. Everything was split between Bill and Agnes. They'd decided to continue farming together. Agnes was a stickler at keeping the books. Having water piped to the cows and heifers had saved a lot of work and the rent money was waiting in the bank. Agnes said she wished Jack had been there to see it. He'd spent the last week in March scrabbling and scraping for the last few coppers every year since nineteen twenty.

The Waterford's sale was set for the last Saturday in March. Brian had known he could get more helpers on a Saturday. It would take about six men to move the cows one by one from the shippen to the sale ring and back again. They hadn't been milked that morning and would be milked straight after the sale. Bill had milked early so that he could go and help. It seemed strange starting work in the dark again when the days were getting longer. He dropped the milk at the station, returned with the empty churns and went straight up the road past Moss's farm towards the Waterford's.

Tom was in a sombre mood when he arrived. All the farm implements were lined up in the front field. Ploughs, harrows, sheep racks and troughs were in rows alongside chicken coops, the dog kennel and the few gates that did not belong to the landlord.

Tom was dumping a pile of firewood in the line when Bill walked up to him. He just shook his head as he pushed the barrow back to the yard. He glanced in the direction of the top meadow where the new tenant was drilling corn.

"There was no bloody need to rub our noses in it when everyone's turnin' up for t' sale."

Horses, carts and traps were appearing along the three roads visible from the farm, making their way towards the gate and turning in along the lane.

Tom was wiping his nose.

"Look. They can all see him up there tekkin' o'er before we've even sold up. We'll be a laughin' stock."

Bill shook his head.

"No, Tom. These people have come to buy and make sure you have a good sale. I think you can be sure whose side they're on."

They went back to the yard where Tom's dad was talking to the auctioneer. Bert Taylor and Tom's younger brother were waiting by the side of the auction ring that had been set up in the middle of the farm yard.

When the sale started the trade was high. Cows were making as much as eighteen pounds each. Bill would have liked to buy one but he hadn't the money. He'd try and buy one of the sheep racks. He needed a new one, and Tom would be pleased if his name was in the sale book.

As the last cows were being sold, Bill went to the kitchen

door. The table had been placed across the doorway and was being used as a counter for handing out tea and sandwiches. Mrs Taylor and Annie Dobson were helping. Tom's mother was nowhere in sight. Bill glanced past the two women towards the door to the front room. It was closed.

Two men Bill didn't know were standing in the queue. One was looking round the yard at the buildings.

"Bloody shame, this. Isn't it?"

"They reckon it's because the lad got caught poaching."

By mid-afternoon the Waterfords' business was over. Cows were being loaded into lorries or walked to the station. The pigs had been shoved up a ramp into a trailer and most of the equipment had gone. Bill said his goodbyes to Tom and his dad. He didn't want to intrude on Tom's mum. He joined the line of vehicles and cattle heading towards the village and turned into his own farmyard. He'd go and see his landlord's agent on Friday.

❖

The back entrance to Friar's Hall led round the edge of the Branthwaite's paddock. A high beech hedge separated the drive from the lawns and tennis court. As Bill walked round with the cheque signed by Agnes, he could hear the thump and thud of a tennis ball somewhere out of sight to his right. The trimmed thorn hedge was beginning to show signs of life, a tinge of green appearing amongst the brown twigs. The smell of new growth filled him with an optimism he hadn't felt since last year.

He was passing the potting sheds and dog kennels when he met Moss coming the other way and stuffing his chequebook into the pocket of his over stretched jacket. Moss feigned surprise to see him.

"Oh. I didn't expect t' see you today. I thought y' might be sellin' now yer father's gone." He was looking hungrily over the hedge towards the park. "It's greenin' up nicely o'er there. I could just do wi' a bit more land mesel'." He cast his eyes towards Bill's farm buildings. "This place 'ud go nicely wi' mine an' all." He wedged himself into a van that was parked behind the potting shed, sparked the engine and drove off before Bill could think of a reply.

Bill looked down at the envelope screwed in his hand. He straightened out the creases and headed for the back door.

Inside, the landlord's agent was waiting. He was sitting behind a large oak desk and wearing half-moon glasses. When Bill crept round the door, the agent sat back, folded his hands across his stomach and looked over his lenses.

"Ah. Young Branthwaite, I think we need a chat."

His tone sent a chill up Bill's spine. The man was out to browbeat him, put him in his place and squash him into a box of his own making. Bill stood. There was no chair. The agent continued.

"The tenancy was in your father's name. Now he's dead it appears that there's no tenancy."

Bill froze. He could hear blood pounding in his ears. He watched as the official behind the desk brought out a file.

"Sir Charles has suggested that I offer the tenancy to you, which is why you haven't received notice to leave."

Bill felt the relief like rain after a drought.

"Thank you. I won't ... ."

The agent held up his hand.

"However, as you're so young, I persuaded him to make out the tenancy to your mother."

Bill tensed. The man liked power. He was using it to humiliate someone he felt was too close to his employer.

"That way, we can make sure that you can manage the farm properly before we commit ourselves. We don't want any incidents like the one Colonel Trewin's had to deal with. You'd better go and send your mother round to sign the tenancy agreement." He was holding out his hand, looking at the cheque. "I'll take that."

Bill handed him the envelope, left without saying anything and stomped back to the house to find Agnes.

He'd half expected Agnes to be pleased. She could have boasted about it to the Laycocks at the very least. It would put her in a position of authority over him again. They'd been working as equals since Jack died. He couldn't understand why she looked worried. When she came back from the Hall she told him she'd tried to persuade the agent to put the farm in Bill's name but he'd told her that Sir Charles wanted an older tenant and if she didn't sign there would be plenty who would. Agnes seemed to be distressed at having committed herself. She returned to her baking with a fury, slapping the dough onto the table so that flour exploded into the air like dust from a falling building.

Lucy had heard the commotion, Bill's curses as he told Agnes about the agent, and the thrashing of baking trays after Agnes had signed the document. She understood Bill's humiliation but couldn't work out why his stepmother was so upset. She was left feeling more perplexed when she went into the kitchen and found Agnes standing at the sink, staring out into the back yard. She seemed to be unaware that Lucy was there.

"Why couldn't they have just given it to Bill?" She wandered towards the pantry, drying her hands on her apron.

Lucy was beginning to feel alone. Bill had hardly spoken to her since his father's funeral, and although Agnes seemed to be losing her sharpness she had a deep side to her that Lucy couldn't fathom. She would talk about practical matters on the farm and in the house. She'd even begun to recall some of her life in Plymouth. It had been a kind of common ground that she shared with Lucy. The big ships made in Barrow were often docked and based in Agnes's home town. Agnes had a remarkable knowledge of battleships. Although Lucy didn't share her enthusiasm for them she'd listened with the dutiful interest that she'd showed to her granddad as he'd talked about big ships being launched at Vickers. Agnes even told her about the *Revenge*, which was the same class as the *Royal Oak* on which her cousin had died.

"The *Revenge* was at Jutland when my father died."

Lucy noticed she showed no emotion, felt uncomfortable and moved the conversation along.

"My granddad helped to build that."

She thought that maybe Agnes was more vulnerable than she appeared. Perhaps the military-like stiffness she showed was a shield. Don't show your weakness and others will think you're strong. She'd seen that in women in Barrow, often the ones who were battling to bring up a family without the help of a husband.

Agnes wasn't quite the same. She'd had a privileged upbringing and had never had a child. She never disclosed her secrets so, although Lucy had warmed towards her, she felt she couldn't really talk to her, even now when the one thing she needed most of all was a mother.

Lucy wanted someone she could confide in, someone like Ruth in Barrow. She decided she would talk to Alice. Alice seemed to have a kind of wisdom that Lucy hadn't seen in girls her age. She'd made Lucy feel welcome the first time they'd met.

The first of May was a Sunday. Agnes had gone to church with Mary and was calling at the Laycock's for lunch. Bill was somewhere up on the lot, checking the sheep. He was always busy now. Perhaps things would change when the cows went out in a couple of weeks. She didn't hold out much hope.

She set off to the Taylor's farm. As she reached the front gate a bluetit flew down from the oak tree with a green grub in its beak. It dipped under the washing line and bobbed into the nest box on the pear tree. Within seconds it was gone again. By the time she'd reached the end of the garden it was back, followed by its mate. The eggs hidden away in the nest must have hatched. They had a family to feed. As she watched them working furiously, flitting from tree to nest and from nest to tree, she wondered how a bluetit would manage without a mate, if the cat caught one. Could the other bird ever hope to feed the chicks alone or would they starve?

She began thinking back, and realised that this was the first time she'd been past the front gate since the funeral. She hadn't seen Alice since January. The flu had taxed her heavily shortly after Bill had been sick and she hadn't felt well for weeks. She was only starting to feel really alive again and wondered how long it would last.

A bumblebee was searching for a hole in the bank. It looped its way along beside her as she walked, the hum of its wings rising and falling as it laboured upwards and stooped down, trying to find a crevice for its eggs. It had survived the winter alone and would soon be starting a colony of its own.

The Taylor's front garden was separated from the road by a flat-topped wall. Someone, a hundred years earlier, had been able to afford to build it from stone, cut smooth by an army of stone masons. As Lucy drew level with it she could see her friend bending over a flowerbed. Alice looked up as she heard Lucy approach. She waved a gloved hand towards her.

"Come on over."

Lucy turned her back to the wall, hitched herself up and swung her legs across. She landed between two shrubs and stepped out and across the lawn to where Alice was dropping weeds into a wheelbarrow.

Alice put her hands on her hips and arched her back.

"Where have you been, Stranger?"

Lucy felt a pang of guilt.

"I've been so busy that I haven't noticed how time was

flying past. Anyway, how have you been?"

"I've been busy, too. Tony's coming round soon, so I wanted to finish here first."

Tony? Lucy didn't remember hearing the name.

Alice continued, "I thought he was a bit quiet at first but he's coming out of his shell."

Lucy remembered: the shy one from the dance.

"I wanted to come and tell you something."

Alice was stooping for the last clump of weeds. She put them onto the pile in the wheelbarrow and began wheeling it towards a heap in the corner.

"I've finished here for now. Let's go inside and have a cup of tea." She breathed heavily as she heaped the load on top of the pile. "I'm just about getting the garden straight now. It's taken me two years." She left the wheelbarrow face down on the heap and dusted herself off with her gloves. "When I was at school we used to have a maid who did most of the gardening. She wasn't very good, and a lot of it got overgrown. She was a terrible girl, always chasing after my older brothers. Bert was scared of her. She started seeing Harry Laycock and someone else besides. In the end she got pregnant and had to go back home to Lancaster."

Lucy's heart sank. Would she be seen as a terrible girl too? She felt her cheeks colouring. Alice was walking in front of her. She held the gate open and fastened it when Lucy had walked through. "I'm glad we got rid of the geese. They were always getting in. Have you any goslings yet?"

Lucy wasn't thinking about geese. She was beginning to doubt whether she could confide in Alice. It had taken her a week to pluck up the courage to come and talk to her. Now she was beginning to long for the life in Barrow where home was separate from work, and people talked about important family matters at home without having to worry about the animals every waking hour.

"I said, 'have you any goslings yet?' Are you all right? You were miles away."

"Oh yes. I'm fine." She was wishing she hadn't come. "Three of the geese are sitting on eggs, and Bill's got three broody hens on goose eggs. They're due to hatch next week." She followed Alice into the house and wondered what she should tell her.

She was disappointed to see Charlie Taylor sitting in an armchair in the kitchen. He looked up from his newspaper and saw the two girls.

"Hello Lucy. How are y' doin? Any goslings yet?"

"I'm doing okay." She knew it didn't sound like it, but Charlie hadn't noticed. "We should have some next week. Bill's tested the eggs in water and they all wobbled."

"That's what I like to see. A good strong kick. You know they've got strength to hatch if they give a good jerk in t' water."

Alice was making the tea. She handed Lucy a cup.

"I'm glad you don't take sugar. Our ration's nearly used up."

Charlie rustled his paper.

"What do you expect? That bloody young feller of yours teks two big spoonfuls every time he has a brew."

Alice glanced across at Lucy and flicked her eyes upwards. Charlie was reading something. "Look at this."

Lucy wondered whether he was talking to them or thinking out loud.

"It says here that Germans are buildin up troups on t' French border. They've another think comin' if they think they'll get past our boys an' the whole French army."

None of them knew it but within two weeks he'd be eating his words.

Alice sat across the table from Lucy.

"What was it you were wanting to tell me?"

Lucy was making a decision.

"I've decided I'm going back to Barrow."

"Why? I thought you were settling down here."

"I'm missing my family."

"What does Bill say about it?"

"He doesn't know yet."

There was a noise from the armchair and Charlie got up, headed for the back door. He stopped and put a hand on Lucy's shoulder.

"We'll be sorry to see you go, lass." He looked up as if he was talking to himself. "They're all findin' jobs wi' more money. Young Phyllis Laycock's got a job in Lancaster as a nurse." He looked back at Lucy. "Come an' see us before ye go." He grabbed his cap from a hook and went outside.

Later that year, Lucy would look back and notice how others' reactions could galvanise your thoughts and decisions, no matter how close or distant those people were. When she'd come down to talk to Alice, she'd expected to be confiding in her about being pregnant. Alice's comment about the maid had put paid to that. When she'd mentioned that she was thinking of going home, it hadn't really sunk in that she was leaving. Charlie's reaction had, in some way, anchored it into her mind that the decision was made and there was no going back.

Alice was holding her hand across the table.

"Don't you think you should talk it over with him? He is very fond of you."

Lucy shifted on the chair, took her hand away.

"He's ignored me since January. He's acting as if I wasn't there anymore. That's why I think it will be better if I'm not."

The door knocked and Tony walked in. Alice got up and kissed him. He blushed when he caught Lucy's eye. She pushed her chair back.

"I'd better be going."

When Alice begged her to stay with them Lucy said that she had things to do before Agnes got back. She left the Taylors' place and headed for the Branthwaites'. Before Christmas she'd almost started calling it home.

✤

It was mid-morning when Bill reached the lot. The hoggs were grazing about half way up the slope. As he approached them they fled in a bunch to the top of the hill. Their long fleeces made them appear like a child's pom-pom bouncing across a rough carpet. Bill rode his pony along the ridge from where he could see the boundary wall at both sides. When he reached the far end he followed the wall eastwards towards Moss's Lot.

An old overgrown lane ran between the two properties and turned down towards Moss's farm when it met the wood where Bill and Dennis had finished putting up the barbed wire. There was something different about the hawthorn bushes that hung over the lane, so Bill eased the pony right up against the wall to take a closer look. All along the lane, overhanging branches had snapped off as if something large had passed along. The track was made of rough limestone. In places it was cut into the rock so as Bill peered over the wall he could see no tracks on the ground, only places where stones had been dislodged or crushed by something heavy. He clicked his tongue and the pony walked on, until a small stream ran from the lot under the wall and across the old lane. He tied the pony to a thorn bush and ducked under the culvert in the wall. The air was damp and his boots sank in the sandy bed of the stream. He stood up in the lane and breathed in the scent of the hawthorn blossom, then looked at the mud where the stream ran across the lane. There were tyre marks in the mud, and at the farm side of the stream he found two potatoes, as if they'd rolled off the top of a load when the wagon climbed the slope from the stream. Further along was another, crushed by the wheels of the returning wagon. He rolled one of the potatoes in his hand, glanced quickly up and down the lane and poked his head between the thorn bushes so that he could see towards Moss's farm. Someone was busy putting up a pole barn. He counted ten poles and saw men up ladders, hoisting up the roof trusses. Moss's stone barn had a new door. Bill thought how strange it looked for a barn door to be closed in good weather. Moss had a team of men working on a Sunday. He glanced back to where the lane wound its way through Colonel Trewin's woods, remembering where it came out on a blind bend about a mile past Tom's old farm.

He stuffed the potato in his pocket and crept back through the wall. As he rode back along the lot Bill kept glancing back at the track to Moss's farm. It had not been used for years. Why use it now when there was a good road through the village? The only reason he could come up with was that Moss was having deliveries that he didn't want anyone to see.

12

Another cause why some wheat is more blighted than
other wheat on the same land, is the condition in which
the insects find it; for the rind of that which is strong and
flourishing is soft and tender; into this they can easily lay
their eggs.

Jethro Tull. The Horse Hoeing Husbandry (1733)

Since Lucy's arrival at the farm, Agnes had warmed to her. The girl always did her work well, and seldom answered back if she was chastised for something. Agnes cringed as she looked back at how she'd treated Lucy when she'd first arrived. She found she had become more tolerant than she was only a few months ago. The hot flushes were not so frequent as they used to be. She put most of her earlier treatment of Lucy down to these, and found she liked herself a lot better when she did. How would she have managed without her during those first few weeks after Jack's death? The house would have fallen apart. Lucy had been doing many of Jack's jobs outside, too.

She remembered her fears when Lucy had first arrived, how she'd been concerned about her getting up to something with Bill. Celia Laycock had warned her about serving girls and had told her about an incident with one of her boys who'd been involved with a girl at the Taylor's farm. She'd tried to trap him into marriage, when all along the father had been some town boy she'd been seeing when she went home for weekends. Agnes could now see that Lucy wasn't like that. At one time she'd begun to think that she might like her as a daughter-in-law, but recently Lucy and Bill seemed to be drifting apart. She wondered if it was anything to do with the Waterford boy. He'd given her flowers on Valentine's day.

Tom Waterford was a nice boy. He was more cheerful than Bill. It was a pity he'd got into trouble with his landlord. He reminded her of her cousin Peter as a boy, a bit too easily led.

The navy had been the saving of him. She remembered the *Royal Oak* and realised the navy had caused his death too. There was too much death in the world. She'd seen war before, and although the politicians talked about fighting for freedom she didn't believe that anyone ever won. Countries and governments could say that they'd won but she'd seen too many families in Plymouth who'd lost. Hers was one of them.

As Agnes rounded the corner in the trap she saw Lucy walking back up the road. She told Mary to squeeze up beside her so that Lucy could climb up.

"Do you want a lift to the top of the hill?"

"Yes please." She pulled herself up beside Mary.

Agnes could see Lucy was tired. She had been looking radiant recently, and Agnes had been pleased to see that she was getting over the flu. It had been over two months, but she'd been run down, sick. The machinery in the older woman's mind began to turn. Things were falling into place: Lucy's vomiting after the flu, the clear complexion and now tiredness. Something was going on inside her that she was keeping secret.

As she recognised the signs, Agnes began to wonder. Was it Bill or was it Tom? Surely it couldn't have been Tom. He'd only been around for a week and only in the days. Lucy had been starting with the flu herself that week and had been struggling to finish her work. Lucy hadn't been out at nights since before Christmas, over five months ago.

The question that was going through Agnes's mind was that, if Lucy was pregnant and Bill was the father, why had they become so distant? A thought flashed into her head and she quickly dashed it away. Of course not. Not Bill.

She remembered a young girl in Plymouth over thirty years ago, trying to hide a pregnancy and ashamed at what had been done to her, ashamed at what they had done to her, all of them, one at a time, holding her down for the next one. The smell of their beer-stinking breath and the scratch of their chins, the jeering, chanting, shouting, the leering, drooling looks on every face as they stepped forward for 'their turn', one of them pouring drink down her while another held her nose, how it burned when it ran into her lungs. She'd coughed and it came back down her nose, burning again.

The girl couldn't remember how many there had been. She'd lost count before she passed out. She remembered the pain. She would never forget that. Nor would she forget that rubbish-filled, vomit-spattered alleyway where she woke up next morning. The bruises, the colour of cobbles, that took a month to fade.

Agnes remembered that girl staggering into the house when her mother was still asleep. The mother who slept a lot just after the girl's father died. The girl, folded in the corner of her bedroom wishing she was dead, staring at the dust under the bed. She never forgot the dust and she never forgot that broken biscuit lying in the corner.

Then slowly, after hours, knowing that she had to live for her mother, the widow on the next landing with the bottles by her bed. She remembered the strength that came over her, swept through her like a wind. It wasn't the warm strength she'd felt as a child when her father praised her and encouraged her, nor was it the hot strength that she'd felt in a rage. This strength was cold, as cold as ice or the water that filled the lungs of dead sailors off Jutland. It blew through her, swept through her and filled her up. She was strong, she was cold; and Agnes Patterson, eighteen, raped and pregnant, went on.

When she sat in the trap, looking at Lucy, Agnes saw the similarities but she also saw the differences. Turning the situation over in her mind did not come up with the answer she expected. Lucy was pregnant. She was pretty sure of that. She hadn't been raped. She was almost sure of that too, but the question remained – why was Lucy hiding it, and why was she so distant from Bill? Perhaps Bill didn't want anything to do with the child. That one didn't seem to fit, either, unless the child wasn't his, and she couldn't really see Lucy as the kind of girl who would have been close to one and getting pregnant with another. The one thought that escaped her was that Bill might not know.

When they were back in the house, Agnes sent Mary to change out of her church clothes and tidy her room. She knew that the child would become distracted and probably spend time playing with the things she was supposed to be putting away.

Lucy always stoked the fire as soon as she came in, so Agnes knew she could catch her on her own in the front room. She waited until she heard the clunk of the coal bucket on the hearth and went in to speak to her.

"Is everything all right Lucy?" Her voice wavered a little and the words came out with a sharper edge than she'd intended.

"Yes. Why?" Lucy seemed to be startled by the question.

Agnes recoiled. It suddenly dawned on her that she couldn't ask the girl outright. She hadn't planned her next question.

"I was wondering if you were happy here."

It was an odd thing to say, especially for Agnes. Lucy stopped and looked at her. Agnes was stumbling over something. She wasn't getting to the point. She was digging, and Lucy began to feel as if her inner thoughts were about to be unearthed.

"Agnes, I've something to tell you. I want to go home." She watched Agnes's face wilt. She'd guessed she wouldn't be pleased. Maybe she would even be disappointed, but the expression she was seeing looked more like deep sadness. Lucy felt something pushing her and continued. "I want to go tomorrow."

"Tomorrow?" It sounded breathless, winded. "Will you be coming back?"

"I don't know. I haven't decided yet." She expected Agnes to ask her how she thought they were going to manage without her, to start listing all the reasons she should stay or demanding more notice. Her voice sounded almost caring, concerned.

"Are you sure it's what you want? You've thought about this?"

Lucy nodded. She wasn't going to let any uncertainty in her voice show through and side with her employer.

Agnes sighed.

"You don't want to talk this over?"

Lucy clenched her teeth, shook her head. Her hands were clasped in front of her.

Agnes was regaining her composure. The logical mind was overriding her emotions.

"What does Bill think about this?" When Lucy didn't answer, the thought forged itself into shape. "You haven't told him."

Lucy's answer was short.

"I don't want him to know."

Agnes shook her head. She was trying to think of what to say next, when Lucy stepped past her.

"It's nearly time for milking. I've got to go and change."

Agnes wanted a chance to talk to Bill. She was determined to find out what had happened between the two of them. She guessed Lucy would be staying out of the way tonight, so she would get him on his own after supper.

She was serving out the stew. Bill was searching through the bottom cupboard for a tin of dubbin to treat his boots. She sat herself down on one of the kitchen chairs. He always treated his boots in the kitchen, whether Agnes liked it or not.

There was a vicious rapping on the front door and they

both jumped and looked at each other. Bill got up.

"I'll get it. I wonder who that is on a Sunday night."

It was Moss. As Bill opened the door he stood there, red faced and raging.

"I've got all your bluffy sheep and lambs in my front pasture. They're eatin all my grass."

Bill remembered Moss's hedge with all the gaps in the bottom.

"It's your hedge Mr Moss."

"My hedge? My hedge? Everyone knows you should fence against your own stock. If you want to keep sheep you should keep 'em at home."

Bill felt himself boiling up inside. He was trying to keep his cool.

"If you think back, it's not so long since we 'ad same trouble wi' your bull."

"I don't know what yer talkin' about. I never saw my bull in your field."

"It's Sunday night, Mr Moss. I'm not sure you'd want to see me doin' extra work on a Sunday. It might not be the Christian thing to do."

Moss was turning redder. He had that wild-eyed look, with white all round his eyes. Bill had seen that in a bull that turned nasty.

"Never mind that. They're all brekkin' through into my field right in front of your landlord's house. I bet he'll 'ave somethin to say about you not keepin' up wi' yer tenancy agreement."

The mention of the tenancy agreement was like a shot in his chest. Bill felt something leaking away inside him.

"I'll come an' get 'em out now." He could see Moss rising in stature. He clenched his fists as he saw the glint of triumph in his eyes. Moss gave a nod of superiority and clambered back in his car. He blasted the engine and shot out of the yard.

Agnes was standing in the passageway. She'd heard it all, and said nothing as Bill went to get his dog. He stopped at the cart shed to get an axe and some leather mittens. He wasn't going to do this twice.

The sheep were settling down for the night. They were mostly lying with their lambs curled by their feet. As the dog ran round them, there was a barrage of deep angry bleats and foot stamping. The lambs jumped up in panic and raced after their mothers through the holes under Moss's shoddy hedging. Bill followed them back into the park and began hacking off thorny branches from the hedge and some bushes by the stream. He channelled his anger through the axe, cutting through most of them with one swipe. He stuffed the thorns into any gaps in the bottom of the hedge and then backtracked to fill some weak spots that might turn into gaps before next year. The whole hedge was over three hundred yards long, and by the time he reached the end it was almost too dark to see. He whistled his dog and trudged back towards the farmhouse. His arms ached and he was beginning to feel that dizzy tiredness that came from working late on an empty stomach.

Agnes wasn't around. The front room door was shut and a towel was hanging on the door handle. She must've been having a bath. He took his plate of stew from the oven, shovelled it down and went to bed.

✥

Spring mornings on the farm had become special for Lucy, stepping out into the inky darkness, with dawn casting a light stain to the east. As she picked up the milking buckets for the last time she felt a heaviness, as if some force was drawing them back onto the bench in the dairy. She was going to miss out on seeing the cows go out to grass. Bill had told her of the fascination it had for him, the way the cows listened as the door and gate were opened, and their excitement about being free again. She would feed the hens for the last time before breakfast and then travel down to the station in the trap with Agnes who would be taking Mary to school.

Tomorrow she would awaken to the sounds of ships, gulls and steam hammers, and she looked sadly at the blackbird that always started his territorial song from the end of the barn. She stopped and watched as he flew over to the oak trees to mark out the boundary of his world. A cock was crowing in the distance at Charlie Taylor's and lambs were bleating from the fields towards the lot.

Bill took a bucket from her and started on the first cow. He seemed to be in a bad mood and she wondered if Agnes had told him she was going. He said nothing when she walked past with the stool. Sitting beside the cow, she noticed how the bulge under her jacket tightened as she leaned forwards towards the cow's udder. The animal's flanks felt warm and comforting against her shoulder and head.

The hens were clamouring at the door when Lucy arrived with the feed. She watched them pecking hungrily in the trough, then running out along the paddock when she'd opened the sliding pop-hole. One of them ran after her as she walked back to the yard. She wondered if it knew.

Bill had already left with the milk when she came back. Since the spring work started he'd taken to wolfing down his breakfast and tearing off to the station so that Dennis was ready with another horse by the time he got back. He'd head off ploughing, harrowing or rolling, taking with him a basket and can, and not returning until it was time to milk. Several times, when the weather was about to break, he'd left Lucy and Dennis with the milking and not appeared till after dark. Often his last instruction as he fled from the house was a shouted order to Dennis: "Bring me another horse at dinner time."

Lucy washed and changed, ate a hurried breakfast and carried her bags from her room. Through the staircase window, she saw Bill leading a horse out of the yard. Mary was fastening her shoes at the bottom of the stairs. She looked at Lucy.

"Are you going away?"

"Yes."

"When will you be back?"

"I don't know." She tried to convince herself that it wasn't a lie. If she wasn't coming back she didn't know when she was coming back.

Agnes took them to the village, Lucy sitting in the middle. Mary hugged her before jumping down from the trap.

"See you soon. Have a nice time."

Lucy swallowed hard.

"Goodbye, Mary." She watched as the girl who saw her as a sister ran and skipped into the school yard.

The pony trotted them to the station and Agnes climbed down to carry one of Lucy's bags to the platform. They weaved through men pushing churns. Milk for another train heading in the opposite direction, to a different industrial town where Lucy would never go.

Agnes carried the heavier bag over the bridge and down some steps to the other platform. Lucy felt she should have been leading the way. Agnes dropped the bag by a crate of eggs and turned to Lucy. They could hear the train's whistle as it entered the cutting.

"Listen to me Lucy. Whatever you decide to do," her eyes dropped to Lucy's stomach, "don't do anything rash."

Lucy looked at her eyes. Agnes had guessed.

"No, Agnes."

The train was pulling up at the platform, hissing steam and billowing out smoke. Its brakes screeched and men were shouting. Lucy was aware that people were moving around her. Agnes grabbed her shoulders.

"Listen to me. Nothing rash." Her face was like a rock, her eyes full of tears. "You've no idea what damage those women can do." She shook Lucy, gripped her tight. "Do you know what I'm saying?"

Lucy stared at her. My God! Agnes had no children!

Agnes pulled her close, and Lucy felt the wetness from her face. Doors were closing and the stationmaster was shouting something. As Lucy pulled away she heard the words:

"Look after yourself child."

She grabbed her bags and jumped on the train.

13

The chief art of the husbandman is to feed plants to their best advantage; but, how shall he do that unless he knows what is their food?

Jethro Tull. The Horse Hoeing Husbandry (1733)

The sixteenth of May 1940 was a Tuesday. It was a date that would be rooted in Bill Branthwaite's mind until the day he died. There were no major incidents on the farm on the sixteenth of May. The cows had been turned out to grass the day before. The heifers were grazing on the lot, and this year's lambs were growing happily on a diet of mother's milk and spring grass.

A week earlier, a German general by the name of Erwin Rommel had led a division of tanks through some woods at Ardennes. They had caught the British and French troops off guard and had smashed through the Maginot line. The newspapers and radio broadcasts were full of reports about the invasion of France. On farmland in another country, young men of Bill's age were fighting and dying in a vain attempt to preserve the freedom of Europe.

Bill was fixing a fence. The ewes and lambs had been moved from the park to the hill pasture behind the house. They'd found a way into Charlie Taylor's meadow between a holly bush and an old tree stump. Bill had finished afternoon milking and taken the axe to block the gap.

He'd heard Winston Churchill on the radio on Saturday calling for local defence volunteers. Yesterday, as Bill was returning from the station, Norman Watterson had waved across to him from over his garden wall.

"Hey Bill."

Bill had leapt down from the cart, gone over and asked Norman how he was.

"Not bad, lad, not bad. What does t' think about joinin' us in t' volunteers?"

Bill had already decided.

"We're meetin' at Friar's Hall at seven tomorra. If tha's got a weapon, bring it. Sir Charles 'as given us use of gun room. We're on parade out back."

Bill had nodded

"That sounds good."

"If tha' asks me, Sir Charles wants 'is house protectin'. It's as good a place as any though."

"Seven o'clock?"

"Aye."

Bill had left Norman feeding his pig and had ridden back wishing he had a gun.

As he wove holly branches into the gap, Bill was wondering who else would turn up. How would he fit in his duties around hay time, and what it would be like facing German tanks that could ride over hedges and blow holes in the solid stone walls of Sir Charles' mansion?

Underneath his concern for the farm and worry about the war, a resentment was still rumbling. Lucy had left without saying goodbye. She'd given no notice and lumbered him and Dennis with extra jobs. Mary was helping Agnes with as much as she could. She'd even started feeding the hens, but she was at school all day and the farm was two hands down.

Bill didn't consider Lucy's reasons for going. His head was full of day-to-day tasks and planning ahead for the next of the season's jobs. She'd deserted him, and that's all there was to it. Whenever he thought about her he found himself cursing under his breath. She was just another bloody town girl who'd gone back to her own kind. Most of the time he could convince himself, but in the brief moments that his resentment subsided he found himself wishing that he had her address.

He looked round for Flash. The young dog had got bored

waiting and, being within sight of home, slunk back to his kennel. Some of the hens were crowding round the hut but a few were still scratching out in the paddock. He wouldn't be able to shut them in until later so he cut across the stack yard towards the house, stopping to close the coop for the broody with the goslings. She had five and although they were less than a fortnight old they were already pushing up through her feathers and peering out from above her wings.

He wasn't sure what to wear for parade. He had nothing that looked like a uniform. As he rummaged through his wardrobe he decided on his auction suit and best boots. He shaved off three days' stubble and set off to the hall. Over the next five years he would follow this path several times a week, often not returning until milking time the next morning, but he always remembered the evening he went to join. It was like his first day at school or the day he walked out of the classroom for the final time.

Bert Taylor was passing the farm gate as Bill stepped out onto the road. He noticed that Bert had slowed down so that they could walk round to the hall together. He seemed a bit nervous. He had a pitchfork over his shoulder and carried it like a soldier marching with a rifle. He was older than Bill, tall and broad, but his voice sounded like a child.

"I've never been to Friar's Hall before. They say it's a posh place. You don't mind if I walk round wi' you?"

Bill had always looked up to Bert and it felt strange that his neighbour was looking to him for reassurance. He shrugged and let him keep talking.

"Do you know what we'll be doing tonight?" Bert didn't wait for an answer. "I hope they've got rifles for us. I brought this 'cos they said bring a weapon. Have you not brought owt?"

For a moment Bill wished he had. He'd thought about it before he went to change but decided he might look silly if he'd turned up with a slashing hook or fork if everyone else had shotguns and rifles.

Bert continued his chattering.

"I hope we get enough training before we see any action." They rounded the driveway and came in sight of the hall. "Bloody hell. This is a fancy spot. I'd never 'ave guessed it was like this."

The gun room door was open, and Bill led the way inside. Norman Watterson was sitting on a stool wearing his old war uniform. It had three stripes. He had an old rusty man-trap across his knees and was working on the teeth and mechanism with a wire brush and some oil. An old army rifle leaned against the wall beside him. He glanced up at them with a sly grin.

"You're first 'ere lads. I'm just tryin' t' get this workin'. Tha never knows when we might need it. T'owd gamekeeper used t' say it caught em just below t' knee."

Cars were arriving outside. Bill could hear footsteps crunching on the gravel round the front drive. Norman put down the trap and took his rifle.

"We'd better gan an' form up lads. Colonel Trewin'll be wantin' t' inspect 'is troops."

Outside, a group of men were shuffling into rows. There was Mr Finch, Bobby Dobson and James Smith, the new tenant from the Waterford's old place. Vince the mechanic was hurrying round the corner to meet them. He'd left his motorbike by the stables near the road and rushed into line, hot and sweating.

The Colonel addressed the men and told them how important their duties would be. They would be involved in surveillance and guarding the bridge over the river. As soon as they had weapons they would receive weapons training. Until then they would be employed making a firing range, and guard duties would be drawn up for each night at the hall. They would be on lookout for planes on their way to bomb the shipyards at Barrow.

The word hit Bill like a bullet. He found himself thinking of Lucy again and the bitterness swelled inside him like a dam ready to burst.

The Colonel inspected their weapons: four shotguns and two rifles. He told Bert his pitchfork was too long and sent Norman Watterson to get some garden tools, hoes, rakes and brushes for weapons drill. Norman was to keep his rank as sergeant, and reluctantly handed his rifle over to Smith.

Bill noticed how the older men knew exactly what to do, and he made a point of following what they did in response to every command. He was surprised to see the Colonel not watching their efforts with derision but wearing a thoughtful concerned mask as if he was wondering how to get the best from this bunch of farmers, shopkeepers and old men.

When they were dismissed, Bill walked home with feelings of apprehension about how they would cope in an invasion. They were amateurs who knew more about lambing and ploughing than they did about warfare. The enemy was pushing through France, sweeping away the best troops of two countries with long military histories. How on earth could a band of green volunteers like this possibly stand up to bombers, fighter planes and Panzer tanks?

Over the following weeks he threw himself into his training. When rifles arrived they started target practice in the park. Bill had never shot anything before and although he soon found that he could hit the target he tried not to let it enter his mind that one day there could be a man in the sights of the gun.

When it was announced on the radio that Operation Dynamo had been a success, Norman Watterson's comment had been scathing.

"Success? We've just gi'en 'em France. How can that be a success?" He was on guard duty with Bill on the roof of Friar's Hall. The night sky was hung with clouds, and Bill had mentioned Dunkirk, trying to find a note of optimism. The nights on duty were long, with little or nothing to report. Bill would never develop the habit of having a few hours sleep while the other one kept watch. It was rumoured that Bert Taylor was already doing this, and in later years several of the volunteers made it common practice.

Bill's days were filled with thinning turnips and sheep clipping. His back ached and he wondered how he would be able to stand up straight on parade. Uncle Harry had come to help clip the sheep. When Bill offered to help him in return, he put his hand on his nephew's shoulder and said quietly,

"Don't you think tha's got enough to do?"

Bill felt pangs of guilt at not being able to return the favour, but knew that Harry was right. He just didn't have the time to do any more work. He hardly ever saw Mary, and his only conversations with her were comments about the hens when she popped into the shippen at milking times. Agnes was doing her best to keep the house running and looked at him with concern when he came in for tea.

"You're not getting enough sleep."

Whenever he wasn't on duty or working late he flopped into bed straight after supper. He awoke each morning still aching from the day before, and was thinking about nothing but the next day's work and his duties with the volunteers.

Each task took so much of his attention that he wasn't noticing the changes around him. Dennis was becoming more withdrawn. They worked together without speaking. The humour and games that strengthened the bond between them were gone. Instead of his absent-minded staring at the sky and birds, Dennis was adopting a head-down posture and waded through his jobs like a prisoner doing forced labour.

The greatest difference that he didn't see coming was in Agnes. Since the invasion of France she had spent each evening listening to the radio. Bill had caught glimpses of her doing this as he rushed out for parade or heard the crackle and whistle as she tuned it in. He even listened to the drawl of Winston Churchill's voice as he warned of what was to come and skipped over the worst of the bad news. Whenever he caught the news, Bill's ears took in the speeches and reports. He heard new names like Charles De Gaulle and Mussolini. He pictured the German troops marching in the shadow of the Eiffel Tower, but wasn't aware of what was happening only a few feet away from him.

Agnes was sitting on an old dining chair right beside the radio. She was biting her nails like a rat chewing at a skirting board. Her face was drawn and the corners of her eyes had slumped as if an invisible weight was dragging them down. She was nervous. Her teacher's training and naval upbringing had developed in her a way of reading between the lines of newspapers and gleaning information from what was left unsaid in radio reports. Bill, she knew, had none of this skill and simply echoed the grave tones or optimism of the reporters or leaders whose voices he heard. He was uplifted by Winston Churchill's dogged tones. *We will fight them on the beaches ... in our homes ... and until every last drop of blood is spilled.*

The new Prime Minister was his kind of leader. He spoke plainly, with determination. He knew about war, and Bill was learning. Bill had said several times that he was sure that Churchill would find a way of winning.

Agnes was not so sure. She had sat in the same place every evening since France was invaded. She'd listened to the rhetoric, the propaganda carefully spelled out to keep the population focussed and give them hope. She'd read the works of Karl Marx and although she would never be a communist or socialist, she did not trust the Tories, especially one who'd crossed the house. She trusted her own instincts more than any politician or news report. She'd heard her parents' conversations in the early days of the last war and noted how her father's inside information differed from what was being said in the papers.

As a nurse, she'd bandaged the wounds of horribly injured men. Truck loads of them returning from the front had been dumped on the steps of the hospital, to be tended by girls in their mid-teens. She remembered a young man with his jaw bone blown away, trying to drink through what had once been a mouth. Agnes, holding his head and a small jug. It was then that she saw what war really did to young men, not just the tearing and burning of tissues, the smashing and splintering of bone. She'd seen it in his eyes; she hadn't a word for it. She never found one when she was reading English at university. 'Despair' wasn't enough. The young man had a name. She couldn't remember what it was. He was half a face that stood out in a batch of hundreds who'd been admitted on a day when the papers said that the war was going well.

She was still sitting by the radio. Bill was getting up. He had that satisfied look on his face that he carried when he'd been told that everything was all right. He yawned, stretched, and the bottom of his shirt pulled free from the waistband of his trousers exposing a trim stomach. She remembered the young man without a jaw. He'd had no other injuries.

Bill glanced at her and pulled his lips tight together.

"I guess we just keep hopin' for t' best." He picked up his cap from the chair arm. "I'll go an' shut hens in, then I'm off to bed."

She felt a surge of anger.

"Don't you realise what's happening?"

He looked puzzled.

She stood up and faced him. All her fears built up over the last few weeks were turning to rage.

"Can't you see how serious this is? They've driven us back to England. They've taken over France in three weeks. Haven't you worked it out that we're next?"

Bill stopped short. His cap was half way to his head. He hadn't expected this. She wasn't waiting for an answer.

"Our troops arrived back with no equipment, nothing. You can't fit a tank in a fishing boat. How do you think we're expected to win a war when all our army's weapons are left in France?"

Bill was thinking. He felt a pricking in his cheeks. Agnes was rounding on him for something that wasn't his fault. At the same time he was seeing things from a different angle.

Agnes was still shouting.

"Do you think that Hitler hasn't planned this? They'll start bombing, then they could be in England any day. Haven't you noticed how they've stopped talking about aircraft numbers and the like on the radio? We haven't got enough."

Something was happening to her. That hard shell of a face was beginning to crack. Her cheeks were changing colour. That almost grey complexion was being replaced by a pink blotchy colour that reminded him of Dennis. "They're rounding up people in France already. They'll do the same when they get here." Her voice was getting higher. "And they will get here very soon. And all you can do is "keep hopin' for t' best"?" She finished off with a mocking tone of his voice.

He was missing something. He felt his anger rising. She'd started on him for no reason. Agnes always seemed to know more about what was going on in the world than he did. She could argue a point quoting all sorts of facts and using words that he didn't know. Like the British army, he had few bullets to fire. He remembered overhearing her conversation with his father. The day the policeman called to question her. He shot at her with the only ammunition he had.

"I don't know what you're so worried about anyway. Rest of us are t' ones who need to worry. I heard you talkin' when Sergeant Jackson came. You're half German." He rounded it off with a nod. He'd got information that she didn't know he had. He expected her to cringe back and look shocked, guilty.

He didn't get the response he'd pictured. Her eyes filled with tears. She slumped back on the chair and shook her head. Her voice was almost a croak.

"He took all my details, everything. They put them in a file in God knows where, so anyone can look at them when they're found."

"There. You're in the clear. Under Churchill, you're half English and under Hitler you're half German. You're t' one who's got it sorted. Hitler's goin' t' shoot any volunteers who resist. Where does that put me?"

"Oh Bill, if only you knew." She leaned her elbow by the radio on the cabinet, rested her head on it and sighed. "You just don't get it do you?"

"Get what?" He was definitely missing something.

She sat upright, put her hands in her lap and looked up at him.

"My father was English, a sea captain. You know that. My grandparents, my mother's parents, came over from Germany before my mother was born. They were dead before the last war started, or they'd have been interned. My grandfather's name was Heinrich Scheffel. My grandmother's name was Maria Kretschmann. She was Jewish."

Bill found himself lost for words. He listened as Agnes told him about her cousin who'd been killed on the *Royal Oak*. His sister had written regularly to Agnes and had kept in touch with the Jewish side of the family in Germany.

They used to write to her a lot. They were very worried about the future. Hitler was stirring up hatred towards them. Then suddenly the letters stopped. There was nothing. She wrote again and didn't get a reply. Since the letters had stopped coming she'd tried everyone she knew. She'd written so many times to Germany that she'd lost count. She was wringing her hands. She got up and paced across to the fireplace. "I can't stay here Bill. I can't."

"But this is our home. We've only just taken on the tenancy."

"Why do you think I wanted you to take it on? I want to leave now before it's too late."

Bill couldn't speak. He felt as if a huge cobble had dropped into his stomach. At the same time he was empty, drained like a barrel that had rusted into holes. He felt weak. The whole world was pulling against him and his feet were sliding towards the edge of a thick fog that he couldn't see through and didn't understand. Every dream he'd ever had was set at Friar's Holme Farm. His knees wavered and he slumped down in a chair like a lamb that hadn't managed to stand.

Agnes was still talking. Her words were like arrows out of the fog and it began to sink in that she'd been thinking about this for weeks, even months.

"Waterfords had a good sale. You could get a cottage with your half of the money."

He knew he probably couldn't.

"You'll soon get another job on a farm. It will be good for Mary to see the world."

"You want to take Mary?"

"My aunt has a big house in a village west of Boston. She's lonely on her own and she says that we can stay with her." It was that detached voice that she always used when she'd made up her mind and would not be swayed. The gate was closed on any other possibilities.

"You've already planned this?" He was shaking his head. Anger was boiling up inside him. "We're supposed to be partners and you've been plannin' this without a word to me." He was shouting. He stood up, staring her down. A strength was raging through him and he roared at her, inches from her face. "You came here with nothing. You acted as if you were better than t' rest of us an' as soon as y' saw yer chance y' med up yer mind t' sell up an' leave. Who the bloody hell do you think you are?" He was clenching his fists, glaring down at her.

Agnes took a handkerchief from the pocket of her apron, wiped a gob of saliva from her cheek. Her face was still. She got up from the chair and stepped past him.

"I've made up my mind. I'm going to speak to the auctioneers tomorrow."

✜

The next morning Bill was outside before his alarm went off. For the first time in his life he hadn't slept all night. He'd spent the night going over the situation in his mind, asking himself questions. Sometimes he had no answer. How could he keep the farm? He didn't know. Could he persuade Agnes to stay? Did he want her to stay? Could he buy her out? It seemed impossible. He had no sure answers for anything. He was only certain about one thing. He hated Agnes. Her arrogance, her selfishness, the way she talked to him as if he was a child. She was taking his sister away.

At the station he was slamming the churns onto the platform when a voice behind him made him stop.

"Good morning Bill." It was Geoffrey Laycock.

"Is it?" He wasn't in a mood for pleasantries. "Agnes is leavin'. I suppose you know all about it."

"She's what?" He looked genuinely surprised.

"She's leavin. Goin t' live with her aunt in America. Don't tell me she hasn't talked to you an' Mrs Laycock about it."

His reaction said she hadn't.

"I didn't know anything about it, Bill. Where is it going to leave you? I mean, you haven't had chance to get yourself established."

"I don't know. She only told me last night. She wants a sale."

"A sale? You mean she wants you to sell up all together?"

His voice was loud.

Bill sensed someone was listening and looked round. Joe Moss was standing by the stationmaster's office with a crate of eggs. He looked away and carried them round to the platform. Geoffrey Laycock watched him go. He fell silent until Moss appeared beyond the buildings at the far end of the platform.

"Look. I've got to go now but if you want to talk things through at any time, come and see me. I've always thought that you had a lot more about you than most of the tenant farmers round here." His eyes flicked towards the men loading the train. "Any time, Bill. I'll be glad to help." He took a parcel from his car and strode into the office.

Bill got back onto the cart and clicked his tongue at the horse. As he crossed the bridge he glanced back into the station yard. Geoffrey gave him a wave as he climbed into his gleaming Ford.

At the top of the hill, Joe Moss's van roared past, coughing out black smoke. The horse shied towards the verge.

"Whoa. Steady." Bill pulled at the reins and glanced up to see the van turning into the back entrance of Friar's Hall. He wondered what Moss was up to.

14

What can we say then to the salubrity of those roots themselves, bred up and fattened amongst these toads and corruption? The leaves indeed are only discharging some of the filth, when we eat them: but the roots have that unsavoury infected food in their very mouths, when we take them for our nourishment.

Jethro Tull. The Horse Hoeing Husbandry (1733)

Bill rode up to the Laycocks' house in the trap. He noticed how the grounds were laid out in an imitation of Friar's Hall. The driveway swept round the front of the house in an arc to a turning circle by the front door. Like Friar's Hall, there was a fountain in the front lawn. It looked like the fountain had long since stopped flowing but the gardens were well tended, with lupins and delphiniums splashing colour up the walls from the backs of borders.

A marquee had been erected in the far corner by the thatched summerhouse and people were either standing inside or chatting on the lawn holding glasses of what looked like champagne. He stopped the trap by George, the Laycocks' cowman, who was dressed uncomfortably in a suit and looking after the horses and cars.

"All right, George?"

"Aye." The tone wasn't convincing. "I'd rather be ploughin'. Come t' think of it, I'd rather be on me knees thinnin' turnips on a wet day than standin' 'ere like a bloody statue." He ran a rough finger round the inside of his collar, trying hopelessly to loosen the squeeze round his neck.

Bill handed him the reins and took the parcel from the seat. Agnes had found some wrapping paper and tied it with a ribbon. He strode across the lawn to the marquee. Phyllis was inside talking with a group of girls and two blokes in army uniforms.

"Bill!" She pushed past them and rushed over to him.

"Happy birthday." He held out the present and she took it from him and kissed him on the cheek. She smelled of expensive perfume. As she stepped back and pulled at the strands of the bow he noticed how her face had changed. She'd lost the puffy cheeks of adolescence. Her eyes seemed to have lost that cold superiority that he'd last recognised. It must have been a year since he'd seen her. Working in the offices of the munitions factory had changed her for the better.

She opened the box and saw the necklace, looked up at him, her eyes wide. She looked back at the diamonds sparkling against the dark velvet of the box.

"Bill! How could you afford this?"

He remembered what Agnes had told him. *Don't tell her where you got it.*

"It's from both of us. Me and Agnes." It was true. Agnes had provided it, and he had brought it. He hadn't seen it since she'd cleaned it up. Agnes's family must have been skilled jewellers. The silver chain was as fine as thread and the pendant was worked into tiny leaves, with the diamonds set in as the centres of three small flowers.

She thrust it into his hand, "Fasten it for me. I'm going to wear it now." She turned her back to him and leaned back towards him to let him put it round her neck.

He held the two ends between his fingers and slipped the pendant over her head, fumbling with the tiny chain. He turned it over as he worked out the mechanism and was relieved not to see a swastika on the back of the clasp. She straightened up and bent her knees slightly. He felt her body rubbing against his and only just managed to fasten the chain before she realised what effect it was having on him.

She turned round and flung her arms round his neck, pulled him even closer.

"Thank you. Come and meet my friends." She led him by

the hand to the group who had stopped watching and were talking amongst themselves. There were four girls, all from the factory. They turned towards Phyllis and started touching the pendant. The two soldiers were local lads from Lancaster, brothers, on leave for the weekend. They shook Bill's hand and introduced themselves. They hadn't seen any action. One of the girls was their sister. It was the first time they'd met Phyllis.

Bill expected to be met with derision when he told them he was in the Local Defence Volunteers but they were interested in how things were going. Their father was on duty at the castle, manning a searchlight. Bill responded gloomily.

"We haven't got any weapons yet. We've been promised a Sten gun, but it hasn't arrived."

Once the conversation got beyond the war, he found it harder to talk to them. They knew little about farming, and Bill didn't follow Preston North End. They thought it strange that they'd met someone who wasn't interested in football and had never been to a match. Even though the season was long gone and didn't start again for another two months, football was their main passion and topic of conversation. They switched to cricket but Bill had to admit that he wasn't a cricket fan either. He was wondering how he was going to keep talking, when the band started up.

Phyllis rushed over and dragged him into the middle of the marquee. He remembered the last time he'd been dancing. Lucy had taught him the steps and had even helped him practice at home. He felt a twinge of guilt when Phyllis asked him where he'd learned.

"At the village hall and at home." Again, he wasn't lying. He wasn't going to spoil things by telling her who'd taught him, and if Lucy hadn't the decency to say goodbye it was her loss. She wasn't even a farmer's daughter anyway; not like Phyllis.

As more guests arrived, Phyllis would break off to greet them, but she always came back to dance with Bill. He was surprised that there weren't more of her friends there.

She told him that Clarissa hadn't been able to come, and that her mother had written all the invitations. Most of the guests were her parents' friends or relations.

At around ten thirty, Bill told Phyllis he'd have to leave. He'd got hay out that needed turning the next day so he wanted to be up early. Her face drooped with disappointment but she understood and walked with him to the trap. She kissed him passionately and he noticed how sensual she was, how he felt a nervous excitement that he hadn't noticed with Lucy. He wanted her.

She wasn't coming home again from Lancaster for two weeks. He hoped he would have finished the hay by then, and arranged to meet her on the Saturday night.

As he rode back in the dark he thought about the way her body felt against his, the nervousness that came over him when he was with her and how different she was from Lucy. He longed for the weekend after next when he could see her again.

Hay time was hard. Bill still hadn't got used to making all the decisions. He worked from dawn until dusk all through the weekend, sometimes going out to mow at four in the morning and arriving back at six to start milking. Agnes was given the job of taking the milk. She'd find someone to help her at the station. Bill ate his breakfast on the way back to the field to continue mowing. Lunch was a sandwich held in his mouth while he sat on the knife bed of the mower, sharpening the blades until they gleamed like the teeth of a dragon.

He allowed the horse to rest, and took the scythe to mow out the corners of the fields. He had four and then five fields mown at a time, so that from Tuesday onwards he would always have a field of hay ready to clear.

On Tuesday afternoon he arrived in the yard and raced into the house. He hadn't enough men to get the hay in that night. As he walked down the passage to the kitchen, he caught sight of himself in the mirror. His face was grey with dust, turning black round his eyes, his forehead and down his neck where sweat had turned it back to mud.

Agnes was pouring hot water into the teapot

"Geoffrey Laycock's sending two men to help you tonight. Vince says he'll come as soon as he's closed the garage. He's not on duty at the Hall until tomorrow."

"Thanks, Agnes." He wondered how he'd manage without her. He was barely keeping up as it was.

By Friday morning, all but two fields were cleared. Bill set off after milking to scale out the first one. The sky had turned hazy, and wind was whipping dust from the track into spirals, miniature tornadoes that blew grit into his eyes and mouth. Oak trees were creaking and showing the underside of their leaves as powerful gusts battered the edge of the woods around the Hall.

As he worked his way across the field, wisps of hay were being lifted behind him and thrown against the hedge. He felt the hairs standing up on his arms, and rolled down his shirtsleeves. He wished he'd brought his jacket. He was finishing the short rows in the corner when he heard a distant rumble. To the south, it looked as if the clouds had swept down and swallowed up the land. He unhitched the horse, leaving the scaler under a tree, hurried off to get the side rake. He needed to get as much of the hay back into rows as he could. Rain was coming and it would dry better if it could be turned onto dry ground again after the sun returned. If it was left in tight rows it wouldn't catch as much rain.

He'd barely finished the six outside rows when he felt the first splashes of rain on his forehead. Huge drops pounded his back like bullets: missiles from high up in the smoke-black clouds. He left the rake in the middle of the field and fled with the horse towards the cover of the out barn, flung open the wide barn doors and led it inside. His shirt clung to his back and as he crouched in a corner his trousers tightened round his thighs, wringing cold drops from the sodden fabric.

He'd worked all morning and half the afternoon, and for what? The hay was almost ready and most of it was scaled out across the field soaking up water. It would soon rot. He couldn't have left it in a worse state if he'd set out to spoil it. The corner meadow wasn't as bad. The cut grass was still green and might last a couple of days before any real harm was done, but if the rain lasted over the weekend the eleven acres he'd just worked would be black and dusty. He couldn't drag his thoughts away from the ruined hay. The full barn at home didn't seem like an achievement. He'd been lucky. He cursed himself for not rowing up the meadow this morning.

A rabbit ran into the barn to shelter from the rain, saw Bill and fled back outside towards the wet hedge bottom and a flooding burrow. A fork of lightning blazed down from the sky and hit one of the oaks in the park like a shell. One of its huge branches exploded and fell to the ground, splintered like matchwood in the grass. The rain hammered down for almost an hour and Bill sat shivering on the cold barn floor.

As the rain retreated up the valley, Bill led the horse outside and climbed onto its broad back. He set off across the hill to check the sheep. The cows had left the shelter of the trees and were grazing miserably in the park. The sheep by the river were safe on the high banks. If it stayed wet he'd start mowing the thistles tomorrow: a punishment for ruining the hay. He counted the ewes on the hill. They all had twins. He rode back to the house and ran inside for some dry clothes, swapped the shire for the pony and went to check the heifers and sheep on the lot. He looked across the sodden valley. Charlie Taylor was standing in his steep pasture, staring down at a dead cow. Bill hoped his own heifers had escaped the lightning. Relief flooded him when he saw them crowding round the gate, steaming in the sunlight and sniffing at

Charlie's heifers across the lane. He counted the ewes on the slopes towards the scar and headed for home thinking about Phyllis.

She'd told him that most nights she went home to bed early. She was getting bored with life in town. An idea came to him. If he finished early tonight he could take the train into Lancaster and pay her a surprise visit. He didn't know the address, but she'd said she had a room in a boarding house. It was the only street off the road from the station to the castle.

After milking he left Dennis to finish scrubbing the milking buckets and went for a bath. Agnes had been keen on his plan and had the hot water ready. His suit was hanging by the fire and she'd left a clean shirt draped over a chair arm. There was soap and a clean white towel on the hearth, a shabby old orange one on the mat for him to stand on. He scrubbed himself clean and hurried to get dressed, grappled with buttons and his tie. He clipped his trousers to his shins and cycled out of the yard towards the village. The wind blew through his wet hair as he sped down the hill, passing the chip shop without a glance. The train whistled, entering the cutting from the viaduct as he passed the village and he felt the heat as smoke and steam billowed up around him when he crossed the bridge. He rounded the corner into the station and rode up to the ticket office without dismounting.

"Lancaster, please." He was fumbling for his change, handed it over and grabbed the ticket, rode through the door and along the platform to the guard's van. He tossed in his bike and boarded the train.

The station signs had been taken down. He was glad he knew all the stations on the way to Lancaster. The clock at Carnforth said half past seven. He would be in Lancaster before eight. Alongside the track were sodden fields of hay. He wasn't the only one who'd been caught out. Some of the smaller fields had been left in cocks. They must've had more time than him.

When the train crossed the Lune, he noticed how full the river was. Muddy brown water was lapping high against the walls of the quayside. There must have been a lot of rain up the valley. His eyes were drawn to several enormous barrage balloons inching their way on steel cables towards the clouds.

The train slowed as it passed Castle Hill. Bill got up and wove his way through impatient passengers towards the guard's van. He took his bike and carried it up the steps from the platform, wheeled it over the bridge and out of the station building. The air smelled of rain and coal smoke. The cobbles up towards Meeting House Lane were slippery and wet. He passed through the gates and mounted his bike, turned left towards the castle and city. He was surprised to see two roads to his right. The first was a short dead end. There were no boarding houses. She mustn't have counted that one. The next road was long and straight, lined with big houses on the right. He wished he'd brought some flowers, freewheeled slowly down the slope, surveying each house as he passed. There seemed to be so many of them, all packed tightly together in terraces. There could be three hundred people living on this street.

At the end of the first row was an untidy looking house with an overgrown privet hedge. In the window was a piece of brown card with the words ROOM TO LET scrawled across it in uneven letters. He leaned his bike against the low wall and steadied it to stop it toppling into the hedge. He climbed the steps and turned the knob to ring the bell. The paint on the door was chipped and peeling. There was no reply so he rang again and heard curses coming along the passageway from the back of the house. An old man with dirty hair and teeth missing opened the door. The house stank of damp and filth.

"What do want?" his voice was snappy and aggressive.

"I'm looking for Phyllis Laycock. She lives in a boarding house along here."

The old man jabbed his thumb towards the sign.

"You want a room?" His teeth were covered in something that must've been food and his breath reeked of stale alcohol.

"I'm looking for Phyll…'

"If you want a room, come in. If you don't, bugger off." The man wasn't deaf. He'd heard the bell and it wasn't very loud. He was closing the door. Bill stepped forwards. The old bloke looked up at him. "Well? Do you want a room?"

Bill hated bad manners and felt little respect for someone as unhelpful as this. He decided to play him at his own game.

"I might if I find Phyllis."

"Try two doors down."

As Bill stepped away from the door, the old man bawled after him, "It'll be full up an' a lot dearer than this place."

Bill hoped it was.

When he reached the next boarding house, the front door was ajar. The place looked better than the last and didn't smell. He knocked on the stained glass in the door and heard the shuffle of slippers. A woman of about forty or fifty pulled back the door and looked him straight in the eyes, smiling. She was wearing a satin bathrobe and seemed to be half way through putting on her makeup. Her hair was in curlers and she had a tube of lipstick in her hand. A gust of wind blew open her robe revealing the top of her thigh. She made a show of closing it, slowly.

Bill looked over her shoulder.

"I'm looking for Phyllis Laycock."

"Please yourself." Her smile receded and she stepped aside to let him in, nodding towards the stairs. She turned her back on him and swaggered back along the corridor, calling back to him and waving a hand without turning her head. "Keep going. Top floor."

It was dark up the stairs. The walls were painted brown. There must've been three or even four storeys. He rounded the last landing and was about to climb the last flight. A soldier was sitting against the window ledge smoking a cigarette and gazing out of the window. As Bill drew level with him, he stuck his boot hard against the banister rail, blocking Bill's way with his leg.

"Where d'you think you're goin?"

"I've come to see Phyllis."

The soldier stood up and Bill tried to step past him but he put his arm across in front of Bill's face, glanced back up the stairs.

"Hear that fellas? He's come to see Phyllis."

Bill heard a comment from the dark top landing but couldn't make it out. There were several low laughs and he saw the red glow of someone inhaling on a cigarette. Three faces appeared in the circle of light then faded into the blackness as the smoker removed his cigarette. The one on the stairs was standing right in front of Bill and stabbed him in the chest with the finger of a tattooed hand.

"Well, wait your turn like everybody else." He pointed back down the stairs.

Bill felt his face begin to redden. Something was churning in his stomach.

At that moment, the door opened at the top of the landing, flooding it with light. Another squaddie half-tumbled out onto his waiting mates, hitching up his braces and carrying his shirt and boots. He turned back towards the bedroom.

"Busy night, Phy. They're still coming."

There was a laugh from behind the door. Last week he'd found that laugh endearing. Now it disgusted him. He turned back down the stairs. As he rounded the landing, he saw the soldier sitting back in the window, lighting another cigarette and staring out across the rooftops.

By the time he reached the bottom of the stairs he was running. He grabbed his bike and jumped on, cycling furiously up the slope to the end of the street. He turned away from the station and headed down through the town. He didn't want to see or speak to anyone. The streets were getting busy; lots of army uniforms, townspeople doing what townspeople did. Phyllis had turned into one of them.

He felt stupid, small, like a child that's been cheated by someone older. He didn't like towns anyway. He rode across the bridge and out through Skerton, had to dodge a scrap man's dog as it ran out from under his cart. He was sweating in his suit as he rolled over the canal-bridge and looked straight ahead past the army camp. The sky was hidden behind dark clouds and light was fading as he rode over the tops from Halton. Somewhere to the west, the sun was setting.

It was almost black through the woods past the Hall. He turned into the farmyard and felt rain on his back and head. He left his bike in the barn and trudged to the back door. Agnes was getting ready for bed. She called into the darkened passage.

"You're back early. How did it go?" She saw his face in the light from the kitchen. Her voice dropped. "Oh."

Bill threw has cap on the stairs.

"She's a bloody tart."

Agnes knew better than to comment before she'd heard the story.

"You an' your fancy friends. She had 'em queuing on the bloody stairs, an' her in her room, tekkin' 'em one at a time. Half the bloody army."

Agnes stood, said nothing. She was wondering whether to question his account, find out if there was some kind of misunderstanding, but his face told her all she needed to know. The Laycock girl had always been spoilt. She'd thought that when she first met her over ten years ago, a precocious little madam, stamping her foot when she didn't get her own way. Demanding sweets as her mother was serving tea and, to Agnes's surprise, being allowed to have them. The Laycocks had been the only ones in the village who'd really accepted Agnes when she arrived. They'd been good friends to her, but she'd never approved of their ways of dealing with the children, giving them everything they wanted and letting them run riot. Now she was being proved right.

Bill was still raging. He wanted someone to blame, to strike out at.

"You never liked Lucy. You drove her away with your demands and always pullin' her down. Now she's gone, an' you're tryin' to fix me up with a slut who thinks she's better than the rest of us."

"Sit down." Her voice was conciliatory, calm. She was making a cup of tea, handed it to him and sat at the table facing him. "I didn't treat Lucy as I should have done." She was struggling for words. "I know I wasn't fair to her, and I'm finding it hard to deal with."

Bill sat looking at her. He was boiling inside.

"If I'm supposed to feel sorry for you, you can forget it."

"I'm not looking for sympathy, not even forgiveness. I didn't want Lucy to leave. We'd been getting on a lot better, especially since your Dad died."

"Then why did she leave? I didn't do anything."

"I know you didn't. Don't you think that might be the problem?"

"What d'you mean? What did she tell you?" He was shouting again.

"She didn't tell me anything. All I know is that you two had hardly spoken since the funeral, and she seemed to be getting more and more miserable. It was as much of a shock to me when she left as it was to you."

The funeral. He felt himself blushing. "How do you know what it's like for me?"

She shook her head. "I don't. But if you really care about her, why don't you tell her, let her know how you really feel? It can't do any harm."

Bill remained silent. For the last two months he'd been thinking about how Lucy had let him down, how she'd left him without saying goodbye, and how much harder it had been without her help on the farm. It hadn't occurred to him until now that he wanted her back.

Agnes was getting up. She went over to the dresser and searched through one of the drawers. She handed him a letter. It wasn't Lucy's hand writing but the address was in Barrow.

"This is the only address I have. It's from a friend of hers. She wrote asking if Lucy could come and work here."

He was reading it. She handed him a pencil and he wrote the name and address on the envelope, handed back the letter. Agnes took it.

"You could go tomorrow on the train. I'll come to the station with you when you take the milk. I'll bring the cart back and you can be home in time for milking." She wondered whether to tell him about the baby, decided it might stop him going, and kept quiet.

15

*This is certain from all experience, that no vegetable can
live long without leaves, but will very soon die, if the
leaves are pulled off as fast as they appear.*

Jethro Tull. The Horse Hoeing Husbandry (1733)

It was still raining on Saturday morning. The cows came in wet
and dripping. By breakfast time, Bill's work jacket was soaked
down one side. Water from the cows had dripped from his cap
and trickled down the inside of his shirt collar. Mary laughed
at him as she crossed the yard with a bucket of grain.

"You look like someone's tipped half a bucket of water over
you."

He smiled back at her, finished loading the churns, and
went to wash and change his clothes. Agnes was ready. She
handed him some sandwiches and went with him to the cart.
They rode through the village in silence and she climbed down
as he unloaded the churns. He was about to head for the bridge
when she grabbed his shoulder.

"Good luck. It'll turn out all right."

He nodded, tried to smile and mumbled a thank-you. The
train was due any minute so he hurried to the other platform.
When it arrived he found himself a seat and stared out at the
grey skies.

"Tickets please." It was a woman's voice.

He handed her the ticket and went back to watching the
fields go by. He checked his pocket for the envelope with the
address written on the back, realised he'd checked it three
times already.

What was he going to say to Lucy? He was trying to go
over the conversation in his head but found that last night's
experience had taken something away from him. He couldn't
guess what her reaction would be. Had she found someone

else? With each question, he found himself knotting up inside.

As the train slowed at Carnforth, he got ready to leave and wait for the connection. His throat was dry already. He stepped onto the platform and wondered if he had time to get a cup of tea. Across the track, the refreshment room was crowded. Through the haze of cigarette smoke the tables were full. The clock hanging from the platform roof said eight minutes to ten. Only eight minutes. There wasn't time to risk being on the wrong platform when his next train arrived. He sat on a bench and waited. There were signs on the walls telling people to keep mum and warning about spies.

Water was still dripping from the eaves and gutters. There must've been a heavy shower just before he'd arrived. He thought about train journeys he'd taken in the past, a school trip and a day out to Morecambe with his parents when he was six. That had been the first time. He remembered holding his mother's hand, and the excitement of going to the seaside. He wished he could have some of that excitement now. He wanted to see Lucy, to get her to come back with him, but all he felt was pessimism, worry about how the meeting would go. He had to find her first.

The train from Lancaster was more crowded than he'd expected. There seemed to be khaki uniforms everywhere. Bill hoped he wouldn't see anyone from last night. The thought of being recognised by one of Phyllis's acquaintances pushed him down into his seat and he sat looking out of the window with his back to the door. Feelings of shame swept through him, only to be replaced by guilt for being away from the farm when there was work to be done. He'd left Dennis mowing thistles for the day and began to wonder whether he'd think to do anything with the hay if the sun came out and dried it. He consoled himself with the thought that it wouldn't be dry until tomorrow.

As the train rumbled on, he realised he'd better start

counting stations. He hadn't checked how many there were, so it seemed a bit pointless, but he made a guess at the names each time they stopped. After Arnside, the tracks crossed the estuary. The flat land to his right was flooded. Some fields had rows of hay in them, rows of hay with water in between. Flocks of wading birds were standing on the sodden fodder or digging their beaks in the peaty soil. His father had told him what good land it was at Levens and round the Kent estuary. Bill wasn't so sure. The hay at home was wet but it wasn't standing in water.

The carriage was warm and he felt his eyes closing. He shook his head and sat up straight. It wasn't long before he was dozing again.

He awoke with a start, glancing round. There was a woman with a baby sitting opposite. How long had he been asleep? She hadn't been there before.

"Where are we?"

"Just coming into Ulverston." She picked up her bag with her free hand and disappeared into the corridor. Bill got up to stretch his legs, sat back down and opened the window. If he was right, there were only two more stops before Barrow. He wiped his eyes and sat with the wind blowing past his face. Something blew into his eye and he reached for his handkerchief. He closed the window and tried to get the speck from his eye. It stung like hell. At least he wouldn't fall asleep again.

Barrow in Furness was easier to recognise than he'd been thinking. The docks and the shipyards were unmistakable. When the train pulled in he climbed out and pushed through the crowds towards the exit. The town and docks were ahead of him. The address was in his pocket. It couldn't be that difficult to find. He knew it was near the docks so he carried on in that direction glancing up at street signs. At least they were still there.

He crossed a main road and began walking through the back streets. The air smelled of coal smoke, and even though it was Sunday there was the sound of machinery in the distance. Gulls were circling above the rooftops or cackling and screeching from chimney pots. Some boys were playing football in a back alley, so he shouted to them and asked if they knew where Michaelson Street was.

They came over in a group and stared him in the face.

"Who wants to know?"

They weren't like farm kids. Their eyes were filled with suspicion and contempt. They stood in a line, the tallest one bouncing the ball.

"I do."

"And who might you be?"

One of them cupped his hand to the next one's ear and spoke loud enough for Bill to hear him. "He could be a spy."

"I'm looking for a Ruth Mattieson. She lives on Michaelson Street."

They shrugged and looked at each other. They weren't going to help him even if they could. Bill turned and walked away. He'd gone a few steps when the football hit the wall a few feet behind his head. He glared back at the largest of the gang who'd caught the ball and was glaring back. He rounded the corner and left them out of sight. He began to feel threatened. If the kids in Barrow were like that, what were the adults like? He noticed an old woman watching him from a doorway. When she saw him looking towards her she went inside and closed the door.

He'd been wandering the streets for over half an hour and didn't seem to be any nearer finding the address on the envelope. He looked up at a street sign – Dalton Road – and began checking all the streets leading in the direction of the docks. They all had men's names: Thomas Street, Stephen Street, George Street. Michael must be somewhere near, but after trailing the length of them and doubling back, he still hadn't found Michaelson Street. He looked at his watch. Another hour had gone by. He needed to hurry up.

There was a newsagent's across the road. He went across and stepped in. The bell jingled above his head as he opened the door. The shopkeeper, a middle aged man with a nicotine stain in his moustache and into his hair, was arguing with a woman. He was telling her that he hadn't any shoe polish and the woman was wagging her finger at him. Her nose was sticking out from under her head scarf as if she was going to peck him with it. As Bill approached the counter she went silent and headed for the door, pausing to listen to what Bill asked for. The man behind the counter was reaching in his top pocket and brought out a packet of Woodbines.

"What can I do for you?"

Bill thought about asking directions.

"Have you any street maps?"

"Lost are you?"

"I've come to see someone. I've got the address but I can't find the road."

The man disappeared to the back of the shop, lighting his cigarette as he went. He returned wiping dust from a folded sheet of paper.

"I've got one here. It's one and threppence."

Bill handed him the money and the bell jingled behind him. He looked round and saw that the woman had gone.

Outside, the clouds were moving quickly, and as Bill studied the map the sun dazzled him as it reflected off the paper. He started in one corner, going street by street up and across the page. Stephen Street was there and Thomas Street. His finger circled the area, widening each time he checked off the names. His mood was lifting and he felt a burst of optimism as his finger landed on Michaelson Street. It went across a bridge to Barrow Island. No wonder he couldn't find it. He was on the wrong side of the dock.

He looked up to get his bearings. The snipe-nosed woman from the shop was standing across the street with a policeman and pointing in his direction. The policeman was crossing the street towards him.

"Excuse me, sir. Did you just buy that map?"

"Yes. I bought it in that shop. I know where I'm going now."

"Really?" His tone was flat, questioning. "Will you accompany me back into the shop, please?"

"Er, yes." He looked round, puzzled. The woman, her deed done, was hurrying round the corner as if she'd something really important to do. Bill folded the map, wondering what he'd done wrong. The policeman was big and broad. He was standing very close, almost pushing him back through the door.

The shopkeeper had been watching. He stood behind the till, his eyes flicking from side to side. The officer looked sternly at him.

"Did you just sell this young man a street map?"

The shopkeeper's cigarette was wavering on his lip. He stared Bill in the face.

"I've never seen him before." His face was still, trying to look innocent.

Bill opened his mouth to protest but was interrupted by the policeman who was studying the man by the till.

"Do you realise it's a criminal offence to sell a street map?"

"Oh, yes. I burned all mine last October. You can check round the back if you like. You won't find a single map in my shop, neither out front or in the storeroom."

Bill found his voice.

"He just sold it to me for one and .threppence. I came in to ask directions."

The man shook his head. His blank expression was one of a practised liar. The officer turned to Bill.

"Can I see your identity papers please?"

Bill felt something drop inside him, like a stone falling through his stomach. He'd been away from the farm and the village so little since his father died that he'd left them in a drawer at home.

"No identity papers? You'd better come to the station with me."

Bill wheeled round, looking for the woman who'd been in the shop.

"Where do you think you're going?" The policeman slammed him against the doorpost and twisted his arm up his back. Bill felt something hard click around his wrist. He heard another click and he was handcuffed to the policeman. His mind was racing as he was pushed out of the door.

"There was a woman here, the one who was talking to you. She saw me b... ."

"Shut it, laddie." The officer was reaching for his truncheon with his other hand.

Bill fell silent and he hung his head in shame as he was marched through the streets towards the police station. They passed the boys with the football and he heard one of them rounding on the others.

"See. I told you he was a spy."

The station was four streets away. People were stopping and pointing. A man with a handcart leered at him as he passed. The handcuff was tight and he felt his fingers going numb. He reached with his left hand to try and stop the pain around his wrist.

"You won't get that thing off. The key's at the station."

When they reached the police station Bill was pushed inside. A constable behind the desk looked up and the officer handcuffed to Bill began telling him his version of events. Bill waited for him to finish speaking, listening to all his alleged offences. The officer took the map and placed it on the counter.

"He claims he bought it from a newsagent, but the bloke in the shop says he'd never seen him before."

"I did buy it from him. He brought it from the back of the shop."

"Quiet, sonny. You speak when you're spoken to."

"My name's Bill Branthwaite. I live at Friar's Holme Farm at Sandholme."

"Quiet." The officer cuffed him with his free hand.

"Wait." The constable behind the desk was writing. "Can anyone verify that?"

"Sergeant Jackson at Hornby police station knows me."

"Hornby? Where's that?"

"In Lancashire, north of Lancaster." At last someone was listening to him.

The constable went over to the phone and began talking to the operator.

"She's putting me through." He waited with the phone to his ear. "There's no reply." He put down the receiver.

Bill remembered it was Saturday afternoon. The sergeant was probably down the garden waiting for his pigeons to come home.

"I'll try him later. You'd better put him in a cell." The constable came round from behind the counter with some keys and Bill felt himself drowning in failure and shame as he was marched down a corridor. It was a relief to be free of the handcuff, but as the door slammed shut he began to wonder how long he would be held prisoner. He sat on the bench resting his elbows on his knees. It must be after one o'clock. A drunk had woken in the next cell and was hammering on the door to be let out. Footsteps echoed down the corridor with the promise of jangling keys. The sounds passed only to return accompanied by another set of shuffling steps. The drunk was muttering something as he passed the cell.

Bill paced backwards and forwards, frustration mounting

and no way to relieve it. He thought how little time he'd had away from the farm since last summer. The hours since he'd boarded the train seemed all the more valuable, and now they were draining away. He began to wonder if the officer at the desk had forgotten about him, so when he heard someone in the corridor he knocked on the door. His knuckles seemed to make no sound at all so he banged the side of his fist against it. A flap opened and the desk officer looked in at him.

"What do you want?"

"Have you talked to Sergeant Jackson yet?"

"He wasn't in. This isn't a hotel y' know."

"What time is it?"

The flap closed and footsteps faded along the corridor. Bill laid on the bench and waited.

He awoke with a start, wondered where he was. The day's events came back to him in a series of blurred flashbacks. The angle of the sun through the window had moved. He must have been asleep for several hours. Someone was outside the cell. The door opened and the policeman who'd arrested him stood in the doorway.

"You're free to go."

He picked up his jacket and stood up. The officer sneered at him as he stepped into the corridor. "If I were you, I'd get on the next train and don't come back. Your Sergeant Jackson's let you off the hook this time, but I don't want to see your face again."

He'd been half expecting an apology. He saw that he wasn't going to get one. The desk officer had gone home, so he thought it best to get out of the police station as quickly as possible. He hurried down the steps and headed for the station. It was half past four.

16

The profit or loss arising from land, is not to be computed only from the value of the crop it produces; but from its value after all expenses of seed, tillage etc. are deducted.

Jethro Tull. The Horse Hoeing Husbandry (1733)

Bill closed the barn door. The last of the hay was inside, black with mould, and dusty. He'd wanted good hay for the heifers. Until last week he'd expected to have it. His father would have made some comment about the barn full of fodder by the house, or consoled himself by looking at the hay left over from last year. Bill was different. His only thought was that he'd failed. He would push himself harder to get it right next time, the thought of the failure with the last field eating into him like maggots in the belly of a sick ewe.

The summer of 1940 would be embedded in his mind as a time of failure and loss. As the years passed he would remember his journeys to Lancaster and Barrow with the bitter taste of bad decisions. Every detail of the humiliation would be stored, to reappear in a flashback at moments of regret. The faces of the soldiers on the stairs, the stale smell in the boarding house, even the pattern of flaking paint in a corner of the cell in Barrow stuck in his memory. If he'd been asked, he could have quoted the dates.

He always remembered coming back to the house on Monday evening after working the ruined hay, the reports on the radio of a huge battle in the skies over London. Whilst the south of England cowered from falling planes, the RAF had gained the advantage over the Luftwaffe.

Bill remembered that the battle he'd been fighting was already lost. It had taken two days to dry the crop, and by the time it was carted inside it had shrunk to barely above half of what it should have been. He could recall any of the events during the first ten days of July, but without talking about them to anyone they became jumbled. The order in which things happened shifted in Bill's memory, and since it was never questioned he began to blame himself for the spoiled field of hay. He had gone to see Phyllis in Lancaster, he'd taken the Saturday off to find Lucy and the weather had broken. As he got older he would never forgive himself for leaving the farm and letting the hay spoil. It never once entered his mind that the hay was spoiled before he boarded the train.

He focussed on his immediate problems. The country was at war. Agnes was leaving and he needed to secure a tenancy. He'd hardly enough time in the day and he hadn't enough money to start farming on his own. Sir Charles's words came back to him. "I'd be happier if you were married."

Bill was losing patience. He couldn't keep everyone happy. He threw the pitchfork back in the cart and rode back to the farm. He would see his landlord tonight before parade and explain his position. He wasn't married, and wasn't likely to be married. If Sir Charles didn't like that he could lump it.

When he arrived at the hall, the housekeeper let him in and showed him through to the study. He stood by the desk in his uniform, waiting for Sir Charles to appear, like a soldier awaiting the arrival of his superior officer. The door opened behind him and Sir Charles entered, carrying some papers.

"Bill. Nice to see you." He shook Bill's hand and pointed to a chair.

Bill sat down with his beret in his hands, and Sir Charles took a seat behind the desk. "What can I do for you? I take it this isn't a social call."

He stammered over his answer. "I ... er ... Agnes wants to leave."

Sir Charles nodded slowly. "Word seems to have got around. What do you want to do?"

"I'd like to take on the tenancy."

"It seems you're not the only one." The landlord looked

down at his desk, turned a pen over in his hand and gave him an upward glance. "I'd prefer to let the farm to you. I've had someone here today trying to get in first."

Bill clenched his teeth. "Joe Moss?"

"No. Moss found that taking on another farm would take his rent over three hundred pounds. He'd have to start keeping accounts, and I don't think he wants anyone meddling in his business at the moment."

Bill remembered the trucks using the old lane. Moss's business was being talked about too.

Sir Charles was watching him closely. "I may as well tell you. I've had an offer from Brian Waterford."

"Brian Waterford?" He didn't want to believe it. He felt the blood rushing through his veins. His fingers tightened around his beret.

"I'm afraid so." He put down the pen, looked straight at Bill. "He needn't think he'll be getting a tenancy from me. As I said, I'd prefer to let the place to you. The question is – do you have the means to take it on?"

Bill felt his cheeks burning. He shook his head. "I've got some but not enough."

Sir Charles thought for a moment. "I may be able to help you there." He spotted Bill's gaze towards the papers on the desk, drew his hand over them and slid them in a drawer. "It just happens that I've got surplus cash at the moment." He looked guiltily away, stood up and glanced out of the window.

Bill followed him with his eyes. There was something that didn't meet the eye. He seemed nervous. Perhaps Joe Moss wasn't the only one in the valley who was heavily involved in the black market.

Sir Charles sat down again. "Have you fixed a sale date?"

"I can't risk a sale. I can't." The word made him nervous. "All the hay goes in a lottery. Moss is putting lots o' tickets in, dozens sometimes, in all his family's names; every sale that comes up. I could end up wi' no feed for winter. I need to pay Agnes out an carry on as I am, or it won't work."

Sir Charles wiped his hand over his chin. "Very wise." He stood up. "I could lend you the money. Do your sums and let me know what you need, then we'll see if we can make it work." He paused. "I'd be grateful if you'd just keep this arrangement between the two of us."

Bill nodded, shook Sir Charles's hand and left.

✛

During drill he'd been distracted. He was slow, something which he'd never been reprimanded for since he first joined the volunteers. His mind kept wandering to the face of Brian Waterford. Bill and Tom had been mates, as close as you could get ever since they'd dammed streams and chased rabbits together in the stubble fields. Brian was coveting his farm. How could someone he'd regarded as a friend be so underhand?

Norman Watterson pulled him aside.

"Look. Whatever's botherin' you, lad, channel it. Use it to yer advantage. Bloody krauts won't wait till yer on form before they invade." He marched them to a clearing in the woods where dummies had been set up for bayonet practice. Hessian sacks stuffed with straw were hanging from a pole stretched across two posts. At Norman's command, they charged, three at a time, and thrust their bayonets into the soft bellies of the sacks. Bill imagined himself, not spilling the guts of Hitler or his square-headed followers, but driving the blade through the overalls of a fifty-year-old Lancashire man who'd had the misfortune to be turned off his farm. He saw his face twist and fall still, terror turning to agony and despair, dying with a last expression of guilt and regret. Brian Waterford was his enemy and would be dealt with in the same way as anyone else who tried to take his farm from him. Later, he would see that same face in a target on the rifle range and hurl dummy grenades at it over walls and banks in the grounds of Friar's Hall. Once, he'd felt guilty about picturing Moss as the enemy, but now the emotions were simpler: hate, rage and determination.

When he was away from the training ground and rifle range, Bill found that the anger wasn't so intense. The red heat that washed over him seemed to cool when he was back on the farm. The steely resolution that he'd felt, hardened into his sinews like wire. He would keep the farm, whatever it took. As he sat at the kitchen table working out the value of cows, sheep and machinery, he began to develop that cold business mind that would one day see him buy the farm off a landlord ruined by gambling debts. There would be no sentimentality in the running of his farm. If he couldn't trust his best friend's father he doubted whether he could trust anyone.

Sir Charles wasn't doing him a favour. He was just using him to hide money that he couldn't let the tax man see. There was no use in asking where it came from. That was no concern of his. It was well known that Friar's Hall had been bought with money from textiles and hardware. Perhaps Sir Charles was selling faulty goods to the army or putting in claims to the government for shipments of supplies that didn't exist. Bill knew he wasn't in a position to do anything about it. *Beggars can't be choosers*, his father used to say. He wasn't begging, but he knew that at this moment he didn't have a lot of choice. He'd use his landlord's money for as long as he had to and no longer. He'd learn the man's ways with money and one day he'd be free of the whole damned lot of them.

He ran the blunt end of the pencil down the line of figures. The total money needed was almost three thousand pounds. He'd have to borrow over two thousand from Sir Charles. If he was ever going to pay it back he'd need to keep a close eye on finances. He took another sheet of writing paper and began to calculate his income for the rest of the year.

17

The house had gone to bring again
To the midnight sky a sunset glow.
Now the chimney was all of the house that stood,
Like a pistil after the petals go.

Robert Frost. The Need of Being Versed in
Country Things (1949)

Agnes left at the beginning of September. Bill had envisioned the day since she first mentioned it at the start of summer, suitcases packed in the front room, Agnes dressed in her best clothes, and Mary tearful and wanting to stay. He'd imagined his stepmother cold and determined, thinking about nothing but herself and the journey ahead. The spaces on the mantle piece where Agnes's clock and candlesticks had been, and probably even one two of his mother's things missing as well. There would be a train to catch and a connection to Liverpool with a ship to America. He'd played the scene over in his mind so many times that he thought he knew exactly how it would go. He was poised for an argument.

Like so many of the events that summer, Agnes's departure bore no resemblance to the image in Bill's head. The harvest was almost finished, and the searing heat of August had given way to still autumn days. Uncle Harry had come to help finish carting the oats to the stackyard. He'd brought both his sons, his cowman, a tractor and an extra binder. Bill and Dennis were sitting at the table with the other four men and Agnes was serving out mutton stew. Mary was finishing mashing the potatoes and listening to her cousins' jokes when a car drove into the back yard. Bill stretched his neck to peer out of the kitchen window. He didn't recognise the car. A policeman and an official in plain clothes were marching towards the back door.

Agnes scooped the last of the stew onto Bill's plate. "I'll

get it." She hurried along the passage and Bill strained to hear what was being said. His cousins were still talking. Agnes gave a high pitched wail and the kitchen fell silent. Bill heard a man's voice.

"We'll give you five minutes to pack your bags."

He jumped to his feet. Agnes was wandering back along the passage, dazed.

"What's going on?"

She muttered something he couldn't hear and stumbled towards the stairs. Uncle Harry was pushing past him and charging towards the back door.

"What the bloody hell's goin' on?"

There was a clatter from the kitchen and Mary raced upstairs. Bill heard the man's voice again.

" … internment of aliens."

"You can't do that." Uncle Harry was shouting. "This family's been through enough this year."

Bill steadied himself against the passage wall. He could hear Mary crying upstairs. He glanced back to the kitchen. His cousins and Tommy the cowman were staring at him. Dennis was hunched and hiding his face. He looked back towards the shadows from the back door and felt stuck as if he was standing in a bog. He felt distant, watching a scene that was being played without his participation, as if the whole world was turning more slowly and he was powerless to change things like a child trapped in a dream, unable to either move or wake up.

On the floor at the end of the passage a battle was raging. Three silhouettes from outside clashed on the stone flags. Uncle Harry, his arms grappling with a shorter man, and a policeman to one side, moving towards them. Uncle Harry's voice was loud.

Bill broke from his trance, stormed round the corner and between the three men. There was space between them. He grabbed the small man by the lapels, slammed him against the house wall, the rat face staring back at him in panic. Reddening.

"Get off my farm and leave my family alone."

There were hands on his shoulders: Uncle Harry.

"Nay, lad. This isn't the way. Leave 'im. Let 'im go."

The policeman, pushing between them, grabbing Bill's arm.

"Calm down, or I'll arrest you for obstructing the police."

The small man was straightening his jacket, pushing his glasses up his nose. He jabbered a speech about his authority and penalties for not cooperating. Bill's strength was seeping away.

Agnes appeared in the doorway wearing a coat and carrying a suitcase.

"I'm ready. Shall we go?" Her words were wilted, resigned; her face drained. Bill pictured her standing over his father's body. The expression, the voice were the same. She climbed in the back of the car and the policeman released Bill and followed her. The small man turned back at Bill, stared: a polecat ready to spit. He took his place in the passenger seat and the driver reversed out of the yard. Mary was sobbing deeply into Bill's chest. Uncle Harry was trying to look hopeful.

"I'll ring Mr Barrington. We'll soon 'ave this sorted out."

Bill could see the solicitor already, surrounded by dusty law books, feigning knowledge and exuding incompetence. He could quote land law until your eyes glazed, could probably write a title deed from memory, but internment and emergency regulations were as alien to him as the workings of a Spitfire were to Bill.

18

A man investing several thousand pounds is entitled to a home possessing comforts which he would expect were his money invested in another business.

Walter James Malden, Farm Buildings and
Economical Agricultural Appliances (1896)

When Jack Branthwaite had died at the end of January 1940, the household at Friar's Holme Farm seemed to develop a kind of dementia. Jack's memories of the farm's history were lost. His knowledge of the course of drains and how to repair clogs on the broken last in the shed was replaced by Bill's fumblings and mistakes. His father could remember when each field had last been spread with lime, who built the dairy, and what type of wood was best suited to each purpose around the farm, from cart bottoms to fence posts and stall partitions in the out-barn. Bill found himself asking advice from whomever was available, the joiner who repaired the cart with inferior wood, his landlord's agent who produced a grossly inaccurate map of land drains, and Agnes whose knowledge stretched back no further than his. It was as if the farm and family had lost a vital piece of its collective brain. Any loss to the family was a loss to the farm and any loss to the farm left the family suffering greater hardship. The two were so inextricably linked that the edges were blurred like an old photograph, and Bill never really knew where the boundaries were, if they existed at all.

Since Lucy had left, he felt as if the household had died. The cheerfulness she brought had boarded the train with her and disappeared, leaving an atmosphere dominated by Agnes's austerity. The lighter moments had ended in disaster and humiliation. The time Agnes had encouraged him to pursue Phyllis, and her suggestion that he went to find Lucy, had both gone so badly wrong that Bill pushed them to the back of his mind. They were foolish errors of judgement; mistakes to be buried and forgotten, like the four dead Clydesdales entombed in lime in the corner of the eleven-acre meadow. (Norman Watterson had told him the story about the previous tenant's son who'd left a gate open allowing them to stray into the churchyard and browse amongst the yew trees.)

Happy memories at Friar's Holme Farm were disintegrating like the carcasses of poisoned horses, only to be remembered by neighbours who weren't overwhelmed by their loss.

When Agnes was taken away a silence had descended upon the household. Auntie Doris had insisted that Mary went to live with her and Uncle Harry. Uncle Harry had explained the situation to Bill.

"A young lass growin' up needs a woman t' guide 'er. There's things she'll need to know that you won't be able to tell 'er."

Mary had left in the back of Uncle Harry's car with her head bowed. She'd barely been able to wave to Bill and Dennis. She would have to go to a different school and make new friends.

The first few days after Agnes and Mary's departure, Bill found himself guiltily aware of the advantages of living alone. He could work late, and come in for meals when he felt like it, without having to suffer a reprimand from his stepmother. He could leave his wet coat to dry in front of the fire without Mary complaining about the smell. He was never asked to move any furniture or help carry out a carpet for Agnes, and also the grocery bill was less. He could get used to not having Agnes's cooked meals. He'd survived on field rations when training with the Home Guard, and his senses were so tuned into his running of the farm and guard duties at the Hall that the finer flavours of Agnes's cooking had gone unnoticed for months.

After almost a month of his solitary life he began to see the need for some help around the house. The farm was running as well as could be expected, and the continued high price for food meant that there was spare cash. A jug of sour milk left in the pantry, a pile of dirty clothes on his bedroom floor and caked in soil on the doormat, were the first signs he noticed that he was beginning to live in squalor. He'd taken extra help on the farm. James Smith's youngest son Gerald had left school and if one of the older boys wasn't to be called up he'd have to find a job on another farm. Bill had talked it over with James after parade and Gerald had started work at Michaelmas. He was moody and did his work without comment, only ever responding with a grunt when he was spoken to.

When Bill appointed Mrs Coburn, the cobbler's widow, as a housekeeper he began to take pride in the smooth running of the house as well as the rest of the farm. His clothes were always clean, there was always a meal waiting for him, whatever time he came in, and the house was clean. He rarely saw the housekeeper. She finished work at twelve and often the only time he spoke to her was when he paid her wages each Friday. She went about her tasks like a woman tending a grave, in subdued silence, keeping everything neat, avoiding conversation and leaving unobtrusively as soon as the work was finished.

As the year drew to a close, the farm was making money, the house was well kept, and since the battle of Britain people were talking less about invasion. If the household had died when Lucy left, Agnes's departure had buried it, and Bill had replaced it with efficiency and routine.

He began to define his life in terms of success. Happiness was a good yield of barley from the field across the road, a high price for a newly-calved cow sold at Bentham auction, or a slump in the trade when he was buying ewes at the autumn sales. He counted pennies. The geese sold well at Christmas.

Joe Moss called in late one night when Bill and Dennis

were finishing dressing the last birds, offered him a meagre price for the three he had left unsold in the loosebox. Bill laughed and told the racketeer to go and rob someone else.

Moss began haggling, offered him a higher price.

"I've got customers waiting. Sir Charles's cousin wants three extra tomorrow."

Bill told him to see Charlie Taylor. His old breeders were still wandering around the sports field. When Moss had left he went out to the loosebox, caught and killed the three young geese. He worked all night, had them plucked and dressed by milking time, delivered them to the Hall before breakfast. He heard later that Moss had turned up at the Hall the next afternoon with three scabby old geese and asking for more than Bill had charged for the young ones. Sir Charles had sent him away, saying he'd buy them all from Bill Branthwaite in future.

The business became a game, to be played like cards, watching the other players' faces. He would learn who was hiding good fortune and who was about to go broke, who was desperate enough to sell at any price, and who had cash to spare.

Agnes's misfortune had been Bill's gain. There was no half share to pay out, no loan to service, and every penny made on the farm was Bill's, at least for now.

Sir Charles was spending money. The textile business was booming. An expanding army needed uniforms, and the looms in Blackburn were kept busy. When Bill went to see him at the Hall he made sure the agent was away. He sat back in a chair opposite his landlord, lit a cigarette.

"I need to expand."

The landlord leaned closer.

"I'm going to need a bigger granary, and a pole barn for the straw. I haven't got the money to build them myself, but I could afford a bit more on the rent." He watched the way the man moved, the tension in his jaw as he considered the options.

Sir Charles clapped his hands together, leaned back and spoke with a finality as though it was all his idea

"I could put them up for you. My estate staff could do it in spring." He paused for a second. "We might have difficulty getting the cladding."

Bill wasn't going to let the older man talk himself into changing his mind.

"Joe Moss seems to be able to lay his hands on anything. He has contacts for steel, feed, even women's clothes." He noticed a slight twitch in the other man's eye. Was it guilt, a reluctance to get deeper into illegal activity? Could it be a last remnant of Sir Charles's aristocratic scruples? The man had cash to invest. Perhaps he was concerned about mixing business that was visible with dealings that were hidden. Or was it that Bill had pushed too far, overstepped the mark by suggesting where his landlord spent his money? "If a man like Moss can get building materials there must be plenty available. WARAG committee are advising everyone to grow more and put up new buildings."

"Quite so." The landlord stretched. "I'll talk to the agent tomorrow. By the way, I was talking to my cousin yesterday. He said to compliment you on the goose he had for Christmas. He asked me if you could supply turkeys as well."

⁜

The agent called the next day to take measurements for the new barn. He rolled out a tape in the paddock and began taking notes.

"We'll put the barn here. It will save money on found-ations." He was wielding power, showing the tenants he was still in charge.

Bill pointed to the other end of the yard.

"I think Sir Charles would prefer it over there, out of sight from the Hall, and in a more convenient position for the thresher."

The agent continued with his calculations. "I'm sure Sir Charles will see the sense of having it here."

He returned in the afternoon to take measurements in the stack yard. Bill watched him just long enough to let him know who'd won and, as he left, pointed out that the opening needed to be towards the yard with the covered side facing the wind.

"I do know what I'm doing. I don't need some youth to tell me how to build a barn."

"Aye." He wasn't going to kick the man when he was down. There was no harm in letting him know that he could. "When do think you'll be able to start?"

"You don't need it till harvest. It'll be at least three months before you sow the corn."

"I was just thinkin'. When yer other tenants find out, they'll all be wantin' one. I wouldn't like t' think you were goin' t' be rushed off yer feet buildin' all summer."

The agent's eyes flicked from side to side. "You'll get it when we're ready. And don't go telling anybody about it. We've enough to do. There's a war on you know." He rolled up his tape and strode back to the Hall.

The game became a sport, to be played out all day and every day. Jobs on the farm were contests to be won, races against the seasons and the elements, to be completed skilfully and artfully with the style that would impress a crowd. Gates that had been tied with string were given new fasteners. It saved time. Cart wheels were kept lubricated to reduce wear and save effort for the horses. The squeak of the muck barrow was choked by monthly applications of grease, and Dennis commented on how much easier it was to push. He lost his hunched gait and set about his jobs with a new enthusiasm, changing his routine so that he finished each one at the right end of the yard to start the next.

When Uncle Harry called to see Bill one afternoon he stood in the dairy doorway surveying the yard.

"This place is a credit to yer. an' that Dennis … . I wish I could get my lads to work like 'im. He's never runnin' empty. If he's not pushin' that barrow he's carryin' summat."

"He's just finished diggin' a channel between the stream an' the hen house. We've got runnin' water fer the hens. We're thinkin' o' puttin' up four more cabins next time an' keepin' a lot more. I reckon if we can save time at everything we do we'll be able to keep more stock."

As Churchill inspired the nation, Bill inspired his staff. They worked together as a team. On the coldest, wettest days through February and March they finished the hedge laying and muck spreading with a sense of achievement. Chapped knuckles and aching backs became battle scars, trophies and medals to be worn with pride at completing the month's work before the neighbours.

James Smith had complained that Gerald was coming home with too many ideas about how they could improve the running of their own farm. Even Dennis began to nurture an air of superiority over the other farms in the valley. He would return from his mother's cottage saying that none of the fields towards Hutton Roof was as green as the ones at Friar's Holme Farm, and Walter Newman's sheep looked thin.

Whilst the three of them were working efficiently, Bill was also playing the game at the auction mart, at the village club, and when he took the milk to the station. The day after the agent had taken the measurements for the new barn he'd been helping Bert Taylor roll some churns onto the platform.

"Thanks, Bill. How's everythin' goin'?"

"Not bad. Landlord's buildin' us a new barn."

"He's what?"

"He's buildin' us a new barn. I told 'im I needed one, an' he's puttin' one up." Bill saw the flush in Bert's cheeks, the slow turn of his head that he remembered from school when someone else arrived with a new pencil box or better sandwiches. "We're getting' a new granary as well."

Bert didn't answer. He slammed the empty churns from the platform into the back of the buggy.

The next afternoon Sir Charles's agent stormed into the yard.

"Who the hell told the other tenants you were getting a new barn?"

Bill shrugged.

"I dunno. Maybe one o' the lads let something slip."

"They're all wantin' one now. Sir Charles is furious."

"Yer can't blame Dennis. He wouldn't realise, an' Gerald's dad isn't one o' your tenants."

"He's told us we have to start on yours right away so we've got a chance of finishing them in time for harvest. Five new barns. Wartime as well. Young Bert Taylor's a jealous little bugger. He's insisting on a new granary, just because you're having one."

"I'm really sorry Mr Finchley." Bill pointed towards the site for the barn. "We'll clear away that pile o' stones before milkin' so it's out o' yer way ready fer tomorrow." Then, as the agent skulked away muttering about all the jobs that needed doing around the Hall, "Send someone round when you want the poles draggin' down from top wood."

19

The re-erection of farm buildings is a most important point to be settled between landlord and tenant .... Until this is done on every farm in England the agriculturalists must be considered as in the rear of their rivals, the manufacturers.

G. H. Andrews. A Rudimentary Treatise on
Agricultural Engineering (1852)

Each season in the valley brought its own sounds, sights and smells. The rhythm of the mower and the smell of newly cut grass marked the height of summer, interspersed with the chatter of newly fledged swallows and the grate of angry partridges as their grassy hiding places were demolished for hay. Autumn brought the crackle of burning leaves and honks from migrating geese as they crossed the sky in a huge V, pointing their way towards warmer feeding grounds, the phenol-creosote smell of newly dipped sheep heading to and from the sales, and the clatter of bullocks' hooves as they scrambled into railway wagons.

Winter had its different moods. The rage of storms that rattled shed doors, whistled through gaps in window frames and blew bitter smoke down chimneys, rasping the lungs of sheltering cottagers and blackening the whitewashed walls of living rooms and kitchens. It could be still and calm, with the rancid vapours of muckheaps wafting across bare fields, the bleat of hungry ewes echoing against naked trees. At times it gave a hint of spring, a warm day, early snowdrops or the birth of an unexpected lamb out of season.

All these sense images became interwoven in the sinews of the inhabitants, marking the passage of time and shifting their dispositions like a changing dose of herbal tonic. Villagers who moved into towns often lamented that each month seemed the same. Their bodies' clocks had ceased to function in a climate of smog, grey walls and mechanical workings.

In the late winter of 1941 the air around Friar's Hall was filled with different sounds. The chop of the woodsman's axe became a familiar rhythm, like the ticking of a clock, each hollow note followed by a deep belly grunt as the ageing lumberman tried to recapture the power of his youth. He kept his axe sharp, sitting on a stump to hone the edge after each tree. He could no longer afford the wasted effort of swinging at a trunk with a dull blade. His patience was tested to breaking point. His well-worn routine of sawing out rails and posts for repairs on the estate, topping up the store of firewood and crafting gates and stiles for the footpaths, had been replaced by a factory schedule of churning out poles and beams for barns.

As each spruce crashed from its anchor, his assistant would yell, "Timber," in a long drawn out tone gleaned from a western movie at the picture house in Kirkby Lonsdale.

"Shut yer mouth y' noisy bugger. Where do y' think you are?"

The youth persisted. Baiting the old man was the best sport he had. It relieved the boredom of hacking branches from felled trees and peeling bark from trunks. On the third day the woodsman snapped. He grabbed the boy and flung him against a tree, gripped his neck with a callused hand, the boy turning to tears as the broken ends of dead branches stuck in the back of his head.

"I've had about enough of you. Yer stupid comments about mekkin' logs and flickin' wood chips at me when me back's turned. I've bin givin' you all the easy jobs so y' can learn." He held up the axe and the boy's face twisted, felt him slipping down the trunk as his knees buckled. "It's time you got what's comin' to yer." The kid was struggling to hold his piss, his arms in front of his face. "Have a bloody go." He thrust the axe into the boy's hands and let him slide to the floor. "This one 'ere."

The boy was fighting to get up, kept dropping the axe, a jelly trying to be solid. He staggered to the tree and took a swing, tried to prise the axe from the bark. He swung again, made another nick.

"No. No. Like this." The old woodsman dragged him aside, took the axe and swung twice, sending a large chunk from the trunk. "One up, one down, and take out a chip wi' every two strokes." He handed him back the axe and sat on a log to stoke his pipe, turned his head to one side as he studied the boy's action. Chips were beginning to come away. "Keep swingin'. It's no use rubbin' yer arms. They'll only get better wi' more work. Now tek a bit more out o' that side an' we'll finish it off wit' saw."

When the tree was felled the boy reached for the axe and set about the next one. The woodsman began peeling the lying trunk. The kid was stupid, but he could work when he wanted. Before the recession the woodsman had had two assistants. One of them had died at Dunkirk. The other was on his way to Africa. He'd have to make do with this one for now. After all, he wasn't the real cause of the trouble. The real culprit was Bill Branthwaite.

When he heard the clink of chains and the stomping of hooves the woodsman stood up, replaced the lid on his Billy can and left his half-eaten sandwich on the log where he'd been sitting. He peered down the bank, could see nothing but bare branches, so he bent almost double to peer under them and saw Bill Branthwaite climbing the fence and making his way towards them. He was in no mood for conversation, so when the farmer reached the cleared patch of woodland he pointed to a pile of poles.

"Them's yours. Twelve. Help yersel'. We 'aven't got time to shift 'em."

"All right?" There was no answer. Bill looked at the pile. The poles were about a foot in diameter and eighteen feet long.

If he swung the ends round he could slide them end first down the slope and let the horse drag them through the fence. The old bloke seemed to be in a bad mood, so he'd get them all to the bottom and stay out of his way.

He was about to move the last one when he noticed how slender it was.

"Hey. This one's too thin. It's only nine inch thick at the widest end."

"Yer'll 'ave to mek do wi' it. There aren't enough big uns t' go round."

"It won't last. It'll be rotten in five years. That one you've just cut'll do instead."

"Didn't you turn out t' be a clever little bastard. Yer father would've tekken it and said nowt."

Bill didn't reply.

"Yer father was a decent bloke. Allus did things proper way. Stooked 'is corn, muck 'eaps in good straight rows in all 'is meadows. It didn't tek long fer you t' tek lazy way out, spreadin' it right out o' back of t' cart."

"It saves time." Bill lifted the end of the newly cut pole and slid it down with the others. "I'll peel this 'un myself."

✣

The tin sheets arrived on a steam lorry the next day. It chugged to a halt, hissing out steam that sent the cat running for cover. The driver scratched his head and looked round the farmyard.

"Ist' boss around, laddie?"

"You're talkin' to 'im."

"I'm lookin' fer a place called Friar's Holme."

"You've found it."

"It's a bloody queer place t' build a factory. My boss sez these are a priority order fer a War Office contract. Seabrooke Mills."

"It's a storage building, away from air raids. Sir Charles

Seabrooke owns this land."

"They should've built it near a railway sidin'. It's a bloody silly idea if y' ask me."

"Nobody did." Bill began dragging the tin sheets from the lorry. The driver gave a grunt and helped to unload. The engineer climbed down from the cab and wiped coal dust from his eyes. He climbed on the back of the lorry and began sliding the sheets to the other two.

"Does this road lead to Over Keer?"

"About four miles straight on." Bill raised his eyebrows. The men were from East Lancashire. "You know the place?"

"That Moss bloke lives somewhere near here, doesn't he?"

"Next farm. How do y' know Moss?"

"He come o'er our way buyin' stuff last month. He's dealin' wi' some right rough sorts an' all." The engineer handed the driver a corrugated sheet and waited for him to carry it across to the pile, leaned closer to Bill. "I don't know what's goin' on 'ere," glancing down at the sheets, "but tek my advice lad. Don't get involved." He was looking Bill straight in the eyes. "Have nowt to do wi' it."

The driver was coming back.

"What're y' sayin'?"

"Oh, nowt much. Just givin' this fella a bit of advice." He handed Bill the last of the sheets. "Have y' got any eggs, lad?"

Bill leaned the sheet against the wall and went over to the house, brought back two paper bags with six eggs in each. He handed one to the driver who was waiting by the lorry, and reached up to the cab where the engineer was stoking the boiler.

"Here." He nodded, held up his hand when the man reached towards his pocket. "And thanks."

✦

When Bert Taylor rode up with the cart to collect the poles for his barn he was overflowing with pride. The new building was his idea, not his father's or some inevitable consequence of following the same traditions for generations. He'd been complaining for years that the barn by the house was too small. Hay and straw had been stacked over winter in the yard, spoiled by rain and blown in drifts from the pigsties to the back door into the kitchen. Charlie had agreed to the suggestion without an argument, without any alterations to Bert's plan and with an acceptance that Bert saw as recognition that he was a man now. He was fulfilling his ambition. He was going to be the boss.

The barn would be twice the length of the one at Friar's Holme Farm. It would almost twice as wide, and it would be higher, standing at the end of the yard as a testament to his vision and skill as a farmer. If Bill Branthwaite could manage a farm, he could do it better. He would milk more cows, keep more sheep and grow more grain. He already had a tractor and was driving a car.

When he arrived at the plantation he strode over to the clearing where the woodsman and his apprentice were splitting logs for the hall.

"Are they ready?"

"Aye. They're all stacked up over there." He pointed to the pile of newly peeled trunks, all cut to the same length and all the same thickness as the one Bill had rejected. Bert looked from the pile to the woodsman who was shaking his head. "I'm sorry I couldn't get you any thicker ones. Bill Branthwaite took all t' best."

Bert bit his teeth together. The heat was flushing through his veins. He said nothing. The woodsman dusted pine needles from his breeches. "I'll give you a hand to load 'em."

As Bert rode away with the poles the old man turned to the boy. "There's nowt wrong wi' showin a man what his neighbour's really like. You watch old Daniel and you'll learn how to get on. Now start cuttin' out some o' those thicker ones fer Walter Newman. He doesn't get on wi' Taylors. They don't speak an' Bert'll never see what his barn looks like."

✦

Friar's Holme Farm was busy. When the other tenants had asked for new buildings Sir Charles had conceded that his staff did not have the time to erect them. He would supply all the materials and the farmers would have to build them themselves. Norman Watterson had been drafted in to help. He passed on his joinery skills to Bill, Dennis and Gerald with the patience of an old master, working seven days a week and only missing a day when it rained or if there was a grave to dig in one of the surrounding villages.

When the first pole was upright in its hole and they were ready to fill it with concrete, Dennis produced a shoebox and placed it in the bottom. Norman watched him

"What're y doin? What's that?"

"A dead pigeon I found behind the barn. I thought it 'ud make you feel at home."

There were jokes about the size and depth of the holes.

"Hey, Norman, don't dig it as long as you usually do." And when it was finished. "You'll have to put coffin on its end in this un."

Gerald joined in. "These poles ud be a lot easier to lower into 'em if they had brass handles on 'em."

Norman took it all with good humour. "Hey, lads. I've dug a lot bigger trenches than owt y'll see in a churchyard." The boys were working and keen to learn. Only when he caught Gerald bowing his head over a 'grave' and muttering did he call a halt to the leg-pulling. "Hey. That's church business." His voice was stern. When he saw the guilty look on Gerald's face he winked, patted him on the shoulder and glanced skywards. "How's he gonna know when yer bein' serious? This war's not o'er yet."

Bill was standing by the end of the house when Bert Taylor rode past with the second load of poles. He put his hand up, waved.

"All right, Bert?"

Bert tilted his head slowly towards him, his mouth twisted into a sneer. He turned straight ahead and rode on.

Bill shrugged. Perhaps he was in bad humour. He would catch him on a better day.

As the frame went up, Norman taught them how to hoist up the roof trusses. Bill and Gerald worked on ladders. Dennis was kept on the ground. When one truss became jammed Bill edged his way onto a spar connecting two posts. Norman rushed up the ladder to help. They slotted it into place and Norman drove home the bolts.

Dennis was by the shippen wall searching through a box for some washers and nuts. A large car drove into the drive and parked beside the stable. Two men in suits got out and looked around the yard. Gerald grinned across at Norman.

"Some fancy fellers here."

"Shh." Norman was watching them, the way they lumbered over the cobbles, one of them blowing his nose with his finger. They rounded the corner, saw only Dennis.

"Where's Moss?"

"Dunno."

"Don't get clever with me." One of the men slammed Dennis against the wall, choking him with his forearm. "I won't ask you again. Where's Moss?" The other one was leaning in close.

Dennis was shaking his head, trying to mouth something.

Bill froze. Norman lifted the lump hammer and hurled it, caught the thug between the shoulder blades. He spun round. The yard was empty.

"Leave that lad alone."

The thug looked up and Norman slid down the ladder with the agility of a man half his age. The two men were coming towards him. He ducked behind the wall and reappeared with his rifle aimed at the first one, only six feet away. The man stopped.

"Don't think I wouldn't. I lost count at the Somme." There was murder in Norman's eyes. The thugs looked at each other. Norman was ready. "Don't even think aboot it. I'd git yer both. I've done it afore." They shrank back. The first one was holding his hands out in front of him, stepping back.

Bill was holding onto the top of the ladder. His knees were shaking. He looked down at the joiner. He was rigid, poised, shouting. "Moss doesn't live here, never has. You've got the wrong place, an yer dealin' wi' the wrong man. Now on yer way." He jerked his head towards the entrance to the yard and they sloped away, Norman following them round the corner still pointing the gun until the car had driven up the road.

Bill clambered down the ladder and went over to Dennis. Gerald was at his shoulder when Norman came back. Norman put down the rifle and came over to join them.

"Are you all right, Dennis?"

Dennis was rubbing his throat and looking at them from one to the other. "Have … have they gone?"

"Aye. An' they won't be comin' back. Ah don't reckon they were expectin' an old soldier like me."

Gerald was quizzing. "Did you really lose count at the Somme?"

"That's enough o' that. We're wastin' time." Norman turned away and began picking up the nuts and washers that Dennis had dropped.

The barn was finished at the end of February. The roof gleamed white and the tin sheets shone in the sun, Bill found himself walking round it whenever he had a spare moment, or sheltering under it at night when he'd been out to check the cows or was returning from guard duty at the hall. He would light a cigarette and stand beneath its huge covered span as he listened to the wind or watched the stars.

He was leaning against the barn wall watching the full moon and listening to the bombers droning towards Barrow in Furness when he glanced across to the house, all in darkness with the blackout curtains tightly closed. He noticed a lighter patch in the yard where the moon's reflection was cast off the side of the barn. Glanced up at the sky. He ran across the yard and turned. The barn was shining in the moonlight like a huge silver snuffbox. He remembered the story in the paper about a bomber unloading its last bombs on a lonely cottage that was showing a light, his mother rushing to take silver candlesticks from the windows during a thunderstorm. Panic surged through him. He rushed into the old granary beneath Dennis's room, began throwing sacks and buckets that were blocking his way. The barrel of tar was at the back. He rolled the barrel towards the barn and tipped some into a bucket. It was thick in the frosty air, like treacle. The tar brush was hard. He began slapping tar onto the tin sheets. It was stiff like clay, sticking in lumps and going nowhere. It needed to be warm. A gust of wind blew smoke from the chimney and the bitter smell of burning wood hit his nostrils. He raced to the house and returned with a shovel full of burning coals and embers from the fire, piled on off-cuts from the roof spars of the barn and set the barrel above it propped on two bricks, the bucket of tar leaning against the flames. Dennis was coming down the granary steps.

"What's goin' on?"

"We've got to paint the barn. Look. You can see it shinin'."

"We'll never do it. It took all afternoon to paint the old granary." He was shaking.

Bill roared at him. "We can bloody try." He ran for another brush and returned to pick up the bucket of melting tar. The handle was hot and it sizzled as it blistered the skin on his hand. He dropped the bucket and tar tipped onto the fire sending flames up the side of the barrel. The tar in the barrel caught light and the top blew of with a deep thud. Flames from the burning tar were reaching twelve feet into the air, reflecting against the end of the barn like a huge beacon and casting shadows across the yard that danced like demons. Through the roar of the flames they heard the rumble of planes overhead, a change in tone as one altered course. Dennis was frozen, staring at the sky. Bill grabbed his sleeve and dragged him out into the paddock. They threw themselves down behind an old tree stump and lay in the freezing mud. There were shouts of alarm from the roof of the Hall, bellows from the cows in the shippen. They heard machine gun fire from way above their heads and saw tracer bullets flashing from a spitfire as an icy wind blew over them and the flames surged upwards in the barrel by the barn. A dark shadow swept over them and Dennis pulled his arms over his head, blocking the sound from his ears with his elbows. The shadow surged towards the yard. Bill looked up, panting hard. They were still in darkness.

"Dennis." He pulled at his arm but Dennis shied away, gibbering. "Dennis. It's clouds. Look. They can't see us. They've gone."

Dennis was curled up and sobbing into his knees. Bill put his arm round him and held him tightly. "It's all right. We can go."

The next morning Norman Watterson arrived as soon as he'd been relieved of duty at the hall. Bill hung his head and told him what had happened

"What've I told ye aboot panickin'? Ye damn near got us all killed." When Bill remained silent, he took a deep breath. "No 'arm done, an' a few lessons learnt, I'd say. Y'd better git it painted quick though. Thah'll be back toneet." As he was climbing back on his motorbike he shouted over his shoulder.

"Vince 'as a drum in 'is workshop. Don't heat it up as much this time."

Bill collected the tar, and Dennis refused to stop work until the job was done. He ate his sandwiches for lunch with one hand still painting the barn, starting at the apex and working downwards. He finished the last corner by lantern light and went to start feeding the pigs.

⁜

During March Bill watched the slow progression of the Taylor's building. He met Charlie at the station.

"How's the barn coming along?"

"Not too good. I told our Bert he'd be better waitin' till summer but he wouldn't listen. He's in a right mood an' all, blames everybody else an' won't see sense, won't accept help from those who know. I reckon there's a storm comin' as well. I'm stayin' out of it."

Bill loaded the cow on and boarded the train to the auction at Bentham. All day his mind kept returning to Charlie's warning. The sheep were due to start lambing, and bad weather could bring a disaster. The wind began picking up, and the doors of the auction mart buildings slammed and crashed. He looked up as he heard a slate sliding from the roof. By early afternoon rain was hammering against the windows. He collected his cheque, paid it into the bank and hurried towards the station.

On the way home the train stopped as some workmen struggled to clear a fallen tree. It was beginning to go dark when he trudged through the wind and rain past the Taylors' farm. Sheets were rattling on the unfinished roof of Bert's barn as Bill struggled to stay upright on the road. He heard a cracking sound and some joists gave way, sending a section of the roof crashing to the ground. The wind lifted some tin sheets that had been left leaning against a wall. They flew through the air and buckled against a tree in the garden.

He hurried up the hill. He was late for milking but he would need to check the sheep before dark. He would be up again in the night squelching around the paddock with a lantern and searching for new-born lambs dying from the cold.

When he reached the yard Dennis was coming towards him with the wheelbarrow, whistling. Bill rounded on him.

"What are doing? Go and start milking whilst I check the sheep.

Dennis didn't flinch. "No need." He nodded towards the new barn. Some gates and an old door had been tied to the front. The barn's floor had been bedded with straw and fifty ewes were lying in its shelter chewing their cud or sniffing through the bedding for blades of grass.

20

The ox should be as little abused by threats and whipping as by stinted feed and overtasked labour.

R. L. Allen. Domestic Animals (1847)

"Young lambs can stand a lot o' frost if their bellies are full. They can even stand a bit o' snow if they can shek it off their backs, but when it rains they soon get cold and die." Jack Branthwaite had said this so often that Bill had got bored with hearing it when he was younger. He'd seen the truth in it for himself during a wet spring in his early teens. During the last weeks of March and the first week of April it drove him to work harder than ever. The fields full of ewes and lambs were puddled black. The river flooded, subsided and flooded again in less than three weeks, carrying with it soil from eroded banks, trees ripped out by the torrent and carcasses of dead sheep caught in the flood waters higher up the valley. In the kitchen of Friar's Holme Farm the air was heavy with moisture from drying coats and the smell of starved lambs brought in to recover by the stove. Mrs Coburn complained about the mess, and Bill turned on her with a rage that, until now, he'd kept out of doors.

"Damn it woman. We're workin' every hour of the day. Each one of those lambs saved will pay your wages for a month."

"Couldn't Dennis keep them by the stove above the granary?"

"He's got three up there already. He's been feedin' 'em for a week." He stormed out and went to check the sheep across the road.

One of the ewes had been breaking out through the hedge onto the lane towards the lot, taking her lambs with her and grazing the roadside in an attempt to keep her belly full. Bill

251

took his dog and went to bring them back. There was no sign of them on the lane. He followed some tracks that led into a wood, hoping that they hadn't gone as far as Moss's lot. With the wind blowing rain into his face he made his way to the top of the wood and found the ewe and lambs sheltering behind Moss's boundary wall. He glanced over into Moss's field towards an old shepherd's hut hidden in the corner by the trees and the hill. It had been unused since Moss took over the farm, so when he saw smoke coming from the chimney he wondered who could be using it. Perhaps a tramp had found it and was sheltering from the rain, but he struck that thought from his mind when he considered the location, out of sight from anywhere on the lane and almost half a mile from the road. He climbed over the wall and crept up to the window, kept flat against the wall so as not to cast a shadow.

The room was small, wooden walls and a tin roof. There was a table, chair and, in the far corner, a bunk. Sitting on the edge of the bunk, gulping down a bowl of soup, was Bruce Crabtree. His hair hung raggedly over his collar and his clothes were worn and dirty. He was a sorry sight compared with the cocky uniformed serviceman Bill had seen when he went to the dance with Lucy. He stooped over his bowl like a half-starved prisoner, and the fingers of both hands were bandaged. Bill heard a noise to his left, his dog scratching at the door. Bruce jumped from his seat and dived under the bed like a frightened rabbit.

Bill realised he was feeling sorry for him, the local bully, even though he had enough reasons to take satisfaction in seeing him brought down to size. He went round to the door and knocked. He didn't expect an answer so he pushed it open and went inside.

"Bruce."

There was silence.

"Bruce. It's Bill Branthwaite. I know you're there. I saw

you hide under the bed."

There was a shuffling sound and Bruce hauled himself out and faced him. A line of dust and cobwebs was smeared down his left side. A leaf stuck in his hair. He stood with his head down, watching Bill with what Bill guessed was a mixture of contempt and resignation.

"Wha' d'you want?"

"I saw the smoke and wondered who was here. I wondered if you were all right."

Bruce grunted. "Been worse."

Bill found it hard to believe. He pulled up the chair and sat resting his elbows on the back. Bruce looked round at the bunk, slumped down on it and wiped cobwebs from his face. Bill found himself breaking into a smile and saw that Bruce almost did too.

"What happened to the army?"

"Got hammered at Dunkirk. Didn't you know?" He was watching the bowl of soup. Bill raised a finger towards it and Bruce grabbed the bowl and spoon, began slurping it and slopping into the bowl with a hunk of bread.

"How come you're not still in the army?"

"What's the point? We can't win. They're too bloody good. We was beaten from the start."

Bill didn't have an answer.

Bruce stuck the spoon out towards him. "Don't go tellin' anyone I'm here."

Bill shook his head. "How did you get away?" Lit a cigarette, handed it to Bruce.

"I sneaked off, ended up back here."

"You've been in this hut all this time?"

"Nah. Been stayin' at Joe Moss's. Not safe there any more, them blokes ... . Mrs Moss's gone away. Took the kids to 'er sister's."

There was a scratching at the door and Bruce jumped to

his feet, eyes wide.

"It's okay. It's my dog." Bill stood up. "It's time I was going." He took out his cigarette case, opened it and handed two to Bruce.

"Thanks. You got any money?"

"No." Bill left the hut and climbed back over the wall. His sympathy for Bruce was fading. Bruce was a quitter. For the first time he'd been faced with an opponent who was a match for him. He'd lost his bottle and run. Now he was back working for Moss, handling black market goods and leaving the rest of the country to fend for itself. And to cap it all he was begging for money.

The ewe and her lambs were still in the far corner of the wood, nibbling grass that was growing in the shelter of the wall. Bill herded them back down to the lane, marvelling at how the lambs fought their way through the wet bracken and weeds. They battled over branches and clambered through the holes left by uprooted trees. They were less than a fortnight old but they followed their mother at a pace that any general would be proud of. They didn't quit.

21

The products furnished by the carcass of swine are numerous. Every part of the animal is used for food, and it admits of a far greater variety of preparation for the table, than any other flesh.

R. L. Allen. Domestic Animals (1847)

The rain stopped on the thirteenth of April. The wind blew from the east, turning the tips of the grass blue and bringing frosty nights. Bill watched with relief as the lambs gained strength and began playing in the drying fields.

Building the barn had saved him from disaster. He didn't need to imagine what it would have been like without the extra space for the ewes and newborn lambs. He'd seen the heap of dead ewes in Charlie Taylor's yard, some of them huge and bloated with the lambs still inside them. Others, weakened and frail from too much wet weather and a diet of poor hay, had struggled to give birth and succumbed to infection. Their carcasses laid flattened at the bottom of the pile. Leaning against the wall were three large sacks stuffed full of dead lambs. The sight confronted Bert and Charlie Taylor each time they passed the midden, overworked and weary, waiting for a dry day when they had the energy and courage to tackle the job of burying them. Bill saw defeat in their eyes and wondered how they would find the resolve to start again with their own barn.

Building his had taught him new skills and given him the confidence to tackle new projects and try out new ideas. He would grow barley as well as oats. He'd ordered the seed from the merchant, along with enough chickpeas to grow three acres.

The only job he was afraid of doing himself was slaughtering the pig. Brian Waterford had always done the job for the Branthwaites. He had been known as a master of the trade, would arrive in the morning almost in a trance, Tom beside him learning the skills. He would unload the wooden stock, ropes and buckets with the air of a vicar at communion. The knives were unrolled from their wrapping and laid on a barrel, sharp and gleaming, scalpels for the operation. The stock was placed close to the sty and Brian gathered all the hands together to give them their ropes and instructions.

"Remember, it's going to be scared, so don't cause it any more distress than necessary. Everybody do your job quickly and quietly."

The pig was herded to the door and trapped with boards. Tom slipped the noose over its nose into its mouth and the squealing started. Brian took great pride in being able to have the animal roped and tied on the stock with its throat slit in less than four minutes. Bill had seen the expression of relief on his face when the pig died, as if he was feeling its fear, its distress, its pain. Once it was hung up he relaxed. The job of removing the guts and cutting up the carcass seemed like an escape for him from the inner turmoil he felt at taking the animal's life. He had taught Bill how to cure the joints, salt petre round the bones, when they needed more salt if the process wasn't working, and when it was suitable weather to do the job. Agnes had always said she would only buy pork when there was an 'r' in the month. Brian lived by the same rule when he was curing bacon. He wouldn't attempt it in hot weather.

Since Brian had left the village the only resident with the know-how was Joe Moss. The cold spell wouldn't last long and Bill had been unable to find anyone else who could do the job in the next fortnight. He'd asked around, hoping that Moss wouldn't find out, but his heart sank when Moss rolled into the yard with a hungry look in his eyes.

"I hear y' want a pig killin'. Ah'll do it after dinner if y' want."

"We were goin t' move some sheep out o' front meadow. Besides, I thought you were too busy wi' yer other business interests."

"Nay. Nay. Yer can't begrudge a man a bit o' sport. Anyway, it's today or niver. Ah reckon it'll come warm next week. It'll be too late."

Moss had him in a corner. There was no escape, no time to think. Bill agreed, but not without an uneasy feeling in his gut that was shouting *No*.

✣

Moss arrived in the yard and blew the horn. He was out of the van bawling orders before Bill had looked up from sweeping the yard.

"Niver mind sweepin' up lad. There'll be a lot more mess by time we've finished." Two youths piled out of the van. Moss started shouting at them. "Get them ropes. Put that stock o'er there. Where's me knife?" he turned to Gerald and Dennis. "You and you, get in that sty an' rope that pig." And when they hesitated, "Show 'em how it's done, Bernard."

Bernard was a shorter version of Bruce, probably his brother or cousin. He barged into the sty and the pig retreated to the far corner with a frightened squeal. Bernard grabbed it by a hind leg and it pulled away, squealing. Moss was bellowing. "That's it. Mek it squeal. Someone get a rope in its mouth while it's open. Don't stand there. Shape yerselves."

Dennis was looking at Bill, wanting guidance. Moss grabbed him by the shoulders and shoved him into the sty. "Grab that bluffy pig." He was gripping his knife. It was filthy, caked in dried blood and mess. "Get hold of its tail. Shove it out here." The squealing rose to a high pitched scream as they dragged the pig into the yard and shoved it onto the stock. Moss hovered over it, lusting for blood. Gobs of spittle were frothing in the corners of his mouth. One hit Bill in the face as Moss danced round trying to get to the animal's throat. His eyes were white like a crazed bull. The pig struggled and the stock collapsed. It was rotten. Moss hacked the knife into the animal's neck, missed the vein and hacked again. Blood poured. The pig was up, dragging the men and the broken stock across the yard, Moss sliding in the blood, trying to grip its snout. Bernard was gripping its ears.

"Stand still yer fuckin' bastard."

Dennis froze, released his grip leaving the animal and its tormentors careering towards the house. Blood gushed onto the flagstones and slopped against the back door. Bernard struck the pig hard in the jaw with his knee and it fell against the wall smearing more blood across the stones.

Dennis was standing motionless in the yard, his arms raised as if he was about to grip his hair with both hands. Moss roared at him. "Get over here yer dope an' do summat." He was kneeling on the pig's back, forcing it to the ground. It weakened. The squealing grew faint, and the pig died. Moss kicked it in the face and ordered them to drag it to the barn where he could hang it from a beam. He started slicing at its belly as soon as it was off the ground. Its guts dropped on the barn floor in a sloppy, steaming heap. Moss was chopping at a hind-quarter. He tore it off and slung it over his shoulder, started towards his van. The two youths retrieving the ropes.

Bill stopped them. "Where are y' goin?"

"We've finished. You deal wi' it now." Moss threw the ham in the back of the van and started towards the driver's door. Bill seized him and rolled him against the door.

"You're not having a whole ham for that."

"That's me price, laddie. I've killed yer pig." Moss pulled away and climbed in, blood still dripping from his arms. "Come on lads. We've three more to do before tea time."

Bill dragged him out again, slammed him against the van and punched him square in the face. Moss's nose exploded in a mass of red. Bill drew back his arm and was grabbed from behind. Bernard had him round the throat. The other youth was twisting his arm. Moss was shielding his face. When he saw that Bill couldn't move he straightened, came back at him.

"Yer'll pay for that, Branthwaite. Just you wait." He wagged a bloodied finger and climbed back in the van. The youths threw Bill on the ground and jumped in. Moss fired the engine and roared out of the yard. Bill turned towards the barn and went to sort out the mess. The carcass twitched.

22

It profits oft to Fire the Fruitless Ground,
And thirsty Stubble crackling all around:
Whether from thence by Nature's Secret Laws,
Fresh Nourishment the Earth and Vigour draws;
Or that the latent Vice is purg'd by Heat,
And the redundant Humours waste in Sweat... .

Jethro Tull. The Horse Hoeing Husbandry (1733)
(From Virgil's first Georgic)

The last time Bill had hit someone was at school. He was eleven. He was late finishing his comprehension exercise and had stayed inside for the first ten minutes of playtime. It seemed like hours. When he was finally released into the playground he found a group of boys behind the toilets. They were standing with their backs to him chanting. "Sowcroft, Sowcroft." Dennis was in the corner cowering. They'd pelted him with mud. The Barrett brothers were the ringleaders. It was always the Barrett brothers.

"Leave him alone." He pushed through them, shoving bodies out of his way. Dennis shrank further into the corner, more scared than ever. Ken Barrett stood between Dennis and the others. When Bill reached him, Ken pushed him in the chest.

"Stay out of it."

"What's he done to you?"

"He stinks."

"Leave him alone."

Ken pushed him in the chest again and Bill pushed back. Ken took a swipe but missed and Bill swung and hit him in the ear. It must've hurt. Bill's knuckles were sore. Ken's face flushed and he shouted threats. He was going to get him for it, tell his dad and make sure that Bill was in trouble. It never happened. For more than a week afterwards Bill's coat was thrown on the floor each time he went to collect it after school. That was the extent of the bully's revenge.

Bill wasn't afraid of Moss. The man was ugly, deceitful and cruel, but he was too self-righteous to set up a beating or steal anything. It was no surprise, however, when a hundred barren ewes appeared in the field next to the park. Moss knew the fence was weak. He would leave them there until they broke through and found free grazing in Bill's pasture, if he didn't find a shady butcher to take them off his hands first.

Bill satisfied himself that the fence would hold. He'd patched it up last year and sent Gerald to block up any weak spots. He began to believe that Moss had been foiled in any feeble attempt at revenge. The man was avoiding him at the station, always standing talking to the other farmers when Bill arrived and was usually still there when he left. His back was always turned as if he'd seen the horse coming over the bridge and had positioned himself so that there was no chance of Bill catching his eye or seeing the damage to his nose. There were more important things to think about than Moss.

Rent day was approaching, and the rent was higher this year, almost three hundred pounds. Bill hoped he could manage without having to sell any more cows. He was confident that the egg and milk sales would cover the shortfall. He delivered them each day to the station with increasing confidence, milk bound for a dairy in Leeds and eggs for shops and market stalls in Lancaster and Carnforth. He was picking up the empty churns when he noticed an envelope tied to one of them. Inside was an angry note from the dairyman telling him to look inside the churn. He lifted the lid. In the bottom was a dead rat, sodden with milk. He knew it hadn't been in the churn when he filled it and wrote out the ticket. It couldn't have been. His attention turned to Moss, standing by the ticket office door and laughing with the stationmaster. Moss was making himself popular with both the staff at the station and with all his neighbours.

Bill loaded the churn with the others and carried a crate of eggs onto the platform. When he returned home there was a letter waiting for him, payment for last week's eggs. He opened it to find there was no cheque enclosed, in its place an angry letter telling him that the shopkeeper was cancelling his order. Two customers had complained that some of the eggs were rotten. Either the man was just making an excuse or someone had been tampering with the eggs. They were collected and delivered daily. There was no way that they could be anything but fresh.

Moss would be the one who was going to pay, Bill decided. The anger that was boiling inside him would not go away. He wouldn't allow it. He hadn't forgiven Lucy for leaving, and the mention of Brian Waterford's name still had caused him to stiffen and clench his fists until his nails dug into his palms. In the days after the pig killing, however, he found himself looking back at Brian with a respect for his skills and compassion as a slaughter man. His double-dealing was forgotten, not forgiven, just blocked out by the memory of Moss butchering all that was fair and decent. Moss was a pig, worse than a pig. Bill had no words to describe him.

When he rode over the lot to check the sheep he was oblivious to the animals around him, his head turned towards Moss's buildings and his teeth jammed together like the jaws of a trap. There were no words in his head, just hate, charged and waiting: a bomb falling towards its target. He passed some gorse bushes and heard a sound to his left, a hogget stuck in the scrub, its fleece tangled amongst the branches. He leapt from the horse and grabbed it by its back legs, tore it from the thorns and threw it out onto the grass. It stumbled up and limped away.

"Stupid bastard." He climbed back onto the horse and dug his heels into its ribs, turning again towards Moss's farm, this time noting the layout of the buildings and which approaches could not be seen from the house.

The old lane that ran down from the lot was covered in overhanging thorn bushes, bare, but thick enough to conceal. They stopped about thirty yards short of the farm where the lane levelled out and ran in a straight line between two high walls right up to the yard. The kitchen window opened into the yard and gave a clear view all the way to the thorn bushes. To the left was a plantation with spruce and larch trees growing about fifteen feet high. It was shielded from the rest of the yard by Moss's new barn. From his vantage point he could see a dark line stretching across the yard and disappearing behind the dairy at one end and the barn at the other. It was moving backwards and forwards across the yard in a long sweeping arc as if it was anchored at one end; a chain. It slackened, and a huge dog, a mastiff, strolled from behind the barn, dragging the rest of its tether behind it. On such a long leash it had access to the whole yard. Moss must have bought it to guard against the mobsters from the mill town. There would be no way past it. The thought seemed to revive him for a moment and he glanced across to see his dog sniffing at a rabbit hole.

"Fly. Come here."

The young collie turned dejectedly towards him and slunk away from the hole. He too had been thwarted from his quarry.

On the way back to the farm, Bill's thoughts returned to Moss. Ever since he was a child his mind had turned towards stressful events. If something was making him angry it would fill his head with visions of arguments, fights and punishments before any confrontation had taken place. When Dennis had been bullied by the older boys at school, Bill had been so angry during arithmetic that he had snapped his chalk on the slate. Miss Taggart had called out his name, questioning if he was all right and he had sunk into his chair, red-faced and ashamed. In his imagination he had already cornered and beaten up the

263

bullies. Her voice came to him not as one of concern but as a chastisement and a call to the front of the class to be caned for fighting.

This time he wasn't thinking of the consequences. All he could think of was what he was going to do when he caught up with Moss. He could see him pushed against the barn wall, his face becoming bloody as blow after blow split open that fat piggish nose. He could feel the strength in his arms, the impact of his knuckles and the slippery wet skin of the man's face as the blood poured. He would get him. That was for sure. The only questions were how? – and when?

His dreams became filled with images of Moss taking his money, invading his land and his home. He would wake in the night; alone and frightened like a child. At work he was angry. He raged – a bull awaiting his chance.

23

Mountain sheep, indeed, are more likely than any others
to have survived the dangers of a feral state; but this,
again, is mere conjecture. It is at all events inferentially
true that different breeds did live through the period when
wolves were not uncommon in this country.

John F. L. S. Watson. The Best Breeds of
British Stock (1898)

The sheep were ready to be moved from the front meadow.
They were to be taken onto the lot the next morning. Bill had
gone to bed still thinking about Moss. He dreamed about being
chased by hounds, massive drooling beasts that bayed and
snarled as they pursued him. Moss behind them on an
enormous horse. Bill stumbling, his legs failing as he waded
through a bog, the dogs pursuing, relentless, scattering the
sheep and getting ever closer.

He awoke. Where was he? He could hear the dogs and the
terrified bleats of ewes and lambs. Why? He was awake. He
jumped out of bed and ran to the window. The flock was
scattering across the meadow, running blindly as a huge dark
shape tore amongst them: The mastiff. It grabbed lambs as it
ran, shook them like rats and slung them broken backed to the
ground, hardly losing its stride.

He grabbed his trousers and raced outside, pulling the axe
from the chopping block as he passed. When he reached the
field most of the sheep had fled over the brow of the hill. The
mastiff had one ewe cornered by the end of the lane. She
turned to face it and it seized her throat in its huge jaws,
gripped until she died, and began ripping at the flesh on her
flanks.

Bill leapt the gate and reached the dog in seconds. It
turned as it heard his approach and bared its teeth. It was too
late. He brought the axe down, two-handed between its eyes.

It let out a sound that was like a shriek as the axe split its skull, leapt in the air and writhed on the blood covered grass.

Bill was panting hard. He stared at the dog, at the dead lambs littering the field and the torn-up body of the dead ewe. Moss, again. It was always Moss. He grabbed the dog's hind leg, dragged it back to the gate and went for the pony. He threw the dog over the pony's shoulders and rode bare-back up the road, gripping the horse's mane with one hand, the axe still held in the other. Moss would still be in bed. Even Dennis hadn't stirred. From his room at the back of the house he would have heard nothing.

He rode quietly, coldly, at a trot. The road was empty. He took the front entrance right up to Moss's house and stopped.

Parked in the yard was a familiar-looking car. He could hear the tick as the engine cooled. He left the horse in the orchard and crept round the back of the barn, watched the yard from between the wheels of a cart. From here he had full view. The back door of the house was open and there were voices inside, low and determined followed by the high pitched squeal of Moss. He was pleading.

"Ah'll get 'im 'is money. Ah told 'im ah would. It's under me carpet by me bed."

The men were silent. They dragged him into the yard and began pounding him with wooden bats.

Bill watched, his anger turning to satisfaction that Moss was getting what he deserved. When they continued, his feelings changed. This was a neighbour; a bad one but no one deserved to be beaten to death. What could he do? He couldn't overpower them himself. This time they might have a gun. One of the thugs swung hard and hit Moss across the back of the head. He slumped on the cobbles and it was over. They dragged him like a carcass and loaded him into the back of his own van. He looked small, sad. His short stubby arms hung lifeless over the back bumper. The hit men shoved him further inside and drove away, one in the car and the other in the van.

Bill stood up, shaking. What if he was blamed for this? He could be seen to have a motive. He remembered Sergeant Jackson's questions when his father died. He ran to the orchard, dragged the mastiff round to the back yard and dumped it. It was heavy. His horse was covered with blood from the dog. He washed it away with water from the trough, galloped home. Dennis would be up soon. Gerald would be cycling down the road past Moss's farm.

In the house he passed the mirror. His face was splattered with blood. He splashed on water from the sink and changed his clothes, hid the dirty ones in the loft.

24

*Seeds, in their natural Climate, do not degenerate, unless
Culture has improved them; and upon the Omission of
that Culture, they return to their first natural State.*

Jethro Tull, The Horse Hoeing Husbandry (1733)

It was the ninth of May, 1941. Lucy sat on the train, thinking
about Bill and the baby she had left in Barrow. She thought
about what it could have been like, the three of them together.
Would Bill ever want her as a wife? She hardly dared to wonder.
Would he speak to her when she saw him? She tried to relax
and watch the fields go by, but every picture of farm life seemed
to bombard her with an artillery of emotions – rejection, fear
and worry – that churned her insides and reminded her of the
nausea she'd felt during pregnancy.

The train rumbled on, stopped briefly at Borwick station,
then began winding its way round the hills towards Sandholme.
She was surprised when it slowed down to a stop about two
miles short of the village. There was something on the track
that was delaying the train.

She stared out of the window across the rushy fields by the
track and up the hills towards the horizon. She could see a
figure on the skyline walking alone. She recognised that walk
even at this distance. He was either looking the sheep or
staring out to sea wondering what the weather was going to do
– probably both. If she ran now she would catch him on his
own, away from that stepmother of his, so without a second
thought she opened the carriage door, jumped down onto the
track. It was further than she'd thought. The door was almost
too high for her to close.

She clambered over the railings into the flat fields between
the track and the hill. She looked back. No one had seen her
leave. When she reached the gate to the lot she could see that

he must still be up there. His pony was tied to a tree just below the ridge. She raced up the hill. The flat ground at the base of the lot was marshy, covered with soft moss, so she took off her shoes and ran barefoot between the clumps of rushes. She winced as she ran past a holly tree that had dropped some of its leaves into the moss under her feet.

When she reached the top of the scar she could see Bill walking along the ridge towards her. As he approached, the puzzled look on his face turned into a broad smile. He quickened his pace and she dropped her shoes and ran towards him, flinging her arms around him. They held each other, not wanting to let go.

He felt a warmth filling his chest, a happiness that he hadn't known since he couldn't remember.

"I'm glad you came back." She didn't speak. "I came to Barrow to find you, last July. It was the first Sunday. I didn't know where I was going so I asked at a newsagent's. The old man in the shop sold me a street map and I was just leaving when a policeman grabbed me and dragged me back into the shop. They took me to a police station and locked me in a cell all day. They thought I was a spy."

"I always said your English wasn't very good."

"It wasn't funny at the time. I kept telling them to ring Hornby police station. There was no reply. They kept me there all afternoon. I had to catch the train straight back. I didn't get another chance to come; and when you didn't write … ."

They sat on a boulder a few yards from the edge of the scar. Lucy wanted to tell him everything, but could not decide where to start. Every second of delay brought back the barrage of doubt and fear. She sat up straight, breathed in hard.

"I've had a baby." She was looking at the mud on her feet. She glanced sideways watching for his reaction.

"My … our baby?"

"Yes. She's six months old."

"A girl. What did you call her?"

"Dorothy, after my mother."

The thought began to sink in. "I'm a dad. I've been a dad for six months." He looked at her. "You've lost weight. You're not getting enough to eat."

She shrugged, smiled. "It's the rations."

"Who's looking after the baby?"

"My cousin. She was bombed out in Coventry. She arrived last night."

They walked back to the edge of the scar, picking their way over the cracks in the limestone and sat talking over the last year. He told her about Agnes being taken away, about her letters from The Isle of Man, how they had all been opened when he received them.

Lucy described life in Barrow, the bombing and spending nights in air raid shelters. There was a man with an accordion who kept everyone entertained. Dorothy had learned to sleep through the blitz. Lucy's father was working long hours. He'd been concerned that she was bringing up a child without being married. He was overjoyed to be a granddad.

Bill remembered the talk when the Taylors' maid got pregnant. The men in the village had responded with jokes and disgust in equal measure.

"Young Laycock's bin provin' himsel' in t' breedin' department."

"I'd have thrown the little trollop out if she were my daughter."

This man from Barrow had reacted with concern for his daughter and the child. It overrode his personal pride and any thoughts of retribution. Although Bill had never seen him, he was getting a sense of the man. Lucy's father was honest, down to earth and practical.

He stared out across the escarpment, over the fields, the bay and towards the cranes and buildings of the shipyards.

CHAPTER TWENTY-FOUR

"I'd like to meet your dad."

"You would? I'm sure you'd like him."

Bill told her that he was worried about Dennis, who had become more nervous, especially since the night they realised that the new barn shone in the moonlight and could be seen across the valley. They'd painted it black the next day. It was right under the path of the bombers heading for Barrow. Dennis had taken to hiding anything that might shine in the dark, empty milk churns and a new shovel.

Lucy told him that many of the children in Barrow had been evacuated onto farms. She blushed. Looked away. Had he thought she was trying to find her own billet?

"You could come and stay here."

"I wasn't trying … ."

"I know, but it makes sense."

She was twisting the corner of her cardigan round her fingers.

"I'd have to talk to Dad."

The sun was setting, and as they looked across the bay, huge balloons were appearing above the rooftops in Barrow. They heard a droning sound behind them and high up. Bill turned to see the sky darkened with bombers, labouring under their loads and pointing westwards towards the shipyards and town.

"Dorothy!" It was almost a whisper. Lucy watched as the bombers took only minutes to cross the sands, a journey of nearly two hours round the bay by train. She stood at the edge of the rock, clinging to Bill's arm. Watched each flash followed seconds later by a deep boom, distant rumbles merging into one. Her speech was garbled. "Shelters … sirens … I didn't hear the sirens."

"It's too far." It sounded weak. He searched for something to say, a way of reassuring her, couldn't find one.

The bombers disappeared from view then emerged out to

the south of the docks, heading back towards Germany and avoiding the anti-aircraft guns on land. Following them were more shapes in the sky. Spitfires, chasing the bombers away from the town. They heard the rattle of machine guns and saw a bomber losing height about a mile south of them, trailing smoke as it descended in a huge arc. The other planes were still fighting, and something rattled onto the rocks at the southern tip of the scar.

Bill and Lucy set off back towards the pony and the shelter of the trees. Bill looked back to see the stricken bomber still turning and heading back towards them. He grabbed Lucy's wrist and started running across the rocks, leaping over each crevice. The plane's roar was louder, behind them. He pulled Lucy. Ran towards the edge of the scar. Heard a crack, like a breaking branch and Lucy's hand slipped from his grip. He was four steps away before he could stop. He turned, saw Lucy, her foot caught in a crevice, the broken bone sticking out below her knee, the agony, the pleading in her eyes. The huge plane behind her. Something screamed inside him and he threw himself over the edge.

✤

Luther Barrett was up early. He'd seen the plane come down the night before as he stooped over a purse net covering a rabbit hole. The ferret had returned several times, twice on the heels of his stricken quarry, but after half an hour of waiting and seeing only the ferret's twitching muzzle peering through the jute strands he'd had enough. He'd cursed the rheumatism in his knees and gone home. It had been a poor night.

This morning he was hunting for a different prize. The police and firemen had left the crash site late last night. It had been almost dark when they arrived. Luther wanted time to search the area before anyone came back. There could be something useful lying around, a flask for his tea or a German

War medal he could sell at one of the local pubs. Maybe even a gun. It was a slim chance. The plane had exploded on impact so most if not all of its contents would have been destroyed. His only hope would be to find something that had been thrown clear. It could be a wide search.

He scanned round the top of the lot. The stink of smoke and fumes was spoiling the morning air. There was a strange calm about the place, like standing on the edge of a river that had reached the height of its flood. The events of last night had brought destruction and death, but now the air was still. His breath stopped when he saw the crater. It was huge; big enough to turn a horse and cart full circle in the bottom, and so deep that he wouldn't risk climbing down into it in case he couldn't get out. The thought of having to wait down there until someone in a uniform came to get him out turned his attention to the area around it. Huge lumps of limestone paving had been thrown in an arc from the crash site, smaller pieces were spread further along the rocks and littered the grass up the slope, intermingled with chunks of metal and burnt-out bits of canvas and rubber. The debris line stopped just short of the trees.

Luther's eye was drawn to a white scar on the trunk of the nearest tree. A small branch had been ripped away. It was too far from the crash site to have been caused by the blast. He turned, looked around to see if anyone else had beaten him to the spoils. There was no one, just a black pony grazing at the far end of the field. But it wasn't just a black pony. It was saddled and bridled. From the reins trailing beside it hung a piece of broken branch. Had it been here when the plane crashed?

He decided that it was time to go. Someone might be back to check on the smouldering heap in the bottom of the crater or to retrieve the horse. He stepped across the shattered paving towards the edge of the scar and stopped when he saw something glistening in a crack between the rocks. It was the fastener on a woman's purse. He reached down and grabbed the purse. It had five pounds in it so he shoved it in his pocket, glanced around, then climbed over the edge and began making his way down the steep face, using the saplings and protruding rocks to steady himself.

The slope was uneven, with a huge bulge about half way down so that anyone standing at the top could not see to the bottom. When he'd passed this he glanced upwards but he could no longer see the top. Below him he could make out something at the foot of the slope, half hidden by the stunted hazels and gorse. As he got closer and the gradient became less steep, he recognised the shape and quickened his pace. It was the body of a man. The shirt had been almost completely ripped from the man's back and the skin beneath was a sickly blue.

Luther hurried down the last stretch towards the body, skidding along the slope on the damp grass. He could see it wasn't the body of a German pilot. The man on the ground was Bill Branthwaite, and he was breathing.

The nearest farm was James Smith's place, three quarters of a mile away round the south end of the ridge. It was too far to carry Branthwaite's dead weight, so Luther turned away, pushed his way through bushes, scrabbled over rocks towards the farm. By the time he reached the house his breath was whistling from deep inside him, rasping the tissues of his lungs. Later he would ask himself why he'd pushed himself. He had nothing to gain. That man amongst the rocks was nothing to him, would offer no reward. His only thought at the time, and the only answer he could give himself, was that he'd seen life in that body, fragile and slipping away.

Mrs Smith sat him at the table and poured him some tea before he could tell her what he'd found. She went to get James and they left the last cows unmilked, raced across the fields in the cart with Luther guiding them. Bill Branthwaite hadn't moved.

✢

When Bill opened his eyes he was confronted by whiteness, a blur that came gradually into focus and faded back to a sea of cloud. There was softness around him, pierced by a prickly line of pain on his scalp, a dull ache in his head. His limbs felt stiff and there was something unpleasant about the feeling in his lower spine. The whiteness came into focus again, almost grey in places, with irregular lines breaking up the surface. He was lying on his back and studying the way the lines crossed and interwove, hairline cracks in something solid. Some of them formed the rough outline of a bull's head with the horns facing forwards. Two eyes had been scratched on the face with a fingernail. He rubbed the tip of his forefinger with the pad of his thumb, expecting to find something chalky behind the nail and remembered scratching those marks onto that face when he was a child, reaching up and making the bull's eyes appear. He was lying in his bed at Friar's Holme Farm. The animal's head was formed by cracks in the plaster on the ceiling. The sun was shining through the window and he could hear sounds outside; a distant birdsong, a cough from the calf-house and the slide of a dog's chain across stones.

Why was he in bed? He tried to raise his head and the dull ache raged into a violent pain in his temples. He rubbed at it with his hand and felt the shaved line and stitches in his scalp, tried to remember what had happened to him.

In his mind, he could see Dennis pouring milk into a churn, the last cow being released after milking, and the evening light in the shippen doorway, his black pony saddled in the yard. He couldn't remember seeing his dad. Agnes seemed to be absent. Mary? Where was Mary? She was gone. Was she dead? She couldn't be dead. Could she?

Someone was coming up the stairs. The creak of floorboards continued towards the bedroom and when the door opened Mrs Coburn stood open-mouthed, looking at him.

"Mr Branthwaite! You're awake."

He started to speak, paused and changed his mind. Something told him that she was supposed to be there. He remembered seeing her in that apron, not long ago, but far off, in the kitchen washing the dishes, hanging sheets on the line, stoking the fire in the front room.

"What ha ...? Where is everybody?"

"Dennis and your Uncle Harry are among the sheep. Gerald's mending a fence and Charlie Taylor's taken that last batch o' lambs to the auction." She was going to say something else but her face turned serious. "How much do you remember?"

"About what? Where's Agnes? Where's Mary? Why's Dad not here?"

Her hand came up to her mouth. She seemed to realise it was there, took it away and tried to sound reassuring.

"You get some rest. I'll make you some beef tea and you can talk later."

Waiting was torture. What could have happened that had taken away his family and left him injured and struggling to remember the details of his life? He tried putting things in order. He remembered leaving school, working with Dennis, his dad. Memories showed themselves at random and, no matter how hard he tried, he couldn't make his mind work. It was like pushing a wheelbarrow through mud or wading thigh deep in fresh snow. Snow; he remembered the snow and digging out the sheep, rushing through milking and L ... . Lucy. He'd forgotten all about her. She brought them breakfast the morning of the snow. His father was a distant memory but he'd spoken to Lucy some time not long ago. Where? When? He could remember her voice, the touch of her hand and that fresh scent of soap. They'd sat on the grass together talking about … about what? A black fog descended over him and his temples began to throb. He sank into the sheets, closed his eyes and, as the pain subsided, he drifted into sleep.

He awoke to the sounds of voices on the landing: Mrs Coburn and a man's voice replying in 'mm's.

"Doesn't remember … asking for his father … his sister … left months ago."

Mrs Coburn opened the door and stepped aside to let the doctor come in. He had a serious inquiring look on his face, and when Bill tried to sit up he raised his hand.

"No. Lie still and rest. You've had a nasty accident and a very lucky escape. I just want to examine you." He leaned forward, and Bill flinched as the doctor's hands touched the stitches on his scalp. "You still remember nothing about the accident?"

"No." He paused. "Was Lucy there?"

The doctor turned sharply towards Mrs Coburn. She shook her head and her mouth tightened. She must have read something in Bill's face, because when he caught her eye she opened her mouth to speak, then stopped herself. The doctor wasn't a patient man.

"What is it, woman? If you have something to say, he needs to hear it."

Her lip was trembling and her voice wavered.

"Lucy was killed in an air raid in Barrow the same night you fell off the ridge. It was in the *Gazette* this morning."

"But I saw her. I know I did."

The doctor was staring at the housekeeper.

"Are you sure?"

She nodded, hurried from the room and returned with the newspaper, already folded at the page. The doctor took it and scanned the page.

"Is this the Lucy he's talking about?"

"Yes, doctor. She lived and worked here before I got the job."

He looked deeply at Bill.

"Are you sure you're not confusing it with another meeting, some time when she worked here perhaps?"

Bill didn't need to search the haze of memories.

"No. we were sitting on the edge of the scar when Barrow was being bombed. I remember it clearly."

The doctor had made up his mind. He turned to Mrs Coburn, opening his bag as he spoke.

"He's delirious. Give him this. It's laudanum. I brought it specially. I'll see myself out." He placed the bottle on the dresser and pushed past her, striding from the room.

Bill stared at the open door, anger pumping through his veins.

"I saw her. She was there with me." He looked to the housekeeper and saw something he didn't expect. "You believe me. Don't you?"

She nodded slowly, snatched the bottle from the dresser and dropped it in the pocket of her apron.

"You won't be needing this. I do believe you, Bill. You saw her all right." She patted her apron pocket. "I'll be tipping this rubbish down the sink. You can have that beef tea I promised you." She turned from the room and closed the door behind her, glanced upwards and crossed herself. "God preserve us. He's got the gift."

The headline in the newspaper spelled it out: *Fifteen Dead in Bombing Raid.*

The facts were laid out: a direct hit on an air raid shelter, the time of the bombing and a list of names. He raced through them, surnames he'd never heard of, people he would never meet. The last two froze him, took away his breath and drained the strength from his limbs, his chest. Alan Rogan, a shipyard worker and his daughter Lucy, at the end of a line of the dead.

How could Lucy have got back in time? He'd sat with her on the lot but couldn't remember what happened next. If there'd been a train back to Barrow she'd have had to run at both ends just to be in the shelter in time to be hit by the bomb. The train was slow. He knew that. Surely the air-raid couldn't have lasted for hours. Nothing seemed to fit. The throbbing in his head made him nauseous and he reached over to the wash stand for the bowl, retched, and produced nothing but bile. He laid back on the bed gasping for air and closed his eyes.

When he awoke the newspaper was crumpled, with pages strewn on the floor. He gathered them together and saw the list of deaths on one of the back pages. Lucy's funeral was to be held on Friday. He sat up, staggered across the landing and called for Mrs Coburn.

"What day is it?"

It was Wednesday. He hadn't missed the burial. He hurried back to his room and threw on his clothes.

✠

Uncle Harry and Auntie Doris drove him to Barrow. The journey was even slower than the train, and the service was at one-thirty. Bill checked his watch. It was a quarter to one.

"Can't you go any faster?"

"Damn it, lad. I'm doin' o'er fifty." Uncle Harry was gripping the wheel, sweat staining his collar. Auntie Doris protested that they should have used the train. "Ah told yer once. They've bombed the station. Besides, we would've had to wait two hours if we'd caught the early one an' the next was too late."

When they reached the church the service had already started. As Uncle Harry parked the car they could hear the sound of the organ drifting from the church and wavering voices following the tune. They crept through the door and sat at the back, fumbling through their hymn books for the right page. Bill glanced at the board on the wall. It was the third hymn. They'd missed the service. How could they have? They were only five minutes late. Were they at the right church? He looked desperately round for an answer. He'd never met any of Lucy's family or friends from Barrow. No one else from the village had been able to come.

Two coffins stood at the front of the church. At the end of the hymn, the vicar nodded to two rows of men in the choir stalls who took up their positions and bore the coffins from the church. As the congregation followed Bill heard a grey haired lady complaining to the woman at her side.

"Not right moving the service forward like that; even if it is wartime."

The other woman shook her head and they shuffled past clutching their handkerchiefs.

Uncle Harry and Auntie Doris were whispering something to each other. They both looked at Bill and signalled to follow the procession outside. He found a place where he could just see the grave through the crowd of mourners, but heard little of what was said by the graveside. It seemed like there was a conspiracy against him, to stop him learning the truth or even getting the faintest hint of what had happened on the lot the night he'd fallen off the ridge. It angered him that he couldn't remember, and he stood behind the other mourners with their backs blocking his vision, and the stench of the factories in his nostrils.

When the vicar stopped talking, the townspeople began to file past the grave, dropping earth onto the coffin and standing around in groups either talking or hugging each other. Uncle Harry and Auntie Doris were several feet away from Bill, leaving their nephew to his thoughts. Had he been her own son, the farmer's wife would have sensed his feelings, gone over to him and known exactly what to say. She didn't know him well enough. He was different from her own boys; more confident, more outspoken and used to making his own decisions. Whenever he came to visit, his conversations with her rarely stretched beyond a 'hello' and a 'goodbye'. The rest of the time was spent with Harry, either walking round the cows and sheep or sitting by the fire discussing prices and the effects of the war on farming. Harry wouldn't be much help to him either. He had little understanding of anything that didn't involve the running of the farm, and no time for anyone who was troubled by anything other than the job in hand. Since his brother's death he'd never mentioned Jack's name to her or discussed his feelings.

She was watching Bill standing alone by the grave, when she became aware of a tall woman watching her. The woman came towards her and held out her hand.

"Hello. Are you Mrs Branthwaite?"

She wondered how the woman knew her name.

"Yes. We brought Bill along. We're really sorry we were late."

"The paper printed the wrong time. Most people round here found out the mistake from each other, but we didn't really expect anyone coming from Sandholme, what with the war and everything. I'm Ruth Mattieson." She said it as if she expected the name to be familiar. "I guessed who you were when I saw you. You were the only people here that I didn't recognise. Lucy told me a lot about you all."

It suddenly dawned on Doris that Ruth Mattieson thought she was talking to Agnes. She was about to correct her but the woman was welling up with tears.

"I'm sorry, Mrs Branthwaite but it's all so terrible. She was a lovely girl and that awful bomb." She was breaking into sobs. "They could hardly identify the bodies. It's a miracle that the baby survived. The paper went to print before it was found. That poor child has no one." She looked towards the grave diggers who were beginning to shovel soil onto the coffins.

Doris looked first at the grave and then at her nephew. Agnes had told her about the troublesome girl when she first arrived. Bill obviously thought a lot about Lucy and now she'd got herself pregnant to some shipyard worker or sailor in the port. That was one piece of information he could well do without. Least said, soonest mended. That was her motto.

Doris glanced round to see Harry reading the names on a stone several yards away. Luckily he hadn't heard. She doubted whether he could be trusted to keep his mouth shut, so she vowed to keep what she'd just been told to herself. She declined the woman's invitation to go back to the church hall for tea and sandwiches and went to tell Harry it was time to go.

April 1992

25

*No plant can live without Heat, tho' different degrees of
it be necessary to different sorts of Plants.*

Jethro Tull. The Hose Hoeing Husbandry (1733)

The young man looked at his watch and stretched. Tom's
breathing was slowing again.

"Is it time you were going?"

"Aye, I've got to check my own sheep when I get back."
He said goodbye, walked to the door and turned. "I'll call and
see you next Saturday."

Tom's eyes dropped. He looked back at his friend.
"Goodbye, lad." He reached for a glass of water and watched
him disappear down the corridor.

Outside, the air was turning colder. The young man
hopped into the pickup and drove back through the town.
There was less traffic than when he'd arrived. He guessed that
most of the town people had gone home for tea. A woman was
locking the door of her dress shop, and an Asian man was
leaning over the range in the chip shop next door. Not
everyone finished at five.

He took the road back through Halton, watched a man in
a long woollen coat feeding his ewes on a hill three fields away.

Two teenagers had finished laying a hedge. One was
knocking in the last stakes as the other turned over the
remains of a huge bonfire with a JCB loading shovel. The
young man waved to them and they both waved back, grinning
under identical mops of red hair. The one by the hedge hopped
into the machine's cab and they headed for home.

At the junction the young man paused. Although he felt
guilty about sticking his nose into Branthwaite's business his
curiosity got the better of him and he took the lane that led
him round by Branthwaite's Lot. It was crowded with vehicles:

Branthwaite's Landrover, two white ones and a police car were squeezed onto the verge. A group of men seemed to be arguing behind the car. He slowed the pickup and glanced across. Branthwaite was waving his arms. He appeared to be shouting. The policeman was stepping towards him. Branthwaite threw his arms up, barged past the policeman and jumped in his Landrover. The young man accelerated and drove back to his cottage.

There was a roar behind him as he unlocked the front door. He turned to see Branthwaite's Landrover flash past. The man had lost it.

The young man heard a crackle of crunched up paper as he opened the front door; letters on the mat. He picked them up and began straightening out the usual delivery of unwanted offers. They always had his name wrong, probably a typing error on someone's computer list.

One letter caught his eye. It was addressed to Mr H. Tyler. At least someone knew. The postmark was Barrow in Furness. It was from them. They'd found something. His hands were trembling. Should he open it now or ring Julie first? It was her idea. *If they find someone there's plenty of time before Mum's birthday party in October.*

They'd wanted to find something for her fiftieth but it had taken two years to get anywhere with the search.

He turned the envelope over in his hand, decided to read the letter first and tore at the seal. He thought it would have looked more official. He'd expected some kind of document. He switched on the light and sat on a chair, began to read.

Dear Mr. Tyler,

We regret to inform you...

The wind escaped from his lungs. Disappointment was leaking in.

*We regret to inform you that we have not been able
to trace any surviving members of your mother's
family. According to the records it appears that her
mother, Miss Lucy Rogan, died in an air raid shelter
in Barrow in Furness in 1941. Your mother's father
is not registered. Lucy's father, Mr Alan Rogan,
died in the same bombing. Your mother was the only
survivor.*

He folded up the letter. That was that. Julie would be
disappointed. Their mother would be heartbroken. She'd
always believed there was someone. He breathed in deeply, let
it out slowly. Perhaps it was time for all of them to move on.
The light was fading and he still had to check his sheep. It was
getting cold. He'd light the fire before he went out. At least
he'd have a warm house to come back to.

The coal bucket was empty so he took it outside to the
shed. From the shed doorway he could see right into
Branthwaite's farmyard. The Landrover was parked by the back
door. Branthwaite was coming out of the house with his
shotgun. He stormed round the back of the buildings towards
the woods. The young man watched him go. Muttered to
himself.

"Taking it out on the crows again." A shot rang through
the trees and the woods echoed with the cackles of rooks and
jackdaws. "Strange. He usually gives them both barrels."

The cries from the treetops faded as the birds settled back
to roost. The young man picked up the coal bucket and went
inside.

Other Books from
Marius Press

The Moment Captured

*Pages from an
Artist's Drawing Book*

ISBN 978-1-871622-63-8
vii + 72 pp.
Hardback

The Late Roy Clapp was prolific in his
output of drawings, paintings, engravings and
sculptures. The drawings presented in this book
are all taken from a single drawing book and
capture moments in the life of his wife, Jill.
The speed and energy with which the drawings
have been executed are almost palpable, yet the
images express a truly remarkable subtlety of
mood and facial expression.

Yrion

A Tale of Dragons and of Men

Neil Johnson

ISBN 978-1-871622-57-7
vi + 88 pp.
Hardback

A sweeping tale of dragons and of the folly of men, in which the fate of the land of Yrion is determined by the compassion of an innocent child. Told in the form of an epic poem in 150 stanzas, this haunting and unusual tale has attracted a substantial following.

There's a WORD
by Neil Johnson for THAT!

ISBN 978-1-871622-62-1
xiv + 210 pp
Hardback

The sequel to the Author's acclaimed
Dr Johnson's Reliquary of Rediscovered Words
(Square Peg: London, 2008) this is yet another
feast of rare and unusual words, accompanied by
humorous and occasionally barbed comments. In
this book's pages you will discover words you
never knew existed, and rediscover many that
you have forgotten or given up all hope of ever
seeing again.

King and Wizard™

The King and Wizard Stories
NEIL JOHNSON

BOOK 1: *Magic in Vàldovar*

ISBN 978-1-871622-22-0: xii + 116 pp: Hardback

BOOK 2: *Dreams of Vàldovar*

ISBN 978-1-871622-27-0: x + 134 pp: Hardback

BOOK 3: *Wonders of Vàldovar*

ISBN 978-1-871622-28-7: x + 150 pp: Hardback

A series of magical tales for children of all ages,
set in the far-off, tiny kingdom of Vàldovar. King
Ferdinand the Thirteenth solves some tricky
problems facing his country, with the help of his
friend the Wizard-who-lives-in-the-Wood.
Humorous and often thought-provoking, the
King and Wizard Stories have been recognized
as modern classics of children's literature. All
three books are lavishly illustrated with
wonderful watercolours by Victoria Flack.